Take Me In

Also by Sabine Durrant

Having It and Eating It
The Great Indoors
Under Your Skin
Remember Me This Way
Lie With Me

Children's Fiction

Cross Your Heart, Connie Pickles
Ooh La La! Connie Pickles

SABINE DURRANT

Take Me In

MULHOLLAND
BOOKS
HODDER

First published in Great Britain in 2018 by Mulholland Books
An imprint of Hodder & Stoughton
An Hachette UK company

Copyright © TPC & G Ltd 2018

The right of Sabine Durrant to be identified as the Author of the Work has been
asserted by her in accordance with the Copyright, Designs and Patents Act 1988.

A CIP catalogue record for this title is available from the British Library

Hardback ISBN 978 1 473 60835 1
Trade Paperback ISBN 978 1 473 60836 8
eBook ISBN 978 1 473 60837 5

Typeset in Plantin Light by Hewer Text UK Ltd, Edinburgh
Printed and bound by Clays Ltd, St Ives plc

Hodder & Stoughton policy is to use papers that are natural, renewable
and recyclable products and made from wood grown in sustainable
forests. The logging and manufacturing processes are expected to
conform to the environmental regulations of the country of origin.

Hodder & Stoughton Ltd
Carmelite House
50 Victoria Embankment
London EC4Y 0DZ

www.hodder.co.uk

For Barney

'A boy may lock his door, may be warm in bed, may tuck himself up, may draw the clothes over his head, may think himself comfortable and safe, but that young man will softly creep and creep his way to him and tear him open.'

Charles Dickens, *Great Expectations*

Everything starts with a story.

That's one of the slogans we came up with at work. God, we were proud of it. When you first click on the Hawick Nicholson website, the phrase flashes across a slideshow of positive world events: the launching of Apollo 11, Obama's inauguration, Mo Farah breasting the tape. And then underneath, in a solid typeface the designer assured us denoted dependability (Verdana, I think): 'We help you tell yours.'

How arrogant it sounds. And also, how deceptive. Google 'world events'. Go on. See how far you have to scroll to find anything positive; to get beyond 9/11.

Own the story. Something else we were always telling them.

Nothing is so straightforward. I know that now. Experience is messy. No story is any one person's to be owned.

And even if you were to argue that it was, that a single narrative can be unravelled from the chaos of life, like an individual thread from a skein of rope, or a line of ink from a sleeve of tattoos, there's one thing this whole tragedy has taught me. It's not how it starts that matters.

It's how it ends.

FIRST

Him

It was Jeremy, a contact at the *Financial Times*, who had suggested the Greek island. He'd gone there several years in a row when his lot were small. I was resistant. I still liked to think of myself as the kind of person who might holiday in Ibiza: four-poster sunbeds lined up along the beach like pimped-up tanks, the throb of bar music, sangria in glasses pearled with condensation. But Tessa's tastes were always quieter, and we had Josh, so even I had come to appreciate we needed something more subdued. Gently shelving waters: fine. The possibility of other children: OK. A villa with easy buggy access: God help me.

It was the first day of the holiday. We had slapped across the hot sand, cracking the skin of it, to a straggling cluster of olive trees at the far end, and laid down our towels. To be honest, I was knackered. We had hired a small boat to get here – the beach had been recommended on TripAdvisor – which was more of a palaver than I'd anticipated. Sweat had collected in the centre of my chest and I eased my T-shirt away from it, flapping it in and out. I think I might have made a noise, a sort of 'pouf'. Tessa ignored me. She was busy, bustling, as she always was those days, erecting the pop-up tent and taking off Josh's life vest, studiously applying another layer of sunblock to his legs and arms before rolling on a pair of orange armbands. She was wearing a pink sleeveless towelling dress decorated with yellow daisies: the sort of mumsy garment she had started buying online. Her own life vest had left red welts across her bare shoulders. She rubbed at them absent-mindedly.

'I'm going to find somewhere to change,' she said. Her springy curls lay flat against her scalp. Her pale green eyes, which I found mesmerising when we first met, protruded slightly – they tended to when she was tired. I felt a stirring of pity and affection and, as usual, guilt. We hadn't connected for a while. It was almost definitely my fault. Most things, increasingly, were.

I moved closer to her. 'No one's looking,' I said. 'Apart from me.'

'No . . . I . . .'

'Can't you just wriggle your bikini on under your dress? Or I could hold a towel?'

'No – it might slip, and everyone would see everything.'

'There's hardly anyone here. And anyway, a bit of slip-page . . . I wouldn't mind seeing everything.' I put my hands on her shoulders and tried to kiss her mouth. My body next to hers felt fumbly and awkward. She moved slightly and my lips grazed the side of her cheek. I was aware of the warm, salty Nivea scent of her neck, the smoothness of her thigh as I raised my knee to rub against it. Her skin was arousingly soft. 'The more I see the better,' I murmured.

She pulled away, abruptly this time. 'It's a swimsuit not a bikini,' she said.

I let her go and sat down on the edge of the towel, sighing with a heaviness that I hoped expressed a more generalised disappointment. It wasn't just the swimsuit. (Didn't she use to have a bikini? Had she thrown it away or did it no longer fit? Either way, to ask would almost definitely cause offence.) I also felt suddenly lonely, and, childishly, left out.

'I expect there'll be a loo over there,' she said. 'I'll only be a minute.'

'OK.'

I unfolded my own legs into the sun. I decided not to bother with lotion: a small rebellion against the tyranny of Tessa's paranoia. They looked pale and hairless. I should join a gym – my generation's answer to National Service. Or get a personal trainer, like Jeff my business partner, anything to beef up my muscles. Maybe she'd be more attracted to me then. I sighed. Both options were expensive. Even if I had the inclination, the way the business was going, I didn't have the money. Or the time.

'Keep an eye on Josh, won't you?'

'OK,' I said again. And then, when she didn't move, 'Of course.'

We both watched him for a second. He was crouched down at the door of the tent, rolling a small plastic tractor over the pebbles, muttering under his breath in a lilting sing-song – one of his little narratives in full flow.

We smiled at each other, united for a doting moment.

'I'll be back in a minute, then.'

'Righty-ho.'

I watched her as she trod slowly across the beach towards the taverna. I was still stressed, that was the problem, nerves still on edge – the KazNeft pitch had taken it out of me – not to mention the journey the day before. Travelling with a child magnified all the usual shit: the nerve-wreckingly early start, the trolley-jamming queues at Stansted, the queue at Avis. The villa was a disappointment, too. There, I've said it. On arrival, I'd felt a crashing sense of dislocation and discomfort. It seemed unimaginable that we could spend a whole week in this house, so much smaller and less equipped than our own: *seven whole days*. But I hadn't been able to express any of that. It had been Tessa who'd Googled, and sifted, who'd done all the research. She was the one who made it her mission to find the perfect family holiday. So she was the one who was allowed to feel disappointed, to stand in the living room, rubbing her two middle fingers across her forehead, her mouth down-turned. My job was to run around, enthusing. 'It'll be great – he'll sleep in without the disruption of natural light! I love the floor! The tiles are like glass. You can slide across them! Perfect, Tess. Well done. Heaven.'

In reality, it was small, characterless and hot, squashed in by an identical property next door. No view. The whole place smelt of drains. We'd have been better off going back to that hotel in Cornwall.

Fuck it.

Josh, still very visible in his turquoise sun-suit, UVA- and UVB-proof, and his blue and white gingham hat, had found his bucket and was picking up stones and putting them into it, studying them first, still keeping up a cheerful conversation with himself. I felt another burst of pleasure in his existence. He was happy. That was what mattered. The holiday, I reminded myself, was for *him*. If he was enjoying it, then it was all worth it. And he'd loved our little voyage around the bay, laughing at every bump, every splash. So yes, renting the boat had been a good idea, even if there had been some hairy moments – sudden dark drops below, the water beneath us black and deep, jagged rocks dangerously close. But I'd moored it up all right – I'd been worried about that. There it was, safe at the end of the little concrete jetty; it didn't seem to be knocking into the larger, whiter vessel next to it. My ropes seemed to be holding. So. Something in our life was secure at least. That vain attempt to prove my virility hadn't been entirely unsuccessful. I'd got us here – hadn't I?

I looked around. The cove *was* pretty: a lilting crescent of pale pock-marked sand, with a single taverna at the far end and a smattering of villas in the trees behind. Only the serrated ramparts of the vulgar hotel we'd passed were visible on the far headland. It was quiet this early in June, sleepy even. Closest to me, a middle-aged woman with a heavy tan lay on a rush mat, eyes shut, one arm above her head, gold watch gleaming, her armpit white against the rounded teak of her body. At the water's edge, a man and woman were playing bat and ball, her lunges the endearing side of self-conscious. Josh had drawn nearer to them now, attracted by the tock-tock of rubber on wood. They noticed him and bent their shoulders, twirled their fingers in his direction, and for a blissful minute I wondered if they might actually play with him. But no, they resumed their game: of course, they were too in love, too thrilled by their own youth and energy. Along from them was a large family group – a load of clobber, a child's buggy and a beach umbrella, some folding chairs, picnic bags, an ice box, stuff, clothes, clashing colours. English voices, embarrassingly loud. I guessed they had ventured out from the big hotel. A large man with a shaved head, wraparound sunglasses, sleeves of tattoos, chucking a ball to some kids who should surely have been in school. Box fresh trainers. Shiny football shorts.

I looked away. The water glistened pearly blue towards the dark rim of a far-distant horizon. A yacht lay moored out there, sail furled. It was hot, but not unbearable. A small breeze flicked the edge of the towel. Josh was still close enough; his suit looked like dayglo pyjamas from here. Could I relax? I began to feel it might eventually be a possibility. I slipped off my Birkenstocks, and felt the warm sand sift between my toes; the catch of a small curl of dried black seaweed. I took off my glasses and leant back on my elbows, the sun flickering through the olive trees onto my eyelids.

A shout woke me, and then a scream. I opened my eyes, staring for a disorientated split second at the criss-cross of silver-green leaves above me, and then sat up. The middle-aged woman on the rush mat was scrunched forward, one hand clutched to her head. She was looking at me and yelling, pointing out to sea. I followed her finger and saw the yacht that had been at anchor was at a different angle, that it was motoring out around the headland, pulling a line of white froth in its wake, and I was distracted by that. But the woman was standing up now, and shouting more loudly, and the young couple further down the beach hurled their bat and ball to the ground and they were both running, and someone had knocked over an umbrella, others were running too, and at the water's edge, flicked by the lapping waves, a brightly coloured object – a single orange armband.

And still it took a second to realise any of this was to do with me, until I saw Josh, face down, the bundle of turquoise and red, the lopsided flicker of orange in the water off the jetty, some way out, and that's when I moved, down over the towels, half tripping, the sand, the pebbles, pushing past the young couple, stumbling down the sudden rake of the beach until I was wading into the water, up to my knees and my groin, fired by fear and adrenalin and that dread that all parents clutch to their hearts, the inevitability of this awful thing that was always waiting there to happen, happening. I could see the terrible shape of Josh's body ahead of me. I could hear Tessa's voice screaming my name now, see her at the edge of my vision, her frantic arms and her stricken face, her open mouth. But it was stony underfoot, and slippery, brown, brackish slime over hard objects, bricks, and what might have been a pipe, a concealed slab of concrete, and I felt myself slip and go over, a flood on my face, up my nostrils, a sharp stab of pain in my heel and my hand, and I knew even in that instant that this wasn't right, that people claim not to feel pain at such moments because of the sheer panic and yet I did feel the pain and the difficulty of it. I was overwhelmed by the sense that this thing unfolding, this terrible heart-breaking thing, was physically beyond me.

I regained my balance and thrust myself forward, desperate to reach sufficient depth to lunge into a swim, to kick my feet free of the treachery of the bottom. And then came a shout, and a thundering of steps, a white T-shirt hurled, shoes flying, and a short distance to the right of me, I was aware of some-one doing the sensible thing, the obvious thing, which was to pelt up the jetty with such force and speed that it vibrated and set rings of water in motion. He dived headlong into the water at the far end of it, beyond where I had moored the boat, which brought him much closer to Josh. And I stood there, redundant, helpless, a father without skin, as another man saved his child.

That was the first time I saw Dave Jepsom.

Of course I didn't know his name then. I didn't know his full name until later.

But that was the first time I saw him.

An act of heroism.

Our saviour. We thought.

It took the man three strong, noisy strokes, a splashy half-crawl, to arrive where Josh was floating. He reached him and pulled his body around, yanked off the remaining armband, tossing it away dismissively, and then he held his little frame high out of the water. I saw Josh's arms flail, his hands grab the man's head for balance. Afterwards I tried to tell myself it was to reassure, to prove to his parents he had him safe, but at the time it looked like the brandishing of a trophy.

I became aware of people on the beach behind me, of muted cheers, gasps of relief, and of Tessa's deeper ragged sobs. I turned and saw her kneeling in the shallows, pitiful and white-limbed, nakedly exposed in her black swimsuit. I should have waded out of the water and held in her in my arms while we waited. But I let the moment pass and turned back, looking out into the bay, rendered bullish by my own mortification. All I could think of was my father, anticipating the weight of his disappointment, and what felt like the fulfilment of his prophecy. The phrase *not my father's son* came into my head, and I stood there, shaking, waiting for Josh, as the man, his hand cupping Josh's little chin, swam slowly, one-handed, almost treading water really, to the safety of the shore.

When they reached the shallows, the man suddenly reared, became upright, water streaming from his shoulders, and he hoisted Josh into his arms, cradling him across his broad chest, as one would a small baby. And of course it was the circumstances that made him look biblical in size and stature. His red and white football shorts – anyone else who knew about these things would have recognised the team – clung wetly to his powerful thighs. On his arms were sea-scenes and faces: locks of hair entwined, or a snake; perhaps a mermaid. He was only a few feet from me, and he must have known why I was standing with my arms out, waiting to prove I was worth *something*, but he altered course. Tessa said later that he was probably avoiding the concrete slab on which I'd slipped. Whatever the truth, he reached the beach independent of me, so I was forced to follow behind, literally in his wake. Across his shoulders stretched a pair of angel's wings – intricately ink-drawn, da Vinci-like in their detail – a patchwork of webs that looked like tracings of his own muscles.

Tessa ran to meet him.

'Thank you, thank you, thank you,' she said. Her face was red and she was crying now. She tried to take Josh from his arms, but Josh was already struggling and kicking – the man winced as Josh's feet impacted with his armpit and he put him down awkwardly half on the sand, half in the water. Josh had started crying too, coughing and retching, punching Tessa's ankles. Other people had assembled: the scraggly kids in the new trainers; a thin, lined woman with long hair in a stringy polka-dot bikini, surely too old to be their mother; a slight teenage girl with a baby wearing a nappy and frilly pink bonnet balanced on her hip. I realised then who the rescuer was – the large man from the big family group, the one who'd been playing football with the two boys.

'I can't thank you enough,' I stammered when I got there. 'I don't know what happened. It was so quick.' I wanted to fall to the ground and hold Josh and Tessa, to say I was sorry again and again, but I felt frozen with awkwardness. Such intimacy was beyond me. It didn't seem my role to comfort. It was all too much my fault. So instead, I raised my hand and rested it on the man's wet shoulder, above the tip of one wing. His skin was cold and goose-bumped, firm to the touch. 'You were just brilliant.'

'Right place, right time,' he said, nodding. Close up, I saw he was somewhere in his late forties, with deep-set eyes and a prominent forehead, a swathe of stubble.

'I had just gone to change,' Tessa said. 'I was as quick as I could. Should I have been quicker? I could have been quicker. I thought Marcus . . .'

'Little tyke. Can't take your eyes off them for a minute.'

'It was my fault,' I said, longing for Tessa to look at me.

'He could have drowned,' Tessa said, face buried in Josh's hair.

The woman in the polka-dot bikini handed her a towel out of a big laundry bag – red and black velour, depicting Spider-Man – and Tessa started trying to dry Josh's head, to wrap him, to pull him onto her lap. He had stopped crying, but he was still coughing, bringing up little globules of phlegmy sea-water. Her head was still lowered, so her own face was hidden in the towel. I saw her quickly dab her eyes with it.

'Yeah. Problem is,' the man said, 'those blow-up things – false sense of security.'

'Yes. Exactly,' I said.

He gave me a measured look. 'Teach them to swim; that's the best thing you can do.'

'Yup,' I said. 'He's only three, but yes.'

'Can't start too soon,' the man said.

I had been cold when I first came out of the water, but I was aware now of feeling clammy and hot. The backs of my calves were stinging. My face was tight, my legs shaking. I felt as if relief was still at arm's length. I wanted all these people to disappear, all of them, to melt away, so I could concentrate on looking after Josh, and Tessa, to get over the shock, to prove *it hadn't happened*. She was right: he could have drowned, but he *hadn't*. That was all that mattered. Anything else – my weakness and incompetence – was secondary. I wanted us three to go back to our spot in the shade. If we could only be alone, I could make it up to them both, to explain. If Tessa knew how tired I was she would understand. We would lie down in our patch over there and I would put my arms around them both and we could be still.

'Oh bless,' the older woman said, studying Josh. 'He needs something to drink. Mikey, get him a Coke.'

She rummaged in the laundry bag and at the bottom found

a ten-euro note, which she pressed into one of the boy's hands, and both boys sped off, scattering sand from under their feet.

Tessa finally looked at me.

'Honestly,' I said. 'You don't have . . . Please.' But the woman shook her head, raising her hand to halt my resistance.

The man had taken another towel out of the bag and was rubbing it, small and folded, over his shaved head, and along his illustrated arms and thighs – as you might run a chamois over a car bonnet. 'Anyway,' he said. 'What's done's done, eh? No point raking over it. He's all right, that's all that matters.'

Tessa cleared her throat. 'I just can't thank you enough.'

'Thank you,' I managed to say. 'Honestly. It was just . . . I don't know how to express our gratitude. We are eternally in your debt.'

'As I say, anyone would have done the same.' He ran his hand over his head, the tips of his fingers feeling for the bristle.

The teenage girl with the baby on her hip had walked over towards the jetty and bent down. She was heading back now, dangling a shoe from its laces. It was an adidas Superstar; spotless white leather with a strip of Burberry pattern at the back.

'Oi, Dave,' she called. 'How big are your feet!'

'Hey!' He laughed. 'Enough of your cheek. They're only 11s. Where's the other one?'

'Dunno. It was on its own.'

He looked around. 'I kicked it off. Can't you see it? It's floating out to sea probably.'

'Dave,' the girl said. 'You've lost it, you silly bugger.'

There was reproof in her voice. Was she his wife? No, she was far too young. She had a rash of acne around her mouth, dip-dyed hair, braces. Too young certainly to be the mother of the baby. His daughter, maybe. Were they all his kids? It was a big spread of ages but that wasn't so unusual.

'Oh God, I'm so sorry,' I said. 'They look expensive. You'll have to let me replace them. Let me make it up to you.'

It was the first time I mentioned money, or any form of financial recompense, to him, unless you count the earlier use of the word 'debt'. Even then, I didn't use actual words. I made a foolish gesture, tapping with both hands at my pocket-less hips, as if feeling for my wallet. 'Let me . . .' I said, pointing up the incline of the beach to our pile of possessions.

'Nah.' He shook his head. He took the shoe from her and did a little hopping dance, putting it half on and pretending to walk in a comic lopsided manner. 'Couldn't ask you to do that. My fault – should have been more careful.' He laughed, and the girl giggled too. The baby caught a handful of her hair and she bent to extricate it. I was smiling in an encouraging manner, though I felt acutely embarrassed. I wasn't sure whether to insist or not. I looked at Tessa for guidance, but she was curled up a few feet away on the sand, with Josh on her lap, whispering in his ear. He looked pale and exhausted. I realised, with an ache in my heart, that she was still weeping. Dave stopped laughing. He took the shoe off and tried to dust the wet sand from its matt-white sides before letting his hand, and the shoe, hang down.

'Maybe it's still there. Maybe I could swim out for it,' I said.

'Oh, you *can* swim?'

'Yes,' I said, mortified. 'But not very well, as you've just seen.'

'Useless.'

He looked at the horizon and then at the shoe in his hand, and then he hurled it, with a powerful over-arm so that the shoe swooped in the air for 100 metres or so before dropping, disappearing finally with a small distant splash.

'Useless,' he said again. 'A single shoe, I mean. Shoes are like people – better in a couple.'

16

'You plonker.' The teenage girl shook her head. 'You complete and utter plonker.'

I stared at him, shifting one of my feet so it found wet sand. I felt a tiny amount of sea swirl around it; my toes sink. Useless. I'd thought he meant me.

Dave slapped me on the back. 'Better my shoe sinks to the bottom than your little fella, eh?'

The small boys were racing back from the bar now, one of them clutching three bottles of Diet Coke to his chin, the other trying to get them off him.

'Here they are,' their grandma said when they reached her. 'You took your time.'

She took a Coke from the boy, wiped the rim with the palm of her hand. 'There you go, sonny.'

She held it out to Josh, who didn't seem to realise what was happening. 'There you go,' she said again. 'It won't bite.'

Tessa took it for him. She glanced in my direction and I smiled brightly at her, nodding my head. I was willing her to let him drink it, to glug back all that aspartame and caffeine. I imagined us laughing at it later, incorporating it into a post-holiday anecdote: *Of course the most traumatic thing was not the near-drowning, but the acceptance of a first Diet Coke.*

'I'm not sure,' she said. 'It's really kind of you, but I don't think he's thirsty.'

'If he doesn't want it, I'll have it,' said one of the boys.

'Oi.' His grandmother slapped him lightly around the head. 'You've already got one. Leave the poor little mite. He'll drink it when he wants it.'

'Thank you,' Tessa said. I hoped the danger might have passed but Josh made a sudden grab for the bottle and she jerked it out of his reach so quickly and violently a carbonated stream shot onto the sand. Josh wailed, struggled, fought to get the bottle back.

'No,' Tessa said to him firmly, and then looked up, realising. 'Sorry. I just don't want him to get a taste for it.'

The grandmother – if she was the grandmother – laughed and one of the boys let out a yelp, a sort of reprimanding groan. The teenage girl said, 'God, give her a break. Not everyone gives their kids Coke, you know. I don't blame her. It's full of sugar. It rots their teeth. Plus it makes them hyper. If you made those two have water instead of fizzy drinks they might be less manic.'

'One Coke's not going to kill him,' the man said to the girl – as if she were the one who'd been difficult, as if she were the one who was precious.

'It's Diet, Tracey,' the grandmother said to the girl. She turned to Tessa. 'Sugar-free. I was only trying to help.'

'Of course.' Tessa screwed the base of the half-empty bottle into the wet sand, tipped Josh off her lap, and stood up. 'You've been so kind, both of you. All of you. I don't know how we can ever repay you.' I could tell she was finding it hard to get her words out. 'Maybe we ought to get this little man out of the sun now, and let you guys get on with your day.' She gave the older woman a hug, and then took a step towards Dave, raised her arms to the side, and kept them there. 'Thank you,' she said before moving forward and clasping him around his back. She drew away and stood there, her head slightly hanging.

I felt weak with relief then, at the realisation that we were seconds away from leaving them, that we would be on our own.

When I turned to Dave to say goodbye, I realised he was just staring at me. For the first time I noticed the blueness of his eyes. People often describe blue eyes as 'piercing', but there was nothing sharp or penetrating about Dave's eyes. They were like a rinse of colour, something faded and soft, like washed denim, or a hazy sky. His face was angular with heavy brows and a jutting chin, the kind of prominent cheekbones that seem to need the skin to stretch to fit, but his eyes were pure blue, like a baby boy's first jumper. He gave a small smile, with a slight inclination of his head. I tried to read the expression on his face: disappointed, maybe; rueful.

The beach receded. The events of the last few minutes spooled backwards in my head.

Your little fella.

One Coke's not going to kill him.

Oh, you can *swim?*

I took a deep breath, not daring to look at Tess. 'Listen,' I said. 'It's nearly midday. Almost lunchtime. The least we can do is buy you all a drink. Or lunch. I don't know about you, but I'm starving. Josh and I have been up since six.'

I tipped my wrist to look at a watch that wasn't there. How ineffectual my gestures were. Dave's actions were concrete and dramatic. They had consequences. I dealt in air and mime.

The woman glanced across sideways at Dave. He seemed to ponder for a moment, while doing this odd thing with his hands: holding them several inches apart and twirling them, as if typing in the air.

I looked down at Josh, then. He was standing by his mother, his face very still, his mouth drooping. He winched his shoulders up and forward, in an exaggerated shiver. I reached out and laid my hand on the top of his head. It was the first time I'd been able to touch him since I thought he was dead. His hair felt salty and stiff. I wanted to bend down and breathe him in.

There was a tightening in the back of my throat, a gradually sharpening pain. My vision blurred.

'Well, if you're sure,' Dave said, cracking his knuckles and then finally bringing his hands together, like two fists in prayer. 'It would give us a chance to get to know one another.'

Her

I didn't want to have lunch with them. It's not that I wasn't grateful. I couldn't even have begun to put my gratitude into words. I just didn't feel capable. Horrors were still flickering at the corners of my eyelids: the moment I emerged, my eyes adjusting to the brightness, and I saw his blue gingham hat turning over in the waves, and then Josh himself, 50 yards out, his arm flailing in silent, urgent movement. My own scream in my ears, my heart cut open. And the horrific gut-propelling realisation that I'd taken too long in the taverna. I shouldn't have been so long. Now all I wanted was to be on my own with Josh, to look over every inch of his body, to hold him close, to hear him breathe. And then I wanted to lie face first in the sand and wail with the horror and the relief of it.

But Marcus was different. Marcus's response to anything was 'Let's have lunch'. He was pretending everything was fine, that he was relaxed. He wasn't one of those parents who fussed and over-reacted. We weren't those people. Nearly losing your child: just one of those things.

And to prove that, lunch apparently was what we would have.

I just wish we hadn't, that's all.

It was an extraordinary thing Dave Jepsom did for us. But

he was in our life now. And we would soon have cause to wish that he wasn't.

We were sitting at the last table on the terrace looking out over the bay. The water in the cracks beneath our feet was so clear you could see the fish dart. Plastic tables, a white paper cloth flapping like a seagull in the off-shore breeze. Oil and vinegar in matching bottles. A tang of seaweed and salt; the heat of the grill shimmering in the air.

It was the kind of lunch I'd imagined us having. If the circumstances had been different, it could have been idyllic.

I realised my legs were joggling the table, that a weird fixed smile had taken over my face. I remembered a show on Sky Atlantic in which a child had died from the effects of drowning, a few hours *after* being submerged. He'd been rescued from the waves, but had drowned, the sea-water still swilling in his lungs, in his bed. Should Josh see a doctor? Should I keep him up all night? Probably, I decided, it was better if he didn't eat too much. Just a light meal. Fluids; he should have a lot of those.

I tried to engage, to focus, to work out who they were, these people who had done so much for us. The man who had saved Josh's life was Dave and the older woman seemed to be called Maureen. The two boys were Mikey and Carl and the teenage girl was Tracey. At least one person was missing – a Sherry they referred to a couple of times, who had eaten a dodgy calamari the night before and 'was basically spending the day on the toilet'. I didn't know who the baby belonged to. She'd been put down in the buggy, with the seat reclined, but the sun was blazing through the awning onto her face. I reached behind me to move it. No one noticed.

At the end of the table, Marcus was doing his best to keep the conversation going, falsely cheerful, firing off questions as if he were holding a focus group or entertaining tricky clients. They'd been here a couple of days already, Maureen said, and were taking 'the full fortnight'. 'You too?' she said. Marcus told her we were doing a split holiday this year – one week abroad, another week a little later in the summer, in the UK. 'A staycation,' he added, 'cottage in Suffolk. Thought it would be easier with a toddler to do two short hols than one big one.'

'Well, that'll be nice,' Maureen added as if she felt a bit sorry for us.

I should speak to Dave; I knew I should. He was across the table from me and occasionally I felt his eyes on me as if he wanted my attention. I should reach over and take his hand and make a connection. But I couldn't find the right moment or the right words. It wasn't just that I found him physically intimidating – the rigid wall of muscle, the number of tattoos. If I hadn't already been in a state, I might have navigated this better. I might have asked about the tattoos, normalised them – where did you get that one? Was it painful? But I didn't. The truth is, I couldn't bear to look at him. Despite the heroism and the kindness of his act, he horrified me. He was a reminder of what might have happened, of our failings as parents.

Marcus was still asking questions. They'd flown from Gatwick and they weren't staying in the big hotel. 'No, an apartment,' Dave answered. He breathed in loudly through his nose and pulled back his shoulders, pushing his neck forward. It was a statement that didn't beg further question-ing – none of the usual holiday to-ing and fro-ing, comparing notes, storing stuff away, making judgements. He squared his jaw, clamping his mouth shut, guarding his privacy.

'Yes. Us too,' Marcus agreed. 'Or, anyway, a house. Small one.'

Had they hired a car? No. 'Very sensible,' Marcus said quickly. He should have left it there, but he gave them a little tirade on the system. I'd heard it already. It was what had brought his long simmering irritation to a boil yesterday. 'You do everything online and still when you arrive at the desk, knackered after the flight, desperate to get the hell out of there, you have to wait for hours in a queue while everyone ahead who has done the same as you and booked online *still* has to fill out endless forms.'

He was talking too much, trying to prove he wasn't embarrassed, filling the gaps.

The food arrived. Maureen and Tracey ate omelettes; the small boys, chicken on skewers – leaving the squares of green pepper in pools of orangey ketchup. If they'd been mine, would I have made them eat the peppers? I didn't know. Was it OK to let them eat so many chips? There was so much about parenthood that remained uncharted. Marcus had ordered the same as Dave: pork chops which came with rice and chips, tzatziki on the side. He was copying Dave, as if he thought Dave would think more of him for eating the same food. Dave had pulled on a white and navy polo shirt with an outsized logo on the breast – Ralph Lauren, or a knock-off – and he tucked a paper napkin into the neck and paused to smooth it down a couple of times before eating. I watched Marcus do the same. I'm a man about to eat man's food, that's what he was saying.

Josh and I shared a plate of whitebait.

'Look at you,' Maureen said to Josh as he opened his mouth for the tiny flick of silvery herring in my fingers. 'Aren't you grown up?'

'I'm trying to introduce him to as many different flavours as possible,' I said.

Maureen, it turned out, was an assistant in a year 3 class; she knew all about introducing kids to different flavours. The 'Eatwell wheel' was part of Key Stage 2.

'Where's your school?' I asked.

'Ashburnam Primary in Orpington,' she told me. 'Nice enough – except for the head.'

We talked for a bit about that, and I expressed sympathy until she mentioned the head's ethnicity, at which point I changed the subject.

'Sweet baby,' I said, looking behind me.

'You going to have any more?' she said.

I felt a lurch inside, as I always did when people asked. I tried to keep the smile on my face. 'Always wanted a big family,' I said. 'But it wasn't to be.'

I put my hand out – a reflex – and touched Josh's head. I kept it there for a moment, smoothing the back of his hair, then tucking in the label of his UV suit.

'You're not too old, are you?' She made a face like she was doubting me. 'These days, with all those scientific advances. A woman in her sixties had a baby in Italy the other day. I mean that's disgusting, but you're not on that level.'

I kept the smile on my face. 'I can't,' I said. 'I had a tricky birth with this one. Ended up having an emergency hysterec-tomy. Just one of those things.'

'Ah.'

'It's why I gave up work. If I'm only going to have one, I want to make the most of it.'

'That's nice.' She patted my hand. 'Why don't you take Poppy?' She called to the other end of the table. 'Tracey! I've just told Tessa she can take Poppy home with her!'

Dave was laughing. He leant his arm along the back of a chair and tousled Mikey's hair.

'As long as she looks after her,' he said.

'I'll do my best,' I said.

Our eyes met, and I felt something pass between us. He knows, I thought. He knows: my best isn't good enough.

I turned my head quickly away and reached for Josh, lifting him off his chair and putting him on my knee. He settled his face on my shoulder and brought his thumb to his mouth. He was exhausted. We needed to get him back.

I looked across at Marcus and failed to catch his eye.

'What do you do?' he was asking Dave.

'I'm in construction,' he answered, squaring his jaw.

Marcus didn't ask for details. He probably assumed brick-layer or roofer. He was respecting Dave's attempt to endow his job with a certain dignity.

'You?' Dave said.

Marcus told him he was 'in crisis management'.

'What's that when it's at home?'

'He's in PR,' I said before Marcus answered. He had a tendency to big up his job, to make it sound more compli-cated than it was – a defence mechanism but not one that would be appreciated here. 'We both are. It's actually how we met.'

'I help clients with their image,' Marcus continued as if I hadn't spoken. 'With their stories.'

Dave had reached across the table for a chip from Tracey's plate.

He dipped it in the tzatziki. 'It's not what you do; it's who you work for. In my experience,' he said.

Marcus nodded sagely.

'You got a good line manager? Easy boss?'

I stared at my husband, praying he wouldn't say he *was* the line manager; he *was* the boss.

'I guess I work for a lot of different people,' he said, glan-cing up at me, and tapping his fingers on the edge of the table. 'I consult across the board, for a wide range of companies in a variety of sectors. Some of them are good. Some of them are total wankers.'

'Lot of wankers about,' Dave said. 'Who's your biggest?'

Marcus picked up a pork bone and gnawed it to play for time.

I cleared my throat, trying to signal a warning. He should deflect the question. It's what his job entailed half the time, after all.

I don't know why he didn't. I don't think it was arrogance or a desire to show off to this man who had just saved his child. I think maybe he just didn't want to seem standoffish. He wanted to be open. Information about himself: it was all he could give.

He put the bone down, and in a fake gossipy, chummy tone, he told Dave about the racetrack owner with the drink problem, the make-up queen who only drank Voss mineral water served at 42 degrees F, and the Russian petro-chemists who wanted media training, but who needed training in basic human decency. He also outlined his dealings with 'an Irish manufacturer of excavation products' who had recently scored a big contract in the Middle East, and 'let's just say they tread a little too close to the legal boundaries'.

'Paddies?' Dave rolled his eyes.

'Bottom line is, every major company has its secrets. My job is to prevent them coming to light.'

At least, I thought, he hadn't mentioned any names.

Marcus ordered ice cream and coffee and the owner brought out glasses of Metaxa 'on the house'. When we finally left the table Dave proposed a game of football.

'Go on then,' Marcus said. 'Long time since I've had a kickabout.'

He was in goal – or at least standing guard of the sand between two buckets. When he let in the first ball, as Carl collapsed to his knees in whooping victory, he let out a loud theatrical groan. He resumed his position, crouching slightly, elbows braced, his lower lip caught between his teeth and, unwatched by anyone but me, he joggled from side to side, self-consciously at the ready. I looked away in embarrassment. It's not being bad at sport that's mortifying, it's showing that you care.

On a towel between Maureen and Tracey, with Josh asleep in my lap, I closed my eyes for a minute, anger at him and pity mingling with my own shame.

Him

I'd hoped everything would be all right when we were finally alone, that whatever was wrong between Tessa and me would be blown away by the trauma, that we would come together in our shared relief. I'd hoped we might be able to laugh about the lunch, as we had once laughed after a dinner party or a client meeting; to compare notes – was Sherry his wife? – and to re-live the more cringeworthy moments. I ran a conversation in my head. 'So Maureen doesn't like Muslims! And did you notice the reference to "Paddies"?' 'What a tosser!' she'd say. 'Yes,' I'd answer, 'total arsehole, but he did save our son!' We'd both laugh.

But we were silent on the boat ride home. She had clambered in ahead of me and watched as Dave and I shared a manly hug.

'See you later!' I said.

'I'll look out for you,' he said.

Tessa breathed in sharply.

The wind had changed direction – Stavros, the boat-man, had warned us – and once we rounded the headland, we turned into oncoming rolls of choppy waves. The boat broke across them, sea-water spraying across the bows and into our faces. Tessa sat, puffed out in her life vest, white-knuckled, clutching Josh to her shoulder, her expression grim. She protected his head with her spare hand, as if the slightest drop might kill him. It was an over-reaction, but after my terrible lapse of judgement earlier there was nothing I could say.

Stavros was there at the harbour to help us moor up, and then firmly held my arm as I scrambled ashore, as if I wasn't to be trusted not to fall in. Tessa waited with Josh in the car while I shopped for supper in the small supermarket: a bag of pasta, feta, some tomatoes, and a basil plant with small pointed leaves, then we trudged back up the hill to the modern complex on the outskirts of town that contained our villa. In the late afternoon, it seemed even hotter and more claustrophobic. I played with Josh for a while in the pool, while Tessa perched in the small square of shade provided by the single umbrella. Only a fence separated our house from the house next door. There was a couple staying there, younger than us maybe, no kids. You could hear the scrape of their loungers on their matching concrete terrace, cheerful requests from one or other of them to pass sunglasses, or another beer; the clatter of the cutlery in their kitchen.

I cooked us pasta and Tessa put Josh to bed, and later she and I sat outside with our iPads, catching up on our emails. I would say it was companionable but it wasn't. The air between us was heavy with tension. Our next-door neighbours had gone out. I thought about them down at the harbour, sharing food, laughing, getting drunk on a bottle of retsina. I was tense for the sound of their return. I wondered if we would hear them having sex. I had heard the woman giggle earlier – a rising sound like a car's engine before it fires. I'd convinced myself she would sound like that when she came.

With a hopeless anguish, I imagined the week that lay ahead – six more days of politeness and distance. We would talk when we needed to, united only in our service of Josh. We would find a routine and stick to it: a daily walk to the local beach, same spot every day; lunch in a taverna at the harbour – perhaps we would find one we liked best and decide to keep to that. Maintain a routine. Play it safe. We'd spend the afternoon at the pool. We would read. I'd cook supper. We'd go to bed.

In the suffocating heat of our room, Tessa undressed with her back to me, shoulders hunched as she shrugged off her bra and replaced it with a T-shirt. She lay down on top of the sheet and reached for her book. She used to walk around the house without any clothes on, sexily at ease with her body. (There *was* a bikini. Pea-green with a white stripe along the top of the bra. Where did it go?) Everything changed when she had Josh. When I told her I loved the softening of her belly, the lower swoop of her breasts, the pattern of her scars, when I told her she was *perfect*, she shook her head as if I was lying. Our sex life suffered, improved a little over time, but had recently had another setback. My fault? Work? I wasn't sure.

I lay down next to her and crept my arm over the slope of her shoulder. Her T-shirt smelt of the suitcase – stale and slightly synthetic. I had showered, but I was hot again already; I could feel my skin stick to the fabric. I wanted to pull the T-shirt off, to feel *her* skin.

It had been a while. *Months.* The emotions of the day, the turmoil, appeared to have reduced me to a state of needy arousal.

'Don't,' she said.

'Please,' I said. 'I know I let you down. And I'm really, really sorry.'

'Forget it.'

'Speak to me, Tessa. Shout at me. Say something. I am sorry. I know it was my fault and look at me: I'm abject.'

She lowered her book. 'Couldn't we have had this conversation much earlier? Left earlier? Did we have to have lunch?'

'It was the least we could do. I mean, we couldn't just walk away.'

'But all day. Did we have to stay all day?'

'He was nice. He was friendly. He saved our son.'

'I know. He was friendly. Very friendly. It's just ...' She closed the book, her finger keeping her place.

'Tessa. I feel terrible about what happened.'

'I was hardly gone any time. A few minutes. I had to a find a loo, and maybe I was a bit longer than I said. But not that much longer. It wasn't so much to ask, to keep an eye on your own son.' Her voice was breaking.

'I am just so exhausted. But that's no excuse. It was awful of me.'

Even as I was apologising, I felt a flicker of relief. At least we were focusing on the lapse in my attention, not the long cringing minutes that immediately followed, in which I failed to save Josh.

'Tessa.' I leant over her and took the book from her hand. I kissed the side of her mouth, laid the weight of my body upon her, felt her tense, begin to resist, and then the loosening of her limbs as she succumbed. She turned her head to one side, her eyes tightly closed. I buried my face in her neck, and shuddered almost immediately to a finish.

She patted my back and said it was all right, but something had already changed. I felt her contempt – not at this minor sexual failure but at my incompetence when our son's life had been in danger, at the fact I had fallen so wildly short in that vital moment when the big question was asked.

SECOND

Her

'So, how was the holiday?'

'It was lovely.'

He lifted his coffee cup to his mouth, keeping his eyes on mine. 'Weather nice?'

I smiled. 'The weather was also lovely, thank you.'

'And the flight?'

'Yes.' I moved my head slowly in a nod, still holding his gaze. 'The flight was fine too.'

'I'm very glad to hear it.'

His espresso had come in a small glass, the handle a tiny stub, which he grasped between finger and thumb as he lifted it to his mouth. The daintiness of the cup and handle made his hand look even larger and more male, the muscles and tendons tense with the contraction of the pinch. The hairs between his knuckles were tiny gold arches across his tanned skin.

'And what about you?' I said. I dipped my finger into the foam at the top of my cappuccino and dabbed it on my tongue. I felt it fizz and dissolve. 'What have you been up to?'

Words and phrases from his answer reached my brain – a franchise expansion, an issue with marketing, a meeting in Geneva. I was aware only of my own breathing, the flick of my eye movements, each quiver of my mouth. When I bit my lip, I felt as if he was aware of it too, that this is what it was about:

tiny physical gestures that ran taut between us like invisible strings.

He had stopped talking. It was noisy in there; music and chatter, the clatter and hiss and thump of the coffee machine. Chairs scraped, a dog barked. A woman pushed past me to get to the counter. On the next table, a man was doing bird-like taps on a MacBook Air.

'Did you miss me?' he said.

His foot had been resting on mine, but he had taken off his shoe.

I could feel his toes, through his silk sock, sliding up my bare calf.

'Did you miss me?' he said again.

I opened my mouth to say no. This time I had come to finish it. We had pushed things as far as they would go. That first morning of the holiday when I had wanted to hear his voice, and as a result had come so close to losing everything . . . No. It was over between us. There was to be no more talk of missing here.

His foot reached my knee and continued on to my thigh, pushing my skirt aside. A button opened.

The heat rose to my cheeks.

He was smiling at me now.

His toes explored further, skimming the inside of my thigh.

I slid my eyes away from his, biting my lip. 'Yes,' I said, my breath quickening. 'I did.'

'How's your coffee?'

'Lovely.'

'Sure you don't want anything to eat?'

I shook my head.

He picked up the menu and pretended to peruse it while his foot continued to press gently against my knickers, pulling away, returning. 'Smashed avo? Spelt toast with almond butter?'

I could hardly speak. 'You bastard,' I managed to say after a moment.

He put the menu down. His foot slipped back to the floor. 'Come on,' he said, bending to put his shoe back on. 'Let's get out of here.'

He paid while I waited outside on the pavement next to the barking dog. It was a cockerpoo: fluffy and blond and desperate. I stroked its head, and it pulled at the leash to lick my hand, its mouth suddenly wide and wet. Its tail wagged. You and me both, I thought.

He came out then, slipping a card into the top pocket of his jacket. We didn't touch as we walked round the corner to his car. This time he had chosen Dulwich, a residential area several miles from where I lived. It should have been far enough from home to feel safe, and yet the geography, the hardware of the streets, was too familiar: the bossy suburban signage with its parking restrictions and limited zones; the rows of Victorian villas with their off-street parking and basement conversions, the safety-netted giant trampolines you could see, beyond the double sitting rooms, hulked up in their gardens. I was convinced I was being watched, felt eyes on my back like a vibration. The bedroom windows in every house glinted.

Richard didn't care. I was beginning to suspect it was part of the thrill for him: the suburban setting, the risk. When we reached his car – a black Mercedes with tinted windows – he kissed me hard against the passenger door, spreading my arms wide with his hands, his jacket falling open, his tie already half undone. He pressed up against me until I thought I might come, or faint, or both. Then, with a click of his key, he opened the door and pushed me in. There was a comedy moment while we fiddled about trying to extend the seat, lying it almost flat, and then he was in too, bearing down on me, door closed, my skirt yanked to the side, his trousers unzipped, my hands inside the crisp white cotton of his shirt, feeling his skin. Another button flicked and rattled under the seat. My elbow knocked against the gear stick. My neck was tipped back at an angle that was probably painful, though I was beyond pain. I was aware of the half-open car door, of the public nature of this, that I should do something to stop it. But I didn't. I abandoned myself to torment, and pleasure, an explosion of senses, an abnegation of self. Nothing in that moment – no anxiety, no unhappiness, no guilt – mattered but this.

I'd known Richard Taylor for eight years, and had been sleeping with him for three months. He had been an early client at Ekelund – I'd helped launch his first organic pizzeria, long before it was the successful chain it is now. Our relationship was complicated from the start, not flirtatious so much as edgy. I fell for him despite the fact he wasn't my type – too tall, too broad, too alpha. I seemed to prefer men with neuroses. But something about his self-confidence, the way in which he funnelled his power into playfulness – he was always sitting on the edge of someone's desk – led to a crush. Ruby, my assistant, warned me off him. He had a terrible reputation with women, she said. He was bad news. And, although I caught him looking at me broodingly once or twice, it was only when he took me out to celebrate my engagement, raised his glass, gazing at my mouth, and toasted 'what might have been', that I realised the attraction had been mutual.

When he rang me in March and invited me up to his office for a conversation, I was flattered. Someone, I thought, remembers my way with a digital marketing solution. I dry-cleaned my old Joseph trousers, bought a new top to cover the straining waist, dusted off my notebook and trotted up to the West End.

It didn't happen then, or the next time, or the time after. He was patient, I'll give him that. He toyed with my insecurities, boosted my confidence, pretended to listen to my ideas. Each meeting spiralled a little closer – a bit less work, better lighting, more booze. He took me to Nobu, and asked me if I was happy.

'Yes, of course.'

'You don't sound it. I always feel with you – no, it doesn't matter. It's not my place to say.'

'What?'

'As if something was missing.'

I tried not to think too hard. I said, 'I miss work, it's true, and the office.'

'Why don't you go back? Ekelund would have you like a shot.'

'It's important to me to be at home. I want my son to have as happy, as perfect, a childhood as possible.'

'Like yours?'

I didn't answer.

'Really, perfection is over-rated.'

When later he pinioned me with his eyes, and told me he wanted to take me to bed, I laughed as if I thought he was joking. I told him I couldn't show my body to my husband, let alone someone new.

His gaze didn't waver, but his tone was casual. 'I want to fuck you, not undress you,' he said.

When I wonder why I succumbed, I think back to our last day in Greece. Marcus and I sat in our usual spot on the local beach, high up from the water, close to the boats. It was pebbly and you had to be careful not to sit on tar. There was a smell of fish and a couple of plastic bags had caught on the rocks. A few feet away, someone had left a used nappy.

I hadn't been in the water at all, too anxious to leave Josh, but because we were leaving and I realised it was my last opportunity, I waded painfully over the stones, avoiding the sea urchins, until I was out to my waist. Then, ignoring the instinct to recoil, eased myself slowly down, feeling the water hit – the twin sensations of shock and relief. I swam out until Marcus and Josh were small distant figures, and turned over and floated on my back. My mind, which had been knotted with worry, tense with the effort of keeping my son safe, rushing from the dangers of the beach to the risk-strewn journey home, rearranged itself. I stopped brooding and fretting and planning how to make things right. I lay back, my hair brushing in strands against my face, my body opening like a flower, and surrendered to the sea, to forces beyond myself.

I was early to pick up Josh so I sat in the car down the road from his nursery, listening to a report about identity theft on Radio 4. How easily, it seemed, someone could creep inside your life and pretend to be you. Vigilance was all. 'Your identity is one of your most valuable assets,' said a spokesman from the Fraud Squad at the City of London police. 'Make sure you take the necessary precautions.'

I switched off the radio. I hadn't been vigilant. I hadn't taken the necessary precautions. All that work I had put in to create the right identity, all those PR skills I had deployed, spinning the story, perfecting the image – the good wife, the perfect mother – and how close I was to the whole thing crumbling to pieces. I could be revealed for what I was: lust and darkness, ripped clothes, side streets. A woman, a *mother*, who was not to be trusted, not even with what mattered most.

At the edge of my skull, humming deep in the bone, was

the memory of that morning in Greece. The heat of it; the blinding shine of the water, like mercury, as Marcus's boat slid through it; a rope untangling under my feet, thick and wet, like a tail; the sting of the sand between my toes. The sudden darkness of the restaurant; the corridor; the toilet where I had changed; the tang of urine and bleach. Music playing: Simon and Garfunkel. And the scratch of the seat against my bare thighs where I had sat, speaking to Richard, my fingers toying with a piece of loose wicker, my cheek against the phone, my thumb touching my lower lip, as my son wandered alone down the beach.

A wild fluttering started up in my chest. I found it suddenly hard to breathe. I rubbed my head back and forth against the seat, felt the desire to bang it up and down, to feel sharp pain.

Rose walked past the car. I slunk down in the seat. Nell, her three-month-old, must have stirred or let out a cry, because she stopped to rearrange one of her legs at the bottom of the sling, and then used her thumb to separate her cheek from a fold of the fabric, and when she raised her head, she saw me. I forced myself to make an enthusiastic half-waving gesture to show I'd be a minute, then folded myself forward, fiddling around in the foot-well, pretending to be getting something from my bag.

I waited until she had joined the others in the forecourt of the church hall – mothers and carers, au pairs, several fathers, a clatter of Bugaboos and Micro Scooters, and bikes with baby seats, and Babboe cargo trailers: all the usual clobber. I got out of the car, composing my face, before walking towards them. She was talking to Patrick, a stay-at-home dad, and Yasmeen, a newspaper columnist who had recently moved into my street. It was normally one of my favourite moments of the day. Nursery pick-up: that moment of condensed social interaction you come to appreciate when you have a small child, the joy of being without your infant for a few more moments, sweetened further by the anticipation of seeing them.

I felt everyone's eyes on me as I pushed open the gate.

'Look at you!' Yasmeen said. 'All dressed up!'

'Oh.' I should have changed. Yasmeen was wearing shorts and Birkenstocks, Rose was in stripy dungarees and a yellow crop top: her usual charity shop chic. In my high-heeled wedges and denim mini-skirt, I was absurdly overdressed. I looked like ... what? *Like a woman who has just met her lover for sex in the back of a car.* Perspiration made my face feel moist, my underarms sticky. My shirt was missing a button. 'Meeting with a prospective client.'

'Was it blissful?' Rose asked.

Blood rushed into my cheeks. 'What?'

'The holiday?'

'Oh, the holiday. Yes! Sorry. I'm all over the place. Bit knackered. But yes. Yes, it was great.'

'Look,' Yasmeen said. 'This'll make you laugh.' She fiddled with her phone and held it out. It was a YouTube video that had been doing the rounds. I watched dutifully, pretending it was new to me. A woman lay in the bath, drinking wine and eating doughnuts, ignoring – she told us – the washing-up and the laundry. 'Priorities, ladies,' she drawled. 'My kids will benefit more from a semi-calm mom who's in a good mood than they will from a clean house.' I made laughing noises. Yasmeen was gulping along. 'It's good, isn't it?' she said.

'Yes. Yes, it's very good.'

Patrick leant in. 'Does that give one licence for anything?' he said. 'I'm not much of a bath and doughnut man. Would my wife benefit from a semi-calm Patrick were I to find other sources of happiness? A quick daytime bonk with next door's au pair – would that be all right?' He let out a honking laugh.

'Oh shut up, Patrick,' Rose said. She widened her eyes at me. I felt myself flush again.

Miss Jenny opened the door of the church hall then, her charges lined up behind her in their blue and white checked smocks. Josh was trailing at the back of the queue, mucking about with another boy. It took a while for the queue to unravel and when he finally reached the front, he barrelled out, his hair sticking up on top, his cheeks pink. He was clutching a brown piece of paper which was almost as big as he was. 'Can I have a snake?' he said. 'A real one. A yellow one, or a pink one. I don't mind.'

'Have you done a picture?' I said, smoothing his damp fringe from his hot forehead. He was flesh and blood, soft-cheeked, bruised-shinned. He was the picture of health. He was *alive*.

'It's "My Holiday".'

I kissed his cheek, breathing in the smell of him, poster paint and pencil sharpenings.

Rose joined us and we walked along the road, towards my car. Chloe and Josh tore ahead, grabbing little bits of hedge as they passed. It was warm and dry, the air full of dust and pollen, and little bits of privet.

'Holiday not that good then?' she said after a moment.

'Nah.'

'I thought something was up. Was it not the bonding exercise you were hoping for?'

'Not really.'

She paused and bent her head forwards to tighten the pair of small plaits she had braided at the back of her hair. Nell stirred.

'Anything in particular, or just the usual domestics? It's not like you get a proper break with a small child, is it?'

I looked across at her. She looked tired – the tops of her cheeks were pink and slightly puffy. The initials of her children hung on a chain around her neck.

I wondered how much I could tell her.

'It was a disaster really, right from the beginning,' I said and told her about the horrors of that first morning, how I had come out of the taverna and seen Josh in the water.

'Oh my God,' she said. 'What was Marcus doing?'

A weight settled in my stomach, the muscles contracted. 'He'd fallen asleep.'

As soon as I'd said the words, saw the shock on her face, I felt the exhilarating rushing freedom of it. It *was* Marcus's fault. The fact that I had rung Richard was irrelevant. I'd left him in charge. I'd trusted him. 'I thought Josh was dead,' I said. 'I heard the words in my head: "I am a mother with a dead child."'

'You poor thing.' Her mouth had dropped. 'Thank God he was all right.'

'Yeah. A man dived in and pulled him out. Not Marcus.' I shook my head, with a little sarcastic laugh. 'He didn't even get his chest wet.' I turned my face away, remembering how shrivelled and pathetic Marcus had looked, shoulders hunched together, the water like socks halfway up his calves, how diminished he had seemed in my eyes.

'I can imagine how that might have caused tension between you.' She raised her eyebrows. 'Thank God for the other man, eh?'

We reached the car. Josh and Chloe had sat down on the pavement and were feeding stones through the grate of a drain.

'Yes, it wasn't great after that. We tried – we were both doing our best. But it was strained. It would help if he talked to me about work. I know he's worried. But it's like I don't count any more, as if he's forgotten I've got a brain. He won't be straight with me. He's spinning the whole time. We both are. Pretending.'

'Did you at least find anyone to chum up with? Other couples or families? It always helps on holiday, I find, to have alternative forms of entertainment.'

'No, not really. Well – except . . .' I swallowed, found my hand at my mouth, my fingers twisting the middle of my upper lip. 'We saw the guy who rescued Josh a couple of times. We met up . . . here and there.'

'That's nice.'

'Yes.' I nodded, averting my eyes so she wouldn't see I was lying.

We *had* seen Dave again during the holiday, both times at the port. We'd been walking back from the beach the first time, late afternoon, and Marcus had spotted him outside the bar next to the small supermarket in the square. Josh was fretful and I had steered the buggy to the other side of the road. We had waved – Dave had made a gesture like a salute. A couple of days later we saw him again – same bar, but this time we pretended we hadn't seen him and we kept walking, both of us keen, I think, to avoid him. I wished we hadn't now. I was sure he had spotted us, and it must have looked rude. He had asked since then to be my friend on Facebook, and I should probably respond, but so far I'd ignored him.

I knew I was behaving badly, that I should be bending over backwards to express my gratitude for what he had done. Rose wouldn't understand. I didn't really understand it myself.

'Josh – do you want to stop doing that?'

'Yeah. Chloe, stop it. You're getting mucky.'

The two children stared up at us, then at each other and giggled. Josh studied his fingers, which were smeared with dirt. He looked back at Chloe and wiped his hands on his

45

ıloe picked up a leaf and tried to poke that through
: instead.

ou think he might be having an affair?'

When I looked up, Rose's mouth was pinched together in
an odd way, as if she already regretted having asked. The
colour had drained from my cheeks. I turned away to click
open the car door with my key.

'Who? Marcus?' I said. 'No. I don't think so.'

'I'm sorry. I shouldn't have said that. It was just Patrick
earlier. You know, a lot of men do.'

I did know. Firstdate.com was a client at Ekelund. I'd seen
the research – a high proportion of men who signed up
were married and looking for a bit on the side. And I'd been
there when Jeff, Marcus's partner, was caught pissing
around with his assistant. Men had affairs all the time. Was
it so different for women? No it wasn't. Both were as
unforgivable.

I hauled Josh to his feet and persuaded him into the car. As
I buckled him up, I imagined I could tell Rose what I had got
myself caught up in, and that she would make it all right, or at
least give her advice. I would tell her what I had done.

I turned back, the words on my lips, but in that moment she
lowered her chin to kiss Nell, rubbing her lower lip across the
fuzzy nap of her perfect little head, and I realised that I
couldn't.

It was busy in the supermarket car park – vehicles reversing,
sounding their horns, jammed in at angles: that toxic urban
combination of irritation and panic. A space finally came free
at the far end and, once I'd managed to secure it, I thought
about leaving Josh alone in his seat while I crossed the lot to
get a ticket. How long would I be? One minute? Two? Three
at a push? Too long. I couldn't risk it.

I unstrapped him and carried him over on my hip to save time. He struggled to get down and I used my body to keep him between me and the machine while I fiddled with the coins. The first pound was rejected, and then a second. I shifted along to the other machine. Three cars were queuing alongside us, wheels turning, the drivers' eyes scanning for spaces. I was breathless when I finally finished with the stress of keeping Josh from running out between them.

When we reached the entrance to the shop, I realised I should have found a trolley and put him in that before getting a ticket. He'd have been secure then.

I felt a wave of despondent self-hatred. I seemed to spend my life making mistakes like that. I was always trying to do things the right way and failing.

We'd come to buy food for supper. The Ottolenghi cookbook I'd ordered had arrived while we were away. I'd chosen a chicken dish. The list of ingredients was complicated – it included arak, whatever that was – and supermarkets are not forgiving of the hopeless housewife, particularly one bearing a hungry, over-tired child in a trolley-seat. As I wheeled him along the aisles, Josh started reaching for items at random: a bag of beansprouts, an extra-large package of currants, a bottle of Pimm's from a display entitled 'Refreshing Summer'. I felt my jaw tighten, tension stiffening my shoulders.

The thoughts circled in my head. Why couldn't I do this? Why was I unable to complete a simple task like shopping? My terrible housekeeping used to be a joke between us, but after Josh was born, something changed: even I assumed that once I was at home all day I would just do it, as if I'd known how to do it all along and had just been pretending. Now a voice whispered, *Who do you think you are? Stick to the Vesta Chow Mein and the tinned ravioli you grew up on. What are you trying to prove? Give up now.*

I was at the back of the shop when I decided it would be quicker to park him. It would only be for a minute, I told myself. I'd been too cautious out in the car park. We had been to the supermarket so many times. Nothing awful had ever happened here before. Why should it now? I tucked the trolley into one side of the butcher's counter, the side touching the glass of the cabinet. And I made sure I could hear him, his sweetly reedy voice singing 'Wheels on the Bus' above the clatter of metal, the beep of tills, the hum of refrigerated cabinets. I was held up by the cereals, helping an elderly gentleman reach for the last packet of All Bran from the back of the high shelf, and he did go quiet then, but I didn't think anything of it.

When I turned the corner of dried goods, the trolley wasn't quite where I'd left it. It was away from the butcher display in the middle of the aisle now, at an odd angle. Josh had been spun in a different direction; he had his back to me. He wasn't singing and his shoulders were hunched forwards. The light in the ceiling above his head was flickering.

I had this strange feeling as I ran towards him that I'd find somebody else's child in my trolley. Madness: it was Josh's blue and white gingham smock. Josh's mop of hair. 'I'm back,' I said, turning the trolley round while throwing the chicken thighs and the fennel seeds and the clementines into the metal cage behind him.

He twisted to look at me. It was Josh. Of course it was Josh. But he was clutching a huge Toblerone, one of the big bars you find in Duty Free, and chocolate was smeared over his face, across his cheeks, on his chin. He grinned sheepishly up at me. His teeth were brown and gloopy, a big half-chewed chunk still in his mouth.

'Where did you get that?'

'It's mine.'

I tried to get it out of his hand. He had ripped off the top of it, but hadn't peeled away the silver wrapping. It was mangled and chocolatey, pocked with teeth marks. He pulled back.

I looked around. At the meat counter, a young man in a grey hat and apron was chopping a rack of lamb with a cleaver.

'Give it to me!' I said.

I tried to pry it from his hand, finger by finger; he began to scream.

The butcher looked up. A woman steering a trolley past us turned her head. She smiled sympathetically.

'It doesn't belong to you,' I said calmly. 'Did you take it? Where did you get it?'

I was holding it away from him now; he had started crying. 'I didn't take it. The man gave it to me.'

'What man?' I looked around, at the shoppers with their trolleys and baskets, past the butcher to the fishmonger, who was weighing a large piece of bright yellow haddock, holding it up by its tail.

'What man?' I said again.

'It's a present. It's mine.'

He twisted in his seat, trying to reach for it and I took a step back. Behind the meat counter was a bin and, when asked, the butcher took it from me and dropped it in.

Looking back, that was the first incident. The first inexplicable thing. It was trivial. It might have been nothing. And yet it was weird enough to unsettle us both. And in fact the very triviality of it made it more slippery, harder to grasp, or discuss with anyone else. It just left us with a creeping sense of unease.

'And you're sure he didn't take it from the shelves?'

'No. We were miles from the confectionery aisle. We hadn't been down it. And even if we had, they don't stock that kind of Toblerone. It's the first thing I did – go and check.'

'He hadn't just taken the last bar?'

'No. They don't *stock* it. I found an assistant and asked. They only sell the small multi-packs, not the big ones.'

Marcus leant back in his chair. 'You asked him, did you? No one gave it to him at nursery? He could have had it on him since then.'

'I'd have noticed. You know, it was a big bar.'

'But you asked him?'

'Yes. Of course I did. He wouldn't stop crying and then he wouldn't say. You can't exactly interrogate him. He's three.'

'Someone must have given it to him in the supermarket.'

'Exactly. And who would do that? Who would give a child a huge bar of chocolate?'

'Well, people give children chocolate all the time . . .'

'Yes, but not like this. You've got to admit it's bizarre.'

'It is. It's bizarre. But you left him unsupervised for how long?'

I let a beat pass. 'It wasn't long, Marcus. A few minutes.'

He gave me a level look, heavy with import, his brows wrinkled.

I felt a need to defend myself. 'I really don't think a few minutes in a supermarket is even remotely comparable to falling asleep when your child is near water.'

He loosened his tie, grasping the knot in his fist and yanking it from side to side a couple of times, as if it had been restricting his breathing. 'Well at least he's safe.' He picked up his knife and fork and then immediately laid them down again, at a neat angle. 'Just one of those odd things.'

He had finished his green beans, but left the orange pieces and the fennel and most of the chicken.

'You haven't eaten very much.'

'I'm not terribly hungry. I'm sorry. But it was delicious. Absolutely amazing.' Each compliment was a tiny dagger. 'Top nosh. Thank you.'

'It's nothing like the picture.' I pushed my own plate away. 'It's dry, isn't it? I overcooked it.'

'It's *exquisite*.'

'It's not exquisite.' I wished he would be honest. I would feel less pressure if he weren't always going on about things being perfect. It was a game between us, I realised. I spun the story; he bought it.

'No, it's just I had a big lunch. Um, the Russians were in. They wanted to celebrate. We went to The Wolseley.'

He felt guilty – I could tell by the way he was talking, the small flicks of his head. And because he felt guilty I had a nasty need to make it worse. 'You don't mind being seen in public with them then?'

'They're actually quite sophisticated. I know you think they're thugs. But Olaf went to Durham and Dimitri studied Economics at the LSE.'

He stood up and took both our plates over to the sink, ran them under the tap and placed them inside the dishwasher. He paused to re-stack Josh's bowl and cup which I had chucked in earlier. His movements were overly neat, like the precision of his speech. I knew what was wrong now, what was behind the exaggerated facial gestures, the oddness in his speech; he was still, very slightly, drunk.

His mobile phone went and he lunged across the room to retrieve it from his jacket pocket. 'Ah! Mary,' he said. His head was bent and his free hand was kneading his forehead.

I did the washing-up and then I went out into the garden to unpeg the laundry.

It was warm out, still; the sun bursting orange across the vast window of next-door's loft extension. I could smell the synthetic smoulder of a barbecue a few doors down; hear the pick-pock of the table tennis table in the garden that backed on to ours. When Josh was older we'd get a ping-pong table.

And a trampoline. (With a safety net, of course.) It's what people like us did. It's what a perfect family life looked like.

In the shadows, tiny flies whirled. I'd left the sprinkler on to water the flower bed under the cherry tree, and a couple of blackbirds were hopping about, beaks pecking at the earth, up and down, like a wooden toy Josh used to have, where you pulled a string to make the birds' heads move.

How much we had. It had never occurred to me I would have so much.

I didn't deserve it.

'Have the certificates been suspended?' Marcus, still on the phone, had come to stand in the kitchen door.

I watched him.

The first time I met him was in a focus group. I was the account ex and he was the new assistant, older than average; he'd begun a law conversion and given it up. I liked the look of him, with his handsome speccy face, his floppy hair, the habit he had of clearing his throat with his fist in front of his mouth. But it was his concentration that intrigued me; there's a lot of bullshit in our business, but Marcus had an ability to get to the nub of what mattered. 'It's the wrong consistency,' he said to one of the testers, as if he really cared what she thought. 'Who wants to drink melted ice cream?' The tester, who had been painfully shy, laughed.

'And what about Unilever? Have they announced their position?' he continued now. He was absent-mindedly scraping at the wall with his fingernail.

I gathered up the basket of clothes – dry now and smelling faintly of firelighter – and walked past him into the house. I piled the items in the ironing basket, and I tidied up Josh's Lego, which I had failed to do earlier, too busy with the chicken and the arak. Then I poured myself a glass of rosé. I felt the tension in my shoulders ease; I'd got through another day.

Marcus finished the call and tapped the phone in the palm of his hand a few times, gazing out into the garden. He seemed to have forgotten I was there. When he was first setting up on his own, he used to talk to me all the time.

When he still didn't say anything, I said: 'Work?'

He thumbed an email or a text and then put the phone in his pocket, looked up, saw me watching.

'Oh, God, yes. Boring.'

'Not to me, remember.'

'Yes, of course.' He breathed in slowly through his nose, and then exhaled from between his teeth, releasing the air in repeated tuts – either at the situation, or at me for asking about it. 'We've got a bit of a Tilly Elworthy crisis – to do with palm oil and Greenpeace and orang-utans. She's going to have to get out of Indonesia, look into alternative sources.'

'What about looking into her corporate responsibility programme? There's bound to be an opportunity to—'

He cut me off. 'Listen, I'm knackered. I'm going to hit the sack. Maybe watch Netflix in bed. It's been a long old day.'

He left the room, and I stood there for a moment, and then I locked the back door and switched off the lights before following him upstairs. He was already sitting propped against the pillows, in his boxers and white T-shirt, laptop open and glasses on. 'So,' he said absent-mindedly, his index finger giving the mouse-pad quick strokes. 'Those trainers; I think I've tracked them down.'

'What trainers?'

'The Superstars. The ones Dave Jepsom lost saving our son.'

A cold flash. Images across my eyelids. Josh's arm, his white face. The waves turning his orange armband. The sound of my own scream. Dave Jepsom looking at me across the table.

'He didn't lose them. He threw them in the water.'

'White leather with a flash of house-check across the heel. They're called Retford. Fuck.'

'What?'

'They're expensive. £295. They've got them on Mr Porter. Size 11s still in stock. He said he was size 11. I heard him say that, and I filed it away.' He gave his forehead a little one-two-three tap. 'Not just a pretty face.'

'Who would choose trainers with a Burberry trim?'

'It's not a matter of taste.'

'How do you know where to send them?' I said.

'I found his work address on LinkedIn. Jepsom Solutions, Catford. We'll just get them delivered, with a thank-you note.'

'I thought he was in construction?'

'Clearly he's a construction solutioner.'

He was trying to make me laugh, but I didn't. I was thinking about the way Dave had caught my eye when we'd seen him in the port. I thought again about the Facebook request. Why would he have made contact with me in that way?

'It's a nice idea,' I said eventually, 'but let's not. Let's just leave it. It was wonderful what he did, but it's over now. We bought him – and his entire family – lunch. That's enough, isn't it?'

He closed his laptop and folded up his glasses. 'You're right. I'm sorry I mentioned it.'

Him

It was mad-busy at work. I wasn't complaining. It's how it had to be if we were to make any money at all. There were only eleven of us at Hawick Nicholson: as crisis management is our business, you could argue if we weren't on the edge of our seat we weren't doing our job. It was still an upward struggle. Ideally we'd be located in Shoreditch or the West End, addresses providing, in their separate ways, the right sort of kudos, but we were tucked away in a small street in Victoria. The building, a 1960s shop conversion, was as unprepossessing on the inside (open plan, highly chaotic) as it was on the outside, with the exception of the ground-floor reception, which was space-age bright and white, with bamboo plants in Japanese lacquered pots, a series of close-up photographs of waves and a wall-mounted television which played twenty-four-hour CNN. There was a desk and a chair, but we had a buzzer not an actual receptionist. Appearance, as they say, is all.

That Monday morning, my partner Jeff sidled over to my desk where I was frantically catching up on emails. Seven years older than me, short, sweaty and louche, he pretended not to care about much. That day he was looking unusually well turned out: closely shaved, red socks under his wide pinstriped trousers, a new white shirt.

'You're late in,' he said, leaning backwards against the desk, waving across the room to Emma, the youngest of our account executives, who happened to be young and blonde.

'Trains were fucked.'

'Should have driven. You still cocking about in that lady's Fiat? When are you going to get yourself a proper man's car? Something with a bit more status, a bit more muscular?'

'When we pay ourselves more, mate.'

'Holiday OK? Manage to rekindle love's young dream?'

At that moment, Gail, my assistant, called us into the weekly status meeting, and after that I was tied up with Emma, getting an update on our social media presence. I didn't get a chance to answer his question until we were in a taxi to The Wolseley where we were having lunch with clients. I gave him a quick run-down, basically a list of my miserable failings, including my near fatal inability to look after my son, and Tessa's rising irritation with me. Jeff, leaning back in his seat with a self-satisfied air, told me that was natural. 'All family time is misery. Competitive hell. You're engaged in a constant battle with each other as to who is having the worst time. It's an endurance test. All you have to do is stick it out 'til the kid's eighteen.'

'I notice *you* didn't stick it out,' I said. Jeff and Linda had split up five years before, shortly after she found someone else's underwear in their washing machine.

'That's different.' We pulled up outside the restaurant and he leant through the window to pay. 'You and Tess are another story. You're worth it.' He gave a little Jennifer Aniston L'Oréal pout to prove his point.

Olaf Petrov and Dimitri Mikhailov, the joint CEOs of KazNeft, were hunched at a corner table, but they expanded their shoulders when they saw us, gestured us over with shrugs and waves of the hand, curls of their lips, extravagant welcomes. A bottle of Krug was already cooling in its metal bucket. Both men were tall and slim and muscular – they spent a lot of time in hotel gyms – and were always immaculately dressed. Olaf, who was less conventionally handsome with a swarthier complexion and hooded eyes, particularly liked to dress like an English gentleman. Today he was in a pale grey three-piece suit.

I was tense in their company. Jeff, too, I think, which explained the shave and the clean shirt. We weren't in a position to turn down new business, even if this one did make us both uneasy. Something wasn't quite right. They were an oil company, but the details were unclear – sometimes they talked about pipelines, other times 'the refinery' – and they'd hired us to handle their media training, thanks to Jeff's years as an advisor for Number 10. (He, and the prime minister, may have left under a cloud, but it was a role that still gave us a lot of clout abroad.) They had hinted at more work in the future, 'a greater involvement', and it felt as if every interaction was some kind of initiation test.

At first, it was all smiles and chit-chat. Dimitri had read about 'Real Tennis' in the BA magazine and wished for the rules to be explained. We discussed a speech Dimitri was giving the following week, and an interview Olaf had offered an industry magazine. Olaf mentioned a top oil exec who had just died in a car crash in Moscow. 'You have to be careful in our business,' he said, 'there are dangers at every corner. It is not for the faint of heart.' I felt his eyes on me as if he were looking for my reaction, and I pulled my mouth down, nodding my head, concerned and yet unfazed.

And then the waiter came to take our order. Dimitri wanted the Wolseley Fish Stew, which was advertised as a Thursday special. It was Monday and the waiter suggested politely that it might be impossible. Dimitri asked with exaggerated courtesy to speak to the manager. The manager scooted over and agreed almost immediately to ask the chef to make an exception.

Dimitri's peremptory tone, his sense of entitlement, was embarrassing enough, but when the food arrived – the fish stew in its own little pot, crowned with parsley – he sent it away. 'I'll have the fishcakes like my friend here,' he said, pointing at my plate.

I turned my head, wincing apologetically at the waiter, and to hide my discomfort I began talking about the psychology of menus. Tessa and I had done a lot of that, with Richard Taylor and all those other catering clients, when we were still at Ekelund. I rabbited on about unjustified text and missing pound signs, about the special boxes to draw the eye to high-profit items and how, in this case, the fillet steak at £28.75 might just as well be a dummy item to make the Filet de Boeuf au poivre, £24.50, appear cheap.

Dimitri leant back to retrieve the bottle of Krug, poured us all another glass, returned the bottle and then clicked his fingers for the waiter. 'My friend will have the fillet steak,' he said.

'No. No. I'm fine,' I said, pushing my empty plate to one side. 'The fishcakes were very filling. I've had plenty.'

'I am not a victim of extremeness aversion, as I believe that sort of psychology is called,' he said, smiling. 'The tendency to avoid choosing options that are at one extreme or the other – that is not my style. I prefer taking risks. As I hope you do too.'

Jeff caught my eye across the table, held it, a muscle ticking in his jaw, and when the steak arrived I ate it.

I had no choice. It was too late. It was a message. He was showing me he knew I looked down on his behaviour – my wince at the waiter had not gone unnoticed – and this was my punishment. I had lectured him on a topic with which he was already familiar; I had assumed ignorance; he was not to be under-estimated.

We shook hands in the middle of Piccadilly, watched by a couple of heavies. Dimitri and Olaf were in town for another month; we had a meeting scheduled soon. They were both all smiles. Dimitri clasped his arm around my back and pulled me to him. I heard the smack of his lips in my ear. For all his charm and conviviality, we were at the interface of something much darker and unknowable.

I couldn't wait to get home that evening, but if I had hoped to be cheered up, I was to be disappointed. Tessa perched opposite me, watching me eat. I still felt biliously full – the food and the champagne, the Armagnac. I decided not to tell her about what had happened. It seemed so foolish in retrospect, so small of me to have been bullied like that. She'd have told me to extricate myself from the relationship; she hadn't approved of me taking them on in the first place. Anyway, she was wrapped up in the domestic trivialities of her own day – upset because a stranger in the supermarket had given Josh some chocolate. I tried to ape an interest, and then changed the subject. Our new neighbours: Yasmeen and Simon, both journalists; I'd bumped into her out running a couple of weeks before and invited them to supper. It was this Friday. Rose and Pete were coming too.

'What shall I cook?' she said.

I looked over to the shelf of cookbooks. There was yet another brand new tome open on the counter. 'Anything,' I said. 'Something easy. I told them it was kitchen supper.'

'What's a kitchen supper?'

I smiled at her, touched as ever by the gaps in her knowledge. 'It's like home cooking but better. Relaxed, but perfect.'

There was a pause before she said, 'Fuck.'

Mary, one of our account directors, called from the office when we were still sitting in the kitchen. Tilly Elworthy was in a state. Greenpeace had just issued a statement condemning the destruction of rainforest in Indonesia – which is where she sourced the palm oil for her cosmetics. Bill Hayes, her CEO, had told her to sit tight, but she wasn't happy. I had a soft spot for Tilly; she'd been our first client, a start-up herself, when Jeff and I had ventured out on our own, but she could be a little hot-headed. Still, Mary suggested it would be better to find a new supplier – perhaps Nigeria? – particularly if Unilever and Procter & Gamble cancelled their contracts. I agreed.

I hung up and stood still for a few seconds, thinking things through. My eyes rested on Josh's latest painting, which was stuck with a magnet on the fridge. 'Our Holiday', it said along the bottom in teacher's writing. It was crude, but you could just about make out a sandcastle and a small stick figure on top of it. Two figures, Tessa and I presumably, were on opposite sides.

I twisted my head. From that angle, it looked different. The shape in the middle, I realised, wasn't supposed to be a sandcastle. It was a figure. I studied it for a few moments, trying to make sense of it. He had painted a small person on top of a larger person, with two other people in the distance watching. It wasn't a happy family scene Josh had chosen to record, but the moment of his own rescue.

Tessa was talking to me, but I couldn't focus. Poor Josh; he must have been traumatised by the experience. It was massive. I felt a fresh flood of gratitude towards Dave, immediately followed by discomfort. We hadn't done right by him. We'd bought him lunch, yes, but we should have joined him in the bar when we saw him the following day. We should have gone over and invited him up to the villa for a drink, but Josh was crying and Tessa wasn't keen, and the moment had passed. But we should have done. And the next time – what were we thinking when we hid from him? He was sure to have seen us. It was so rude, and unfriendly. He saved our son.

I went up to the bedroom and got ready for bed. I wished there were something we could do – not to thank him so much, but to make amends. As I sat on the bed and unlaced my shoes, I remembered the trainers, the Superstars that had been lost in the sea. Burberry trim. I pulled out my laptop and trawled about until I located a website, Mr Porter, that sold them – satisfyingly expensive; they would do.

Of course Tessa didn't agree, but I ignored that.

When I got to work on Tuesday, I arranged for them to be delivered direct to his office, Unit 53, Moffat Road Business Park, SE6. I looked up the address on Street View – a bland, unprepossessing sprawl of lock-ups and corrugated-fronted 1960s warehouse buildings. I requested a covering note: 'You're right – one is no good without the other. Here are two. With thanks and apologies, Josh and family.'

The rest of the week had its usual knots and stickiness. The palm oil situation turned nasty when a group of London sixth-formers somehow – God knows how – got wind of Tilly's Indonesian connection, and picketed Selfridges. Mary worked with Tilly on a Twitter statement that apologised from the bottom of her heart, proclaimed her affection for the Indonesian orang-utan, and gave away a free Perfect Pout nourishing lip balm for the first 100 retweets. Emma started a #beautyontheinside campaign on Instagram, involving pictures of random acts of apparent kindness within the animal kingdom (two lions rescuing an injured fox, that kind of thing), and by day two, the sixth-formers had slowly trickled back to their common rooms.

What else? Ron McCready, the racetrack owner, was stopped for speeding, which would have been almost funny if I'd stopped to think about it, but I didn't. And the 7Night Group, a chain of motels we were helping reposition, kicked off when they saw the final guest list of a press trip we'd organised. Mary tried to sweet-talk them, but in the end, I took the meeting myself. Of course they wanted *Condé Nast Traveller*, the *Sunday Times*, I argued: we *all* did. Nobody just wanted *Hotels and Motels Today*. But you have to be realistic in this game – which high-end journo is going to want to be shipped out to a motor lodge on the M40, even if Ilse Crawford has consulted on the design?

It didn't go well.

But it was at the end of the week when there were the first stirrings of trouble with our biggest client. McPhee Judd International had recently won the contract to excavate a deep-water port in King Abdullah's planned Economic City in Saudi. On Friday morning, someone calling themselves DigOutTheDirt began tweeting veiled aspersions about their business practices and by lunchtime a reporter from *The Economist* was on the phone asking questions. Fact is, we all knew Tony Judd had greased a few palms, but it's a fine line in the Middle East between bribery and 'facilitation payments'.

I had an uneasy feeling that I was responsible for the rumours. I'd told someone recently about MJI's activities, though I knew I hadn't mentioned any names. It seemed like a nasty coincidence, and reminded me how important it was to keep one's gob shut.

We worked quickly to divert the story with positive news of our own. Basty, the account executive, commissioned an infographic on cubic metres of earth shifted in worldwide construction projects, and threw a series of digger-against-sunset photos on Instagram. Noah came up with an idea for a company-wide Wear Purple Day for bowel cancer. 'Find a disaster somewhere,' I said, as I left the office. 'Get those hydraulic excavators doing some good charitable works. Hasn't there been an earthquake we can exploit? Haiti? Or Bangladesh: there's always shit going down there.'

What with one thing and another, I could have done without dinner on Friday. It was one of the drawbacks of owning your own business, always having to be on the alert, but it was too late to cancel. And anyway, a Sunday columnist and a *Guardian* editor on the doorstep was too good an opportunity to pass up. At Wandsworth Common, where I left the train, I made a short detour up to the Sainsbury's by the traffic lights, and bought six bottles of Peroni, some spearmint gum and ten Marlboro Lights, one of which I smoked on the pavement, looking over the grass and the trees, enjoying the late warmth and the golden pinkness of the June evening before hiding the rest of the packet in my inside jacket pocket. I chewed three strips of Wrigley's as I walked home, masticating hard, really rolling the ball around my mouth, to banish any lingering smell of nicotine. When I reached the house, I took a quick call from Noah who asked if we should change bowel cancer to liver, due to the former's excavation connotations. I agreed. We laughed at our own stupidity. And then I put the key in the front door and let myself in.

A new Diptyque candle ('Baies') was flickering on the shelf in the hall; all the post and detritus that normally piled up there had been cleared away. I could see through to the kitchen, where the lights were dimmed, and out to the garden, where lanterns I hadn't seen before were sparkling across the fence and in the tree. Rumer was crooning through our expensive new Sonos system. The smell was nicely piquant.

Tessa was talking to Josh a floor up – her tone gentle, lilting, as if she were reading him a bedtime story. I took the stairs two at a time, but found Josh alone, sprawled on our bed wearing headphones, watching *Thomas & Friends* on the iPad. I gave him a hug, which he strained to escape. Tessa's voice was coming from the en-suite bathroom. The door was ajar and I pushed it open.

'Hi, honey, I'm home,' I said, American 1950s-style.

A sudden movement of the water.

She was in the bath and she pulled herself quickly together, her knees shooting to meet her chin.

'Sorry, you're on the phone,' I said.

'It's OK.' It was hot in there. The mirror was steamed up. Her skin was pink and blotchy, her hair damp about her face.

'Got to go. Speak later,' she said, her tone clipped now. She put the phone on the shelf behind her. 'I didn't hear you,' she said. 'I was just talking to Ruby – catching up, you know.'

I sat gingerly on the edge of the bath and bent to kiss her soapy shoulder, remembering a time when I would have plunged my hands under the water, run them all over her body; we would have kissed, maybe I'd have even let her pull me in.

She bent herself forward, away from me, to reach for the shampoo. 'They'll be here shortly,' she said. 'I hope you've noticed how tidy it is downstairs.'

'Yes I have. I like the new lanterns. Mail order?'

'Cox and Cox.'

'Food smells nice.'

'It's a disaster. I tried to make pork braised with vinegar from the *River Cafe Cook Book* and I burnt it. I had to rush out to Cook.'

Cook was one of her old clients – a frozen-food company that provided room service for several top hotels. I felt a flicker of resentment; it was an expense we could do without. It was baffling, her inability to throw a meal together. She was always trying too hard.

Still, if she'd kept the receipt, I could claim it as a business expense.

'I don't suppose you fancy getting Josh to bed, do you?'

'Sure.'

I stood up, brushed a couple of suds off my trouser leg and went back into the bedroom. It took a while for me to wrest Josh away from the iPad but I finally got him upstairs and into his pyjamas. I read him *The Tiger Who Came to Tea*, a story I've always found a bit creepy with its greedy and potentially dangerous uninvited guest. Josh was sleepy and rested his head on my chest. When it had grown heavy, I carefully extricated myself from beneath him, only then remembering I had forgotten to clean his teeth. Too bad. As long as Tessa didn't find out, it didn't matter. She was the teeth police. In fact, I realised, these days I thought of her as the everything police.

The bedroom was empty when I came back down. I took off my suit, put on my new Paul Smith beige chinos, and a linen paisley Liberty for Uniqlo shirt. I had a quick shave, clearing the mirror with the side of my hand. She'd left her towel in a wet heap on the floor, the shampoo, lidless and trailing its contents, at the bottom of the bath. *Elle Decoration* lay open on the floor. I smiled ruefully to myself. Typical, really. For all her attempts to 'make house', she was unrelentingly messy. Her phone was still on the shelf, and I picked it up. She had a missed call from 'R' – Ruby? I put the phone in my pocket to give back to her.

I was halfway down the stairs when the house phone rang. This was an unusual occurrence – it was either my mother, who rang quite regularly now my father was so confused, or 'an urgent message' from a cold caller. I lunged into the sitting room, and snatched the receiver off its base.

'Hello?'

I thought I could hear breathing but it might just have been air in the wires.

I said hello again and the line went dead.

'Who was that?' called Tessa.

'No one,' I said.

Rose and Pete were the first to arrive. They had brought two bottles of Prosecco from Lidl and we sat in the garden, the four of us, and drank one of them. They were good company, though I am slightly scared of Rose, as I think men often are of their partner's close friends. It was warm and bosky. I remember noticing that the wisteria had flowered for the first time – it had taken three years since we'd planted it. Birds were singing frantically – that dusk chorus that is most often triggered by the presence of cats. Tessa passed around some 'hand-cooked' salt and pepper crisps and Rose, who was looking even more pert and elfin than usual in a purple dress and pointy shoes, said, 'No offence, but I'm so over posh crisps. Am I alone in thinking there is nothing to beat Walkers?' Pete, a tall, broad solicitor at one of the big City firms (I always forget which), wondered what had happened to Golden Wonder and Smith's. And we launched into remembrances of pocket-money treats past: Black Jacks and Fruit Salads, Caramac. I kept my eye on Tessa. There hadn't been many trips to the sweet shop in her childhood.

She had changed after her bath into a halter-neck black dress. Her feet were bare; her toenails ruby red. She wasn't wearing a bra, which made me feel aroused in a maudlin sort of way. She stood up when the bell rang again, and I watched her as she crossed the kitchen and then as she crossed back, towing Yasmeen and Simon, noting the movement of her body, the sway of her breasts as she opened the fridge to find the second bottle of Prosecco, the swing of her hips as she closed it.

The rest of us got to our feet, and kissed, and pumped hands. Yasmeen in heels, a satin sheet of black hair down her back, was more glamorous than her husband, who was short and wearing khaki shorts and a T-shirt with a design on it of two cupped hands, shaped to look like a vagina. 'I know. I know,' he said, tucking shoulder-length hair behind his ears. 'I didn't even realise. Bought it in this trendy shop near the newspaper. Liked the colour. Now I'm going round with a big pussy on my chest. OK, Yas. I know you hate it.' He poked his chin defiantly at Yasmeen, who defiantly poked her chin back. (God, I thought, they still have sex.) 'What do you want me to do? You want me to go home and change?'

'I like a man with a pussy on his chest,' Rose said. 'It sends out my kind of message. You can sit next to me.' She patted the bench next to her.

'Well, maybe I will.' He threw himself down and launched into a self-satisfied moan about the *Guardian* where he was 'responsible for online content'. It was all hell there, he said, cuts and redundancies. He'd be lucky still to have a job at Christmas. 'Well, if you need an employment lawyer,' Rose said, bringing her husband into the conversation, 'you know where to look.'

'I'm always here,' Pete said affably.

Yasmeen was gazing at the back of the house, shuffling her feet a little to the music, while sizing up the proportions of our extension. I saw my moment and sidled over. I might as well get it over with before I got too drunk. She told me they had put in for planning permission. We discussed contractors. They had a second home in Kent and were hoping to 'coax' the 'wonderful Polish builders' they had used down there to do their London work.

I asked her how often she went into the office. 'Never if I can help it!'

'I enjoyed last week's column.' It had been about the tax-dodging practices of multi-national corporation: I'd done my research.

'Thank you.' She inclined her head.

'It's the lack of transparency that's the main issue,' I said, paraphrasing her argument.

'Yes. Exactly,' she agreed.

'I don't know why the government doesn't bring in the right measures. If Starbucks paid the same tax as you or I, it would sort the NHS out in one fell swoop.'

'It would indeed,' she said.

She smiled at me enquiringly, willing me to change the subject, I think.

I took a sip of my drink. 'I do some work for Chris Longridge. Have you ever come across him? He's the CEO of the 7Nights chain; he's always on *Question Time* – they roll him out whenever they want a businessman who'll argue for high corporation tax.'

'Interesting,' she said, sounding not very interested.

I laboured on. 'They're trying to reposition themselves actually, to imitate the success of easyJet. Style and simplicity rather than tacky and cheap.'

'Carolyn McCall, easyJet's chief executive, she used to be CEO of the *Guardian*. Simon!' she called out. 'You used to work with Carolyn McCall, didn't you?'

Simon swivelled. 'Amazing woman,' he said. 'Tough operator.'

I refilled everyone's glasses and then my own, took a swig, felt the bubbles burst at the back of my throat. 'I don't know if you two fancy it,' I said, as casually as I could, 'but we're taking some journos up to try out the 7Nights experience at the flagship lodge, just close to Bicester, and we've had a couple of cancellations.'

Simon said: 'I never get away these days. Press trips are a thing of the past. I can't think of anyone who isn't desk-bound. Though a night away – Yas? We could try and make it work.'

She swept her hair over one shoulder and said, laughing, 'It's not my idea of a *perfect* mini-break.'

I left it there – the seed had been planted, I could do more work later – and swung down to check on Tessa in the kitchen. She was standing in the middle of the room, as if she had forgotten what she was doing there, and I helped with the food, throwing together a quick salad as she seemed not to have thought of that. She took two large ceramic dishes out of the oven, Moroccan Spiced Harissa Chicken and Minted Couscous, and she'd bought some flatbreads and yoghurt to accompany them. 'Hang on,' she said, as I was about to add the bowl of yoghurt to the tray. She opened the fridge, peeled the cellophane lid off a plastic pot, and sprinkled some pomegranate seeds over the top.

'You're a natural,' I said, and was relieved when she laughed.

'Tra-la,' she said, as she carried the food out into the garden, with me bringing up the rear. We were a little harmonious procession – a happy couple who shared the load. Look at us.

Everyone sat anywhere, before Tessa could get out her seating plan.

'This is delicious,' Yasmeen said, as soon as she started eating. 'It's Moroccan, is it?'

'Yup.'

'Do I detect orange-blossom water?'

'Just a drop,' Tessa said, and caught my eye.

The light sharpened and then began slowly to fade; the evening swam and expanded and then settled. Conversation, which had splintered when we first started eating, came together again. Rose was telling a funny story about a fly-on-the-wall documentary they'd filmed at the surgery where she worked when I realised I could hear something above the chatter and the laughter, the music and the clink of glasses. Now I concentrated on it, I picked out an insistent peal, a finger pressed relentlessly on the doorbell. I made a face across the table at Tessa and she shrugged.

I jogged across the kitchen floor and up the steps into the hall, humming to myself. I felt cheered. The evening was a success. Yasmeen had mocked my 7Nights invitation, but she hadn't actually said no. Tessa seemed more relaxed. She'd been grateful for my salad. She had laughed at my joke. Perhaps later, after everyone had left, we might even have sex.

As I opened the door, I was smiling – expecting, I suppose, to see a delivery man with an Amazon package, or a charity collector, or a teenager wanting sponsorship for a fun run.

A person was standing there with a face I recognised, though it was blank and expressionless, and out of context. He was standing slightly too close to the door, one arm leaning on the frame, and he was taller than me, and muscular.

'Hello, Marcus.'

He re-balanced his feet, evenly placed, like a policeman. 'Don't you recognise me?'

It took a moment for the cogs to click into place. Dave Jepsom. *Shit.* 'Hello. Yes. Yes. Hi.'

He was dressed differently, of course, in a button-down navy shirt and stone-washed jeans. The outfit seemed incongruous; in my mind he was frozen in his football shorts and his bare chest. I tried to make a joke about this – 'Sorry, not used to seeing you with your clothes on' – but he stared at me as if he wasn't sure what I meant. On his feet were Burberry-trimmed white Superstars. They'd arrived then; had he come to say thank you?

'Hi!' I said, again.

A large square object was hooked under his right arm, and he held it out. It was a present, wrapped in gold paper, with a red metallic ribbon stuck on the top. 'For the kiddy,' he said.

'Ah!' I said, as if that explained everything. Awkwardly, I put my hand out to take it, but he didn't let go immediately.

'All right, is he? I've been thinking about him. I wanted to check.'

'Yes. Yes, he is.' Behind me, a tinkle of laughter in the garden. I should invite him in. I was glad to see him. It would be the normal thing to do; it was just the timing . . . 'Josh is asleep but I'll make sure he gets it. Well, obviously I will. He lives here, so he's not going to *not* get it.'

He held on to the parcel for a fraction of a second longer. I felt the resistance in his hand, aware once more of his physical strength. It was apparent in the rigidity of his jaw, the brace of his thighs, the sinews in his forearms. I'd forgotten how intimidating it was to stand next to him. *Did* I have to invite him in? I imagined the scenario with a sinking in my stomach: my embarrassment and high-pitched awkwardness as I explained who he was. No, it was all going so well out there. As we stood, a second gale of laughter, more boisterous than before, erupted. Yasmeen said, 'Shut *up!*' in that new way people have – adopted from the young.

'Honest to God.' Rose's voice now, rising, a peal. 'You couldn't fucking make it up.'

I felt the sudden weight of the parcel as Dave let go.

My breathing changed, as if a hard object was squeezing my lungs. 'Listen,' I said. 'Come in. Come and have a quick drink. We've got some friends round if you can stand it.'

'If it's not a bad time.'

I stepped aside, and he lumbered past me, and stood, too big for the hall. I still felt dwarfed by him, but I was aware also in that moment of a quick shift in power. Once inside the house, he looked embarrassed by his size and I would be lying if it didn't, after everything that had passed, give me a kick.

'Nice house,' he said, staring at the candle. 'Nice area.'

'Yes. How did you find us?'

He shrugged. 'You know. These days – not difficult.'

'Well, clever you anyway.'

'My grandma grew up round here. She gave birth to my father in the old hospital.' He made a circular rolling gesture with his hand, to indicate out beyond my garden, over the roofs, to the street beyond. 'I see there's a fancy estate there now.'

'Not that fancy,' I said, raising my eyebrows. 'A few nice duplexes, but most of it is housing association. Some odd people wandering around. You wouldn't want to venture too far in after dark.' I remembered the Street View photograph of his business address. 'Except at Christmas,' I added quickly. 'A couple of the houses go overboard with the festive lights. There's a ground-to-roof Santa Josh is rather keen on.'

We had reached the kitchen. Out in the garden, Tessa was staring in our direction, trying to work out who was here.

'Can I get you a drink?' I said. 'Red, white or beer? Prosecco?'

'I'll just have something soft.' He tapped his back pocket – to indicate a car key, I suppose. 'Coke. 7UP. Anything will do.'

I opened the fridge, frantically hoping to magic up a can of either.

After a moment, he added: 'Or squash? Orange squash.'

'I'm not sure . . .' I searched a little longer. 'Pellegrino?' I brought out a large half-empty bottle.

He studied it for a moment. 'Tap's fine,' he said.

I poured a glass of tap water, tried to find ice, failed, and then handed it to him. He drank it in one and then put the glass carefully down on the counter.

'OK.' I turned on the tap and refilled his glass, rather as one would for a thirsty dog. 'Well, let's go out. Once more into the fray, old friend.'

He took a step forward for the glass and as he took it, I put my hand on his arm. 'Did you get the shoes?' I said. 'Are those . . .?'

'Yeah. I did. You didn't have to. But—'

'OK. I'm glad they arrived. But, um, if you could not mention to Tess that I sent them?'

He tipped his head to one side and dropped his lower lip as if he might have been about to ask more.

'It's complicated,' I said, and then when he still didn't say anything, 'Come on, then.'

I walked out towards the tinkling laughter, the sparkling lights. Tessa was still peering in our direction. Dave paused in the bi-fold doors. I made a gesture, a beckoning or maybe a shooing.

'Hey, guys,' I said. 'We've got a surprise visitor. Everyone, this is Dave. Dave Jepsom.'

As he stepped forwards a trail of wisteria, one of my precious blooms, caught in his hair, and he tugged it free, rolling it between his fingers and tossing what was left onto the grass.

Her

Had Dave been on my mind that week? Not at all, in fact. After deciding not to respond to his Facebook request, I'd put him out of my mind. Not the episode of course. That was still there. But him specifically.

When I realised who it was, standing in the doorway to the kitchen, I felt once again the horror of that morning flood back into me, the fear and the guilt; it began cold and grew hotter as it rose up my body. I got to my feet, holding the back of my chair for support. I managed to smile. I think I said, 'How lovely to see you. What are you doing here?'

'I've surprised you, haven't I?' he said. 'Yeah. I was passing. I thought I'd drop in – say hello. See how you all are.'

Marcus was holding a package. 'He's brought a present for Josh,' he said.

'I was going to get sweets,' Dave said, looking at me. 'But I know you don't like him having too much sugar. I wasn't sure about chocolate . . . but then I thought a toy.'

I smiled brightly, nodding thanks, my mind racing. Why was he saying all this?

Marcus turned to the others. 'We met Dave on holiday,' he said. 'In Greece last week. He rescued Josh from drowning.'

His voice was oddly clipped, almost off-hand, as if he was trying to get the explanations over with.

'We owe him everything,' I said, to compensate. 'Honestly, Dave, we can't begin to express how grateful we are.'

'Oh!' Rose said. 'Oh – you're the knight in shining armour.'

'Right place, right time,' Dave said. 'I hate to think what might have happened if I hadn't been there.'

Marcus inclined his head and gave a sort of bow. 'Dave,' he said, sweeping the company up in a movement of one hand, 'these are our friends.'

Simon and Pete half got to their feet, stretched out their hands for a pump; solid, bloke-ish. Yasmeen and Rose, staying seated, both said, 'Hi.'

Pete reached for the third bottle of Prosecco, gave a quick inspection of his own water glass, tipping a dribble onto the grass behind him, then offered it to Dave.

Dave looked at the used glass, and then back to Pete. He shook his head. 'I'm good.' He took a sip from his own beaker, holding it at his mouth longer than necessary.

'Lidl,' Pete said. 'But surprisingly good. We buy loads of our booze there – that and smoked salmon.'

'And the occasional incredibly weird item like a wetsuit, or a solar-powered shower,' Rose added. 'I bought an inflatable kayak the other day. £19.99. Rude not to!'

Dave was standing awkwardly. There was no apparent room for him at the table. The others, realising this, began to shift along. 'It's OK,' I said. 'Only one of you need budge.' But it was too late and Dave managed to lodge himself between Rose and Simon in the middle of the closest bench, twisting awkwardly to get his legs in place, and then sitting upright, his elbows pinched to his sides.

'So tell us,' Yasmeen said, when he was finally settled. She had rested her face on her clasped hands, tilting it flirtatiously towards him. 'What happened?'

I pushed back my chair and quickly stood up. 'Let me get you some food,' I said, and managed to get back down the steps and into the kitchen before he answered. I stood braced against the sink, aware of the drone of Dave's voice if not his actual words. The pain deep in my chest increased. I thought about him filling the gaps in the narrative we had already provided. I imagined the reality sinking in, the dawning comprehension in our friends' faces, when they heard in his words how close we really had come to letting our son drown.

I waited as long as I could and then tried to assemble a helping of food. There wasn't much left in the ceramic pots now I looked closely: a few stray strings of chicken, a couple of olives, half a preserved lemon. On the plate it looked woefully inadequate. I took a few deep breaths at the door – surely he'd be finished – and came back out.

Dave was still talking, his voice slow and measured. 'It's the highest – or maybe the second highest, no I think the highest – cause of accidental death for the under-fives in this country. I say accidental because most under-fives who die are murdered. And I know handicapped youngsters, those with birth defects, can die as a result of their defects – of whatever's wrong with them in the first place. But death by drowning is more common than you think. You only need an inch of water. Paddling pools, baths, water butts – they're lethal. Turn your back on a toddler in a paddling pool for even a second, and their lungs could fill with water.'

'Sorry, there's not much left,' I murmured, reaching over his shoulder to put the plate down in front of him.

Everyone had fallen silent. Their faces looked stricken. 'Murdered?' Yasmeen said. 'What do you mean?'

'By a family member. Shaking. Or burning with cigarettes. Starving, sometimes. Often neglect.'

Neglect. He seemed to look at me when he said that.

Something I had nurtured – this evening, this gathering, my sanity – had been ruined. I sat down abruptly.

'We took Skye to Aqua-babies when she was eight weeks old,' Yasmeen said.

Dave had been poking with a fork at the food on his plate, turning it over, but he looked up. 'Eight weeks?' he said.

'You just throw them in, and they learn to breathe instinctively,' Simon said. 'It's wonderfully bonding for mum and baby.'

Dave was staring at Simon's T-shirt. A frown crossed his brow, at the vagina or the information. 'Eight weeks?' he repeated. 'That doesn't sound right.'

'It uses their natural reflexes; they have an affinity with the water. They've been in the womb after all.' Yasmeen spoke quickly to close the gaps. 'Has Nell been swimming yet, Rose?' she asked.

'No, but maybe I'll take her,' Rose said. 'I've heard there's a super private pool in Tooting you can hire.' She really had just said 'super'. Rose was as middle class and Sloaney as everyone else round here. I loved her. I spent my life trying to copy her. All the effort I took to try to match up to her ideals, to mirror her taste, but it was hopeless. I was so far removed – even the crisps I'd got wrong. The rules were too hard to grasp. In that moment, seeing her through Dave's eyes, I felt my own past press in on me. He and I were the same. Neither of us fitted in here.

I glanced at Dave and he was looking at me. I felt the heat rise to my face.

Rose was still talking. 'I just can't face the leisure centre these days, not after it was closed after that d and v outbreak.' She shuddered.

'Rose is a GP, Dave,' Marcus said. 'She's not just being snobby. She knows about these things. She has inside information.'

'Part time.' Rose looked hurt. 'And I'm not sure that I do.'

'So Dave,' Pete said. 'Tell us, where do you live?'

'In the Catford area.' He prodded his food, found a piece of lemon and ate it. He chewed thoughtfully. After a few seconds, he swallowed hard.

'Catford?' Pete's expression was one of polite confusion. 'Remind me – where is Catford?'

'Oh, I know Catford,' Yasmeen said. 'The one with the big cat at the shopping centre. We pass it on our way through to Kent.'

Dave wiped his mouth with a napkin, scrunched it up, and then brought the napkin down to his lap.

Pete started asking Yasmeen about her connection with Kent and she was telling him about the 'bolt-hole' they had recently bought in Deal: 'Tiny, but heaven. It's so nice to escape from London for weekends. It hadn't been touched in twenty years. Lots of tiny little rooms. I gutted it, stripped it down, open-planned the whole thing.'

'You personally?' Pete said.

'No.' She slapped the air floppily to say get away with you. 'We had some wonderful Polish builders, dirt cheap. Half the price of London builders. For once they actually cleaned up after themselves, too. Total gems. We're hoping to persuade them to do our kitchen.'

Oh God, I thought, not this.

Marcus said, 'Dave's a builder. Though not that kind of builder. You're in construction, isn't that right? Or . . .' He glanced quickly at me. 'Building solutions? More grand scheme of things than manual labourer?'

Dave put his knife and fork down, carefully as if not to make a noise. 'I'm more of a trouble-shooter,' he said.

The conversation split then, the spotlight on him temporarily dimmed. Our guests had picked him up and dropped him; duty done, they were talking to each other now. Yasmeen and Rose were discussing Patrick at nursery, and his liking of an off-colour joke. Simon and Pete launched into a discussion about a show on Amazon Prime about a woman's sexual obsession with a Texan artist. It was called *I Love Dick*. I wished, under the circumstances, it had been called anything but that. Dave was rolling the pad of one finger over his gums. Marcus cleared his plate – he had only picked at it; even the lemon, I suspected, was hidden in the napkin – and took it down to the kitchen, returning with the Chocolate and Almond Torte, which he put down in front of me. It was in its packaging – its giveaway plastic shell. I had planned to decant it onto one of our own plates.

It didn't seem important now. I felt as if I had already been revealed for a fraud.

I picked up the knife, ready to cut it, as Yasmeen's face stretched into an artificial smile. 'It must be so varied, your line of work,' she said slightly too loudly, to get Dave's attention.

He turned his head towards her, blinking slowly. 'Sorry?'

'Any big job on?'

'Couple of things. One project that's quite local. Something else in Witney.'

'Oh, Witney – isn't that near Bicester?' Yasmeen said.

'It is indeed.'

'Will you stay over?'

'It's not that far. I'll drive up every day.'

She glanced at Marcus. 'You could ask Marcus to put you up at his hotel.'

'Yasmeen, don't tease.' Marcus tried to laugh.

'When's the 7Nights relaunch again?' Yasmeen was enjoying the sound of her own voice. She was one of those attractive women who thought it was amusing to push the boundaries of acceptable conversation. She was safe to shock, with those lips, that hair.

'Thursday week,' Marcus replied, valiantly. 'Can I put you down on the list?'

'I'll have to consult my busy schedule.' Her eyelashes were fake, I was sure, each one individually glued. 'But maybe Dave could take my place. Or come with, as my date.'

'It's just journos, I'm afraid,' Marcus said, his eyes darting. 'Sorry, Dave.'

His hands were making silly panicked movements, rearranging a glass, brushing invisible crumbs from the cloth. I'm sure he didn't mean to sound snide, for his 'Sorry' and his 'Dave' to sound like two different sentences. Or if he did, perhaps the sarcasm was directed at Yasmeen, not him.

'Perhaps you should re-think your press launch,' Yasmeen said, playfully. 'Perhaps inviting real people, the kind of people who might use the motel, is the way forward. Dave's line of work takes him out and about in the world. He could spread the word.'

'Absolutely, absolutely, absolutely.' Marcus stroked the back of his spoon, replaced it on the table, took a glug of wine. 'Absolutely.'

Dave was studying his hands again.

My knife was suspended above the tart, poised to crack the chocolate casing. The music had stopped. I had the feeling if I could only react in a natural human way, I could retrieve the situation, bring the scene back to life. If I knew what to do, if I had the right instinctive social graces. But I didn't, and I couldn't think of anything to do, or say. I wanted suddenly to run away, away from this party, and this man, and his unwanted intrusion into our lives.

A cold breeze rattled lightly through the apple tree; a few leaves spiralled down onto the table. An exhausted blackbird was still singing, disorientated by the street-lights. The next-door neighbours closed their upstairs window with a pointed slam. I felt a sudden sense of dread, and shivered.

'Shall we take our pudding inside?' Marcus said.

Him

We sat in the sitting room for a bit, but the evening was ruined. If Dave had left then, as we longed for him to do, perhaps it could have been revived, but he didn't, and it wasn't.

Dave asked me for 'the toilet' shortly after we had sat down, and I took him to the foot of the stairs and pointed up. 'The main bathroom's all the way up I'm afraid – on the top floor. Next to Josh's room.'

He was gone quite a while, and I sat talking to the others, while listening out for him. Time seemed to pass. What was he doing up there? Tessa caught my eye across the room. I knew what she was thinking. He wouldn't disturb Josh, would he? *Would he?*

On the pretext of getting more wine, I left the sitting room and stood again at the bottom of the stairs. After a few moments I heard a faraway flush and the sound of the cistern filling, followed by an echoing yanking sound, or like a heavy object hitting metal. And then footsteps. Not on the stairs, but across our bedroom floor.

Just too late, I leapt out of the way, into the kitchen. He was still waiting for me in the hall as I came back out, holding a fresh bottle of wine. 'You've got a dripping tap up there,' he said, flicking his head towards the stairs.

My eyes darted. I felt a stirring of discomfort. 'In our en-suite you mean? You used that?'

'Yeah, sorry. Got a bit lost.'

'Bedroom's a bit of a mess.'

'Yeah, well. Nothing I haven't seen before.'

I smiled doubtfully, still unsettled.

We stood there. I wondered if he might find this a good opportunity to make an exit, but he didn't show any signs of wanting to do so and, after a moment, we joined the others in the sitting room.

It wasn't long after this that Josh woke. Tessa went upstairs to settle him, while Yasmeen and Rose lolled on the sofa, routinely recounting the antics of their own children – a kind of boasting in moan form 'And then she wants me to read her *a second* book. "Another story, Mummy!" And I'm like, "Please go and watch TV like normal kids."'. Pete and Simon debated the merits or otherwise of a Premier League football manager, but it was a conversation Dave didn't seem to want to join. He perched on the armchair, fiddling with his jeans at the thigh, pulling at the seams, occasionally flattening his hand and stroking the denim. I tried to talk but in the end, I gave up, and we sat there in silence, other people's chat floating over us.

Our guests left before midnight, funnelling noisily out into the street. Tessa hadn't reappeared and I stood alone with Dave at the door.

Yasmeen's voice carried from the road. 'Bye, sweeties! Sleep tight.'

The Baies candle had burnt low, and it was flickering angrily against the glass, crackling and spitting.

'It's a bit dangerous, that,' Dave said. 'You shouldn't leave fire unattended, particularly with a kid in the house. You got fire alarms?'

I wet my fingers and pinched the wick. 'There.'

He stood, still staring at it.

'So you drove?' I said, hoping to encourage him out.

'A mate dropped me off. I'll, um . . .' He pointed towards the main road, meaning he'd catch a bus, or a taxi; it was unclear.

He still didn't move, as if he were waiting for something. My wallet was sitting on the shelf next to the candle, and I imagined that his eyes rested on it.

'I might get a cab,' he said. 'As it's late.'

'Yeah,' I said. 'Good idea.' I picked the wallet up, and started flicking through it. My fingers found three twenties.

Dave had crossed the threshold and was standing outside on the mat now. 'OK,' he said. 'Well.'

'Here.' I took a step towards him, and reached my hand towards his. I hadn't properly thought it through, but I had a notion I would press the notes into his palm, that I could do so without either of us registering what had happened. Through the haze of my drunkenness, I thought this perhaps was what he was waiting for.

His face became still. 'What are you doing?' he said.

'I just thought, for the fare . . .'

'You think I want money?'

'We're so grateful for what you did, and you've come all this way, and . . .'

He looked at me without saying anything, and with a sinking in my chest, I watched as he turned his back on me and walked through the gate to the road.

THIRD

Her

Nothing on the surface changed. The things that did were invisible even to us. On the Saturday morning, it was my turn for a lie-in. I woke, immediately alert, at 9 a.m., the bed empty next to me, and reached for my phone. It wasn't on the table by the side of the bed. And it wasn't in the bathroom, where I thought I remembered leaving it the night before.

When I came downstairs, Josh was in the sitting room, leaping across the sofa in his pyjamas, hauling a huge red plastic fire engine – the size of a four-slice Dualit toaster – along the back of the cushions. He was shouting, 'Nee-naw, nee-naw.' Marcus was curled up in the foetal position in an armchair, wearing my Liberty dressing gown. I pointed at the fire engine and made a face.

'Hang on, Mary.' He held his phone out from his face. 'What's the matter?'

'We can't accept it,' I said. 'It's too much.'

'What do you want me to do? We can hardly give it back.'

We glared at each other.

'Have you seen my phone?' I said.

'It's in the pocket of my chinos. Meant to give it to you. Sorry. Yes Mary, I'm here.'

I picked up the wrapping paper from the floor, bundled it into a ball and chucked it into the empty fireplace. Then I

went through to the kitchen. We had done some of the washing-up the night before, but the room had the greasy, vegeta-
tive smell of dirty dishes left to soak. The floor was smeared
with footprints. It had rained overnight and outside were small
signs of devastation – paper napkins sodden under the wooden
table, a bottle of wine on its side in a flower bed. The trees
were dripping.

What a disaster the evening had been. Even without Dave,
I'd got it wrong. The wrong crisps. The wrong people. I'd
been so good with a PR launch – I could make anything look
desirable and good. I'd been trying to transfer those skills to
my own life, trying to spin a story that I was a good mother, a
good housewife. The truth was I wasn't and I never would be.

Sighing, I polished and put away the glasses, scrubbed the
dishes that had been left to soak, and emptied the dishwasher.
The plates had been stacked too close together and food was
stuck to the backs. I rinsed them off, left them to dry, and then
went upstairs in search of my phone – which was in the pocket
of Marcus's chinos as he had said.

A missed call from R.

I sat on the bed, feeling suddenly sick. Marcus might have
felt the phone vibrate. He might even have looked to see who
it was. My heart began to beat faster and I got dressed quickly
and then went back downstairs. Marcus was talking to Mary.
I got Josh dressed and into the buggy and out of the door
within minutes. Marcus held his call to ask where we were
going and I shouted, 'Playground,' over my shoulder, and
then I closed the door behind me.

Our road leads down to the common. The houses aren't
huge but you pay a premium to be so close to green space.
People find it hard to move and instead they add to their
properties – up and under and out the back. It means constant
skips and drilling, blocked drains, builders you see so often

you know their names. It's silly really. The area is desirable because of the peace and quiet, but that very desirability means it's never peaceful and it's never quiet.

That morning, a car was parked outside our house: a black Jeep, the window wound down, and a person in the driver's seat. I didn't look too closely. At the time, I didn't think I needed to.

Further down, an enormous lorry was delivering what looked like slabs of concrete to number 52, its reverse alarm beeping; other cars were stuck, building up behind it, trying to back on to the main road. Chaos.

We got beyond this obstacle and past the cafe on the corner, which was just opening up, and crossed over the main road onto the grass. A Saturday morning football club was in mid flow – small kids in kit, a clutter of mini-goals. Josh leant forward, his attention on a small white dog that bounded onto the pitch to nose a ball. The sky had almost cleared; a pale cold blue, with trails of frantic clouds. Livid green trees and grass, the hawthorn bushes a riot of blossom. These are impressions I can retrieve – though it may well have been another June day I remember. The fact is I was somewhere else completely in my head. My heart had become so shiftless and unreliable, my recollection is not to be trusted.

The ice-cream van was parked up by the pond, a straggle of eager kids queuing. Rose had a rule: no ice creams before lunch. But I got to the back of the line and bought Josh a 99.

'Oh,' he said, comically taken aback, when I handed it to him.

Richard answered on the fifth ring.

'You're alive,' he said.

'Were you worried?'

'You hung up abruptly yesterday.'

A helicopter was circling; a plane had left a white trail in the sky over the pond. A man on a bicycle veered past. From the other direction, a woman in pink Lycra was running towards me. I took a step off the path, onto the grassy verge that edged the wilder undergrowth. I felt the air move, the sound of the runner's breath. She might have been someone I knew. I bent my head and didn't look up. 'I'm sorry,' I whispered. 'Marcus came into the room and I didn't have a chance to ring you back. We had people coming to dinner. Supper. Kitchen supper actually, though we had it in the garden. Is it still kitchen supper if it's in the garden?'

He laughed. 'I don't know, but it sounds ghastly either way. I don't know how you bear it.'

That was the thing about Richard. He didn't *care*. He had contempt for the world in which I lived, the life I was trying to construct.

I felt myself smile, breathe deeper. The tensions of the night before began to seep away.

'So what was it you wanted to say?' he continued. 'You said it was important.'

He sounded anxious. He was worried, I realised, not that I was about to finish it, but that I might be about to leave my husband. He wanted nothing from me.

I sighed. 'I've been trying to tell you I don't think we should do this any more.'

'What if I'm not ready for that?' There was amusement in his voice. 'What if I don't let you?'

'Well, that would be a shame.'

A bush next to me shook and a dog emerged, sniffing the ground. Its owner followed; a woman I recognised, one of the assistants in the chemist. I glanced away, feeling heat rise up my neck.

'Where are you?' he said.

I returned to the path. Josh was still happily eating his ice cream. I looked behind me. Two children were wheeling towards us on bikes. Six women in an exercise class were doing planks on the grass. None of them was obviously paying any attention to me. The back of my head prickled.

'I'm on my way to the playground,' I said.

'What are you wearing?'

I looked down at my tracksuit bottoms, and my old Nikes.

'Nothing,' I said.

Heavy breathing. 'Nothing at all?'

A couple was coming towards me carrying tennis rackets. The woman skipped backwards for a second to say something to him and the man gave a low imaginary swipe of the ball.

I took a step to the side.

'No seriously – nothing. Tracky bottoms and a T-shirt,' I said.

'If I was there, I'd undress you. In front of everyone.'

I could still hear the sound of his breathing. The heat from my neck rose up to suffuse my cheeks. My face felt flooded with blood.

'I'd take you against a tree in front of everyone, strip you bare. That would give all your middle-class friends a shock.'

I'd reached the gate to the playground, and I bent to wipe Josh's face and fingers with a tissue. He strained to get out and I undid the straps. It was seething with kids in there, all over the equipment, charging in different directions like ball bearings. Parents were standing by trees, in groups, or sitting on the big benches, or leaning against the mini ones, sipping coffee from takeaway cups, chatting. Josh charged off towards the climbing frame.

The tarmac was cracked along the railings, and I scuffed at it with my feet. 'You've never seen me naked,' I murmured.

He laughed throatily. 'Yes I have.'

'Not all of me at the same time. It's always bits here and there.'

'Maybe it's time we did something about that.'

'Richard.' I was smiling. 'We mustn't see each other again. You mustn't ring me.'

'What are you doing on Monday? Come to the flat. You've never been. I'd like you at least to see what I've done with the place before you cast me into the wilderness.'

'Mum!'

Somehow Josh had managed to wriggle through the top bars of the jungle gym and was holding on with one hand, swinging.

'Look at me! Mum!'

'I'd better go,' I said.

The council had long ago replaced this bit of tarmac with a soft squidgy surface; nothing like the hard squares of the playground where I grew up. I reached him before he dropped, held on to his feet, persuaded him to let go and guided him down.

As I straightened, I saw Rose standing by the swings, with Nell in the sling. She was watching me.

I swallowed hard, biting down panic, and then I waved and she walked over. 'You all right?' she said.

'Yeah, fine. Just rescuing my son from instant death.'

'I was going to come and chat, but you were on a call.'

'Oh.' I felt for the phone in my pocket, felt myself flush. 'Yeah, sorry. Got a bit tied up. I didn't see you. Where's Chloe?'

She gestured to the other section of the playground, where Chloe was careering back and forth on a rocking goldfish. Rose seemed to study me for a moment. 'Thanks for last night. It was fun. Delicious chicken. You must give me the recipe.'

Why, even then, didn't I tell her it was ready made from Cook? 'Yes of course. Did you have a nice time?' I sounded needy.

'Yes I did. It was nice to meet Josh's rescuer. He wasn't quite how I imagined.'

'It was unexpected. I don't know how he found our address. He was delivering a present for Josh – an enormous fire engine, which was kind, but . . .'

'What?'

'I don't know.' I shivered. 'A bit inappropriate?'

She shook her head. 'No, I don't think so. I thought he was sweet.'

'Not a bit odd turning up like that?'

'He's bound to feel a connection with Josh because of saving his life. It's massive. It's probably one of the most meaningful things that has ever happened to him. He's just being kind. He seemed a bit lonely if anything.'

I was aware of a sinking, a small internal collapse. Had we made him feel at home? Or was I rude? 'He's got a big family,' I said.

'Oh. You didn't mention them. Nor did he.'

I felt a flicker of irritation. She was being judgemental, but she was implicated too, with her 'super' private swimming pools. 'I suppose no one asked.'

'We did our best, but it was a bit difficult. He wasn't very talkative. I know we all kept trying to include him.'

I felt a further loss of bearings. 'I think he blames me for Josh almost drowning. He was there. He saw. I can't get it out of my head.'

'Maybe you have too much time to dwell on things.' She had on her GP face: concerned, but also detached. 'Morbid thoughts can begin to build – you see it a lot with elderly patients.'

'Thanks!'

'You know what I mean. You're in the house on your own all day. *Every* day. I've only been on maternity leave for four months and it's beginning to do my head in. Did anything happen about that prospective client?'

'What prospective client?'

'Didn't you have a meeting earlier in the week?'

'Oh. Yes.' I turned my face away, ostensibly to check on Josh. 'Nothing really. They were just putting out feelers.'

'Maybe something will still come of it?'

Josh had found Chloe and the two of them were darting in and out of the bushes that run along the fence between the playground and the railway line. Chloe was in the lead. Josh was copying everything she did. Stamp. Run. Skip. Copy stamp. Copy run. Copy skip.

'Maybe,' I echoed.

I took a different path on the way back, the track that led along the back of a row of large properties on the other side of the common. One of the houses was covered in scaffolding. Further along some labourers were rebuilding a garden wall. I began to walk more quickly. A project that was 'quite local', Dave had said. I wish I'd asked more questions. At any moment, I expected to hear a voice, a holler: 'Tessa!' Or worse, 'Josh!'

I joined the main track, relieved to cross at the lights and put distance between me and the houses. I paused briefly to exchange a few words with the snake-hipped French bloke at the rotisserie chicken place, who was leaning outside, smoking a cigarette. He was closing, he told me – rents had soared. 'That's annoying,' I said, 'my little cheat gone.' (I often used to pass his roast chicken and gravy off to Marcus as my own.) Then I headed up past the gallery and the boutique, and the flower shop, and the wine shop, and the rash of estate agents, and turned into our road.

The cafe on the end of our road was busy now. On one of the closely packed outside tables, loudly chatting in a group of women, was Yasmeen, and she called me over, leaning back from her bench, like someone listing out on a yacht. I put the brake on the buggy and stepped between the tables. I tried to smile and appear relaxed. A black crow was tossing a crumb in the gutter. Across the road, delivery crates were clattering up the ramp into the small supermarket.

She thanked me for supper, her mouth curling up in a smile. Marcus, she continued, glancing quickly at her friend, had already texted her about the 7Nights thing. I rolled my eyes and told her to ignore him: 'He can be very persistent, my husband.' She didn't mention Dave Jepsom, and nor did I.

My eye had only been off Josh for a few seconds, but when I stepped out from between the tables, he had pushed himself forward against the foot rest, half standing, and was staring hard at the shop window opposite.

'What?' I said. 'What is it?'

He sank back into his seat, and turned his face shyly into the fabric of the hood.

I looked back across. The sun was hitting the glass and I couldn't see through the window, just a reflection of the street where I was standing, and a movement of clouds. Was there someone there, looking out, a figure maybe? Was I imagining a fuzz of grey-blond hair, broad shoulders, inked arms?

Laughter broke out behind me. I glanced round quickly, just to check, and the woman with Yasmeen was staring across at me, sizing me up. I smiled questioningly, but she didn't smile back. I looked over again at the shop window. The shape had gone, but the door was opening and there was a shadow behind it, about to exit onto the street.

It took me a moment to free the brake. I set off quickly down the road, speeding up, almost tripping over the wheels. I got to the gate of my house, struggled through it, down the path, and then fumbled for the lock.

Once inside, breathless, I leant against the wall for a few seconds and then double-locked and put the chain across the door.

Him

It was the weekend that Tony Judd was arrested in Riyadh. The Department of Public Safety had cited 'improper conduct', and had clearly decided to make an example of him. Saudi was working on its own image problem. They obviously had someone handling their PR.

I spent the Sunday pounding the phones trying to clear it up, but by the time I got to the office on Monday morning, the company's stock had fallen12 per cent, to its lowest share price since 2008. I took a conference call with other members of the board in which I strongly recommended 'an immediate restructuring of the management team', code for 'fire the cheating bastard'. It was rash and unthinking of me. Mike McPhee and Tony Judd had been at primary school together. I was the one who was going to be restructured if I wasn't careful.

'Fuck, fuck, fuck,' I said, leaving the meeting room where I'd just been briefed. 'Fuck and shit and fuck.'

My assistant Gail caught my eye, inclining her head towards a young girl who was standing by her desk.

'Marcus, this is Jemima, remember?' And then, as I stared back blankly: 'At school with your niece? You've offered her work experience?'

'Ah. Of course,' I said, vaguely remembering then: various emails from my elder sister Sarah in which I'd agreed to help out. I bowed my head and shook the girl's hand. Her grasp was soft and limp. The usual type: long blonde hair, too much make-up, eyebrows plucked into thin lines. She was wearing a navy suit and black tights that were too hot for the weather.

'You're in Izzy's class, is that right? Want to go into PR?'

The girl, Jemima, turned up one side of her mouth, half shrugging, as if even she couldn't quite maintain the fiction.

'Yeah,' I said. 'I know. They force you to do this to get you out from under their feet after GCSEs. You don't know what the fuck you want to do. Why should you? You're only – what?'

'Fifteen,' she said. 'Sixteen next month.'

I thought about Tessa for a moment; at sixteen she was already working her way up. I felt a rush of the old admiration for her.

I smiled: 'Exactly.'

'And when you've got a minute,' Gail interrupted, 'Jeremy Pickens at the *FT* wants to talk about Judd. And Owen Johns from the *Evening Standard* rang for you too.' She was reading from a spiral notebook. 'The third time this morning.'

'Did he say what about?'

'Something about Ron McCready's speeding offence. I said I'd ask you to ring him back.'

'Who in hell's name leaked that?' I thumped my palm dramatically against my forehead. 'I thought we'd contained that one at least.'

'Clearly not.' Gail was about my age, but often made me feel like an over-excited schoolboy. She turned back to her screen. There was only so much of my showing off she was prepared to be part of.

I rolled my eyes theatrically at Jemima. 'Sometimes I feel as if I'm being fucked with, as if someone knows exactly how to ruin my life and has set about doing it.'

'Really?'

'No. It's what the job is.' I perched on the edge of Gail's desk. 'These things find a way out like water.' I leant closer and lowered my voice to signal the fact I was about to impart a jewel of wisdom. It came easily to me – I'd trotted out almost the same words to someone else recently. 'Any company that's been around for any length of time has its secrets. It's how many layers down they go that matters.'

'Scary,' she said.

I cocked my head and clicked my tongue against the roof of my mouth. It's possible that I was overdoing the man-of-the-world thing. I slipped off the desk. 'You said it, not me.'

I took her round the office, introduced her to everybody, and then found her an empty chair in a corner. 'There'll be something for you to do later, I'm sure,' I said. 'But for now, maybe watch, drink in the atmosphere, work out if it really is the career for you. Just don't tell anyone else what goes on in here.'

And then I forgot her.

The important thing at moments of press interest, which I could have told Jemima if I had thought to take her presence seriously, is to keep in touch with the journalists. Jeff told me this on my first day at Ekelund. Silence infuriates them. Ring them, he said, every hour. Don't apologise, but show you are taking their concerns seriously. Bore them into submission if you need to. That morning, I rang Pickens and Johns, and in both cases I found a line and stayed consistent. Yes, it was true; yes it was a matter of concern to the shareholders. Yes, I would keep them both informed as soon as I had any information they should be informed with.

Once I got into my stride, it was the kind of morning I rose to. At moments of crisis, it doesn't matter how badly you feel you're doing your job, how insecure you are as a son, or as a

99

father, or as a husband, how distant your wife, how shit your weekend. It's about fast reactions, doing your best for the client in the moment. There is no time for anything but action, and any anxieties about self-worth go out of your mind.

That afternoon, Sam and Basty dug up a Royal Society for the Prevention of Accidents Gold Award MJI had won the previous year and announced it as if it had just happened. Emma got to work moving the Wear Purple for Liver Cancer day forward, and made headway with a bridge in Haiti that the government was willing to use MJI's equipment in rebuilding.

'Poor old Tony,' Emma said at one point. 'I hate to think what it's like inside a Saudi jail.'

You want to know the truth? In that week, that day, that moment, in that *mood*, I didn't care. It wasn't my problem. I know I was fulfilling the male cliché; cauterising emotion, channelling my aggression and disappointment into work. But someone else could take responsibility for the human side. The hard bed. The small window. The beatings. My prize, the only one that mattered, was the long-term reputation of the company.

Her

The rest of the weekend was a struggle. I am not proud of myself. I hope I have made that clear. There is nothing I wouldn't change about my behaviour, thinking back – and I'm not saying it just because of what happened.

You think that if you put yourself in a situation in which a choice is integral that you'll know what you want, but you don't. You have *no idea*. You lose perspective. You think an affair takes you somewhere else, out of your life, but it's a trap – you're stuck, legs flailing, like an insect in honey. Infidelity is selfish. Does that sound trite, too obvious to need saying? Perhaps the very fact that I *feel* the need to say it, that it seems to me like an insight, is just another facet of the solipsism of my situation. I understood the banality of extra-marital sex, the damp predictability of it. And yet I felt I was different. I meant it when I told Richard it was over, but as the weekend progressed, as the house got messier, as Marcus ignored me, as Josh played up, as I felt less and less in control, my mind began to seek out Monday morning as an escape. I had no intention of sleeping with Richard. Probably, in fact, I would finish with him. Do it in person. By the time I texted to say I was coming, I had, like so many adulterers before me, executed a neat U-turn. What harm would it do to see his flat?

On Monday, Marcus left for work early – some crisis that had been bubbling all weekend. He didn't volunteer any details and this time I didn't ask.

Josh slept in, so I took my time getting ready. I had a bath, and rubbed on body lotion, and blow-dried my hair. I felt the relief of adopting a role I knew how to play. It wasn't so different to going to work. I chose my clothes carefully – fancy lingerie from the back of my drawer under a simple dress. I laid out my make-up and tried out different eyeshadows and liners on the back of my hand. When Josh still hadn't stirred at 8.15 a.m., I sat at the kitchen table, and worked how to get to Richard's flat, scribbling some directions to myself. At 8.30 a.m., almost ready to go, I went into Josh's room.

He was awake, lying on his side, his face flushed and pillow-creased, staring at the door.

'Oh poppet.'

I felt his forehead. It was warm. He coughed, half raised his head, and then laid it back down. I sat on the edge of the bed, slipped off my heels and put my arms around him. He was ill. That's why he had been so difficult the day before, so tearful and bad-tempered. Poor little boy. How could I have thought to leave him? As I stroked his hair, I was aware of disappointment, but also relief.

I gave him some Calpol, and a cup of warm milk, and then, when he said he was hungry, I wrapped him in his dressing gown and carried him downstairs. While I was making porridge, he began to play with his fire engine on the floor. He sneezed twice and I wiped his nose. He tried to push me away. It was a cold, that was all.

He ate enthusiastically, and then almost immediately struggled to get down and play, picking up his fire engine and bashing it against the table leg. 'Hey,' I said, 'let's do something quieter.'

He ignored me.

I tried to take the fire engine from him. He had broken off one of the wheels. But he yanked it away, scraping the plastic against my finger. It hurt, and with the pain, a little pilot light of frustration flared inside my chest.

I looked at my watch. It was only five past nine. I still had time to get him to nursery.

It didn't take us long. At quarter past we were in the car, and were driving down to the church hall. At the door I gave him a cheery goodbye, got back in the car, almost breathless with the combination of anxiety and release, and drove to the Tube.

I couldn't find a parking space and drove several times around a tangle of side streets until I found a spot quite a distance away on the other side of the High Road. I just managed to squeeze into a slot at the end of a row of houses. I ran back down to the station, out of breath when I finally got on a Northern Line Tube to London Bridge. I emerged from the escalator to an overcast sky, and a throng of touts in masks and bloodied white surgical gowns carrying placards for the Jack the Ripper tour. I couldn't find the envelope on which I'd written the directions – I must have dropped it running to the station – so I used my phone to navigate a web of side streets, in which old printers' yards were now craft beer centres and cobbled streets led to artisan coffee shops.

 Richard lived in a warehouse conversion squeezed between taller modern blocks. An arched entrance opened into a court-yard where olive trees stood like sentries; the building, all glass and steel and sand-blasted London-stock brick, loomed up on four sides, an intricate pattern of pulleys and fire-escapes, balconies and window-boxes. I pressed a button in a wall and a door lock released with a click when I pushed.

His flat was on the top floor, the penthouse – of course it was. The lift opened directly into a shot of light, an enormous open-plan room. The walls were white-painted brick, the floor pale wooden boards. A kitchen area took up one corner; an L-shaped sofa facing a modern fireplace another. There were glass vases of elaborately arranged flowers and copper pans hanging from a wrought-iron rack, and a bronze sculpture of a rearing horse. Most breathtaking of all was the view: a wrap-around terrace, where beautiful pale pink terracotta pots frothed with plants – white blooms, all shades of green – and then sky, layers of cloud and rooftops, grey and black and silver, the distant crenellations of Canary Wharf, the spike of the Shard.

I stood for a moment. I knew he was successful (the pizzerias, the sushi bars, the fastfood Chinese ... a branch of Noodle Palace alone sat on almost every high street in Britain), but until this moment I hadn't translated that success into money. I felt foolish, as if I'd been deceived.

'Hello. Just give me one minute.'

His voice came from an office to one side. I took a few steps towards it and stood looking in. He was sitting with his back to me at a huge glass table, tapping on a tiny laptop. For a moment, I felt the force of what I was doing. I should just leave. I should turn round and get back in the lift and be taken downstairs and walk out into the street and go home, pick up my sick son, resume my life. I should do it now. Before it was too late.

'There you are.' His chair swivelled and he got to his feet, coming towards me with his arms out. 'Angel. How lovely you look. How fuckable.'

He was wearing navy suit trousers and one of his crisp white shirts – he had recently told me he owned thirty. The three top buttons were undone. On his jaw was a tiny speck of shaving foam.

He took off his glasses and they dangled in his hand against my back as he kissed me. The other hand was in my hair. He tasted of coffee and mint. I couldn't leave once I had breathed in the smell of his neck – soap and vetiver; sandalwood. I had no resolve for anything at all. He pushed me backwards and we stumbled and I heard myself laugh.

'I haven't got long,' he said. 'Sorry to say that straight away, but I might as well be clear.' He winced. 'I've got to be at Cannon Street by eleven thirty.'

His bedroom was stark white and dark grey; a velvet head-board loomed high above the bed. 'Sheets and blankets,' I said, as I fell backwards into the pillows. 'I didn't know anyone still used those.'

My clothes lay strewn outside the lift. His mouth was at the top of my knickers. He raised his head. 'I'm old-fashioned,' he said.

'But no curtains.'

'I like to see the sky.' He lowered his head again. I heard a scratch against the glass, like a fingernail. A plant – a magnolia – was reaching to get in. I looked beyond it, at the terrace and the clouds; at the buildings, below and above – all that glass, all those mirrors, all those other windows.

'Can anyone see us?' I said.

He didn't answer. I closed my eyes, and forgot everything.

I must have drifted off, just for a few moments, and when I woke he was staring at me.

'Your mouth was quivering.'

I wiped my hand across it. 'Was it? Sorry.'

'And now I've seen you naked,' he said.

He traced his finger along my cheek and down my chin, and slowly followed the curve of my neck, dipping down to my breast. He bent his head and I thought he was going to kiss my nipple, but he licked his finger instead. I arched my back and closed my eyes. I didn't feel self-conscious at all, not about my stretch marks, or the looser skin on my thighs. I'd forgotten it could be like this, that I could be this person. My senses were alert to nothing but his touch.

Afterwards I thanked him and told him he was very considerate. He was leaning on his elbow, still looking at me. I was half joking; I'd said 'considerate' in an accent, a little bit Frankie Howerd. But he didn't laugh. His eyes seemed very dark. Behind his head was an expanse of naked glass and the sky and all those tall buildings, all those windows.

'Are you sure we're not being watched?' I said.

'Would you like it if we were?'

'I know you would.' I sat up and swung my legs over the side of the bed, eyes scanning for my clothes. 'But I wouldn't.'

'Stay here while I go to my meeting,' he said. The idea seemed to come to him; a whim, like a child deciding they want an extra ice cream. 'I'd like to think of you lying here naked in my bed while I'm talking to the men in suits.'

'I can't. I've got to get back.'

He grabbed my arms and pulled me back down, holding my wrists above my head and pressing them into the pillow. 'I might keep you here,' he said. 'Your husband wouldn't be able to reach you. You'd be mine to do what I like with.'

I struggled, laughing. There was a moment of resistance and then he let go. 'Thank you for the thought,' I said, sitting up again. 'And thank you for the orgasms.'

He smiled. 'You're welcome.'

I felt his eyes on me as I walked around the room and into the hallway, collecting my clothes. But by the time I was dressed, he had stopped looking at me and was looking at his phone instead.

'Fancy dinner on Thursday?' he said, glancing up.

'I'm not sure I'll be able to get away.'

He shrugged, as if it hardly mattered. 'Let me know.'

I parted with him at the entrance to his building – casually, a bird-like kiss on each cheek, in case anyone was watching. I still felt as if someone was. He rested his hand on my neck as he said goodbye, his thumb pressing on my collarbone, and then he let me go. Then, hoiking his leg over the saddle of his steel-framed bike, he scudded off towards Cannon Street. I watched him until he disappeared.

I turned and began walking back to London Bridge and the feeling was upon me immediately. I felt as if I were being followed. The crown of my head tingled. There was a pressure on my shoulders, an elastic tug at my heels. I anticipated a pull on my upper arm. I imagined a voice calling my name: 'Tessa. *Tessa.*'

I wasn't concentrating and took a wrong turn, which led me into a cul-de-sac and the London Bridge Hospital. Retracing my steps, I found an entrance to the Tube and descended the escalator to my platform. I was acutely aware of the passengers around me. I felt primed to catch sight of someone I knew. I hadn't been sufficiently careful.

A signal failure at Camden was causing delays and when the train finally arrived it was packed. I stood in the middle of the carriage, hemmed in, holding on to the pole as the Tube listed and lurched. At Borough a woman got on who I thought was my mother; the same dyed mahogany hair, the same rounded shoulders, with that odd raised lump at the base of her neck. I recognised the tasselled shirt, the spindly heels.

But when the woman turned, she had a different face – too young and serene. And anyway, it couldn't have been my mother. She'd been dead for years. I could see, past heads and bodies, through the dividing door to the next compartment, swaying limbs, faces that jerked into view and then out. A young woman with a scarf tied around her head like a turban blocked the window, but as the train pitched to one side, she listed and behind her, for a split second, I saw his face.

Dave Jepsom.

He was wearing a cap, his broad torso in a white T-shirt, his arm raised. He was staring right at me. His eyes were in shadow; his mouth fleshy, open.

I shifted back on my heels. The train braked as it rolled into Stockwell. I steadied myself and when I looked back the turbaned woman refilled the space.

Several people got off and as I moved out of the way to make room for them, the seat next to me came free. I slid into it, out of sight.

I tried to breathe, concentrating on filling my lungs.

I leant forwards. I wanted to check. I had an acute need to be sure. The turbaned woman had got off. The next carriage was now half empty. Had he sat down? There was a bald man in a white shirt standing, legs apart, at the far end, but he wasn't wearing a cap, and it wasn't Dave.

I must have imagined him. I relaxed into the seat, slipped my hands under my thighs, pushed slightly, dug my nails into my flesh – grounding myself. How could it have been him? He'd have had to have been following me.

The train drew into Balham and I got out and walked along the platform towards the exit. An ad for a Sandals holiday filled one wall: a man dressed in white holding a woman, also dressed in white, against the backdrop of a turquoise sea. 'Love is all you need' the strapline read.

On the escalator, an intense memory came into my head: the darkness of the taverna after the brightness of the beach, the sweat along my upper lip, a smell of tomatoes and oregano, the elastic tight feel of the Lycra against my breasts, the need to tug it to sit down, And then the sense of manufactured excitement as I searched for Richard's number on my phone, the breathlessness in my chest as it connected.

But this time, a new detail. A dark figure walking through the door, leaning in. The slap of notes on the counter, the clink of bottles, and a man's shape, tall, bulky, against the light. The smoothness of his head as he turned to watch me. Was it Dave Jepsom? Had he seen me on the phone? Did he know that's what I was doing when I should have been watching my son?

I was hit by a blast of cold air as I touched out through the barriers, and the stench of the Subway franchise at the top of the stairs. As the signal returned, my phone began to vibrate. A missed call, a voicemail. I listened to it with a rushing in my ears. It was the nursery. Josh had a temperature. I put the phone back in my pocket, speeding up with alarm, contrition, a desperate desire to hold Josh in my arms. As I did so, I sensed someone coming behind, taking the stairs two at a time; heavy, determined, gaining. The figure brushed past me and bounded away – just a lad in school uniform. My nerves lurched. The muscles in my stomach clenched.

I ran from the station to the street where the car was parked, tense with panic, flooded with horror at what I'd done. The air surged in and out of my nostrils, the blood pounded in my ears.

I could see as I got close that I had parked badly. I was several feet over the line, partially across a drive. There wasn't a ticket, thank God. I'd blocked in a white 4x4; somewhere in the house I could hear the barking of a large dog. But there was no sign of anyone. The front door was closed, and shutters blocked the windows. Also I was only a few feet out of the box. If they had really wanted to reverse out, and if they had someone to guide them, they could possibly have managed.

I turned back to the car, reaching for my key. There was something on the driver's door. What was it? A chalk mark? Dust? I stepped closer. No, scratches. It seemed to be a word. I bent down to wipe the abrasions with my finger, realised they were deeper and more prominent than I'd realised, and then reared back.

'SLAG'.

The letters were deeply scoured. I couldn't rub them away. Another long mark ran down that side of the car – an angry, jagged gouge in the grey paintwork. I felt sick. The owner of the white 4x4 expressing their anger? Or was someone telling me that they knew?

The car was facing the wrong direction; it was a busy road and I waited for a few minutes, my heart still pounding, for it to be clear in both directions. Finally there was a space; I indicated, spun the wheel and quickly pulled out into a three-point turn.

I was halfway across the road, and had put the car in reverse, when I glanced in my rear-view mirror and caught sight of him in the corner of the frame. He was standing on the pavement, a little further down from where I had parked, watching me. A cap concealed the upper half of his face, the brim down over his eyes, but I would recognise his stance anywhere – the way he stood firmly with his legs a measured distance apart, the fold of his hands. And there was something about the posture. He was too still, close to a tree, as if hoping not to be noticed. I felt transfixed for a moment, paralysed, and then heard a car-horn, and looked ahead and realised a car was waiting to get past me. I reversed, finishing the manoeuvre, until I was no longer an obstruction, then I turned my head to look over my shoulder. If he walked towards me then, I decided, I would ask him why he was following me.

But now I could see properly, with the full stretch of the pavement in sight, and there was nobody there.

Him

That Monday night at supper, a tragic lamb chop she had nuked, Tessa was quiet. She was wearing an unusual amount of make-up, a dark purply eyeshadow which made the lids look bruised; she looked brittle and unhappy. Josh had come home from nursery with a fever, and I assumed she was anxious about that.

'You all right?' I said, hoping she would pretend she was. I'd had a stressful day. I was tired. So, please not *now*.

She fiddled with a necklace at her throat. 'Do you still re-live the moment you saw Josh in the water?' she said. 'Do you still have flashbacks?'

'I do,' I said. 'Yes.'

'Do you think they will ever go away?'

I opened my mouth to answer, but the house phone rang and I hurried through to the sitting room to answer it. There was no one on the other end when I picked up – another silent call – and when I came back into the kitchen, the moment had passed. I tried to hug her, and to say something I hoped was consolatory, but her shoulders were stiff and I let her go.

I busied myself about the kitchen instead, concealing my guilt. I didn't re-live the moment Josh almost drowned, but the opposite: I did everything I could to keep it out of my mind.

I was taking out the rubbish, putting the kitchen bag into the dustbin at the side of the house, when I saw the scratch on the side of the Fiat: a deep, jagged cut that had been caused by a key, no question. I walked around the car, inspecting it carefully. 'SLAG' had been delightfully engraved on the driver's door. She'd tried unsuccessfully to cover it with something; there were flakes of a different-coloured grey – it looked like poster paint – in the gouged letters.

'What happened to the car?' I said, going back into the house.

She flushed. 'It was like that when I came back from nursery this morning.'

'While it was parked on the off-street?' I said.

She nodded.

'Bloody hell.'

'I thought I might be able to cover it up,' she said. 'I tried nail varnish. But it didn't work. I'm sorry.'

'You don't have to apologise. You don't have to hide it from me. It's not as if it's your fault.'

I felt confused and also sheepish, as if somewhere in the past, I had bullied her without realising; why else would she try to hide the damage?

I put my arm around her; her shoulders moved up a fraction and we stayed there for a moment, her sitting, me standing next to her. She smelt different, of lavender, maybe not a new perfume, but a different washing powder.

'It seems so personal,' she said. 'I feel as if it's directed at me.'

I laughed. 'Who would call you a slag?'

Her shoulders shifted sideways. She was picking at a piece of skin at the edge of her thumb. 'I know you'll say I'm mad but I've got it into my head that it was done by someone we know.'

'Tessa. Of course it wasn't. Which of our friends would do that? Even as a joke. *Babe.*'

'I wasn't thinking about a friend. More someone like Dave Jepsom.'

'Dave Jepsom!' I dropped my hands and looked at her in astonishment. 'Why on earth would you think that?' I said.

'I don't think he likes me.'

I tried to stay reasonable, trying not to think of the last episode. I'd hoped we had got to grips with her anxiety issues. 'He's got no reason not to like you. What have you done to him?'

'Or he feels that I'm a bad mother.'

'You're being absurd.' I bent to kiss her head and took a step towards the door. 'Too much time on your hands. It'll be random. There are a lot of psychos out there.'

The next day, Tuesday, I took the car into the authorised Fiat garage in Battersea on the way to work. I was anxious to get it done by the dealer rather than some independent outfit, even though I'd pay more, get ripped off. Of course it's smoke and mirrors – I'm sure all you need is a mechanic and a forecourt. When I was growing up, my father was forever tinkering around under the bonnet of his car. He had had contempt for my lack of practical auto skills. Maybe that's why I'm so bullish on the matter. At least I can throw money at it. At least I can pay for home delivery and an official sticker.

A man in a tight suit made me a coffee from the Nespresso machine while the damage was being inspected. In that sort of macho environment, I tended to find myself playing a certain role. With Jeff's words ringing in my ears – he was right, wasn't he? It was time I found a car more suitable for my status as a company director, a 4x4 or something – I asked about trading the car in, or at least selling it on. Secondhand Fiat 500s were an easy enough sell; I knew that. But he was all wear and tear and bodywork and 'the issue with that particular model', blah blah. They make it up as they go along. I know the type. I'm one myself.

I took an Uber to the office as I was running late and I raced straight into a meeting to discuss an upcoming pitch: Prospecta, a multi-product software provider that wanted to 'redefine its internal and external communications strategy'. We were down to the final three.

I didn't notice until I came out that the work experience girl was still sitting on the chair where I'd left her the day before. She was swivelling back and forth, kicking against the floor with her toes, her mouth down, eyes glazed: an expression of absolute boredom.

'Oh my God, have you been there since yesterday?' I said.

'I went home for the night.' Her tone was deadpan.

'That's something.'

'It was the least I could do.'

She bit her lip, looking at me through her eyelashes. She was mocking me, not quite flirting. It showed spirit.

'Indeed. Indeed! Now we must find something for you. A project!'

I glanced around the office. Mary and Shreya were both on the phone; Emma was putting on her jacket, about to head off. Only Jeff looked at a loose end. He was sloping out of the meeting room with the air of a man in search of a cigarette.

'Jeff!' I beckoned him, and he weaved across the room. The pouches under his eyes suggested a heavy night. 'Hail,' he said to the girl.

'Hail,' she replied.

I was beginning to like her.

'Jeff,' I said. 'Am I right in thinking you have the Citrus Burst Grand Prix sponsorship meeting this morning?'

He nodded.

'OK if you took Jem with you? It'd be more interesting than sitting here.'

He made a courtly bow and, without saying anything, crooked his elbow, inviting her to link her arm through his. She slipped off her chair, her youth revealed in a sudden blush, and the two of them left the office.

It wasn't a conscious decision to put Jeff in charge of the intern. It happened just as I have said. If she ended up shadowing him instead of me, well, mea culpa. Hands up. I was lazy and thoughtless here, as I was in so many other aspects of my life.

I should have anticipated the dangers. But the tide was against me. Who wouldn't have preferred hanging out with Jeff to me, who wouldn't have gone with his nonchalance and charm and self-confidence, his BMW, his proper *man's* car: of course it would appeal.

I don't see why I should be held responsible.

Her

Josh was still poorly on Tuesday. I rang Yasmeen to cancel the playdate we'd planned that afternoon. He lay on the sofa most of the day, drowsily watching *Octonauts* on CBeebies. I curled next to him, regularly checking his forehead, kissing his damp brow.

I felt both guilty and acutely anxious. He had been sitting on Miss Jenny's knee when I'd arrived to pick him up, his cheeks flushed, his eyes bleary. Her expression told me what she thought of me and she was right. I'd abandoned him for Richard. I should never have gone to his flat. I don't know what I had been thinking. I *hadn't* been thinking – that was the problem. I was dangerously out of control. I wouldn't see him for dinner on Thursday. Of course I wouldn't.

Slag. The writing on the car – it seemed so personal. Marcus had said it was random. He didn't know the truth: that I'd blocked someone's drive. I couldn't have told him, or he'd have wanted to know why I had parked down at the Tube; where I'd been going. So many layers of deception. Now I thought about it, though, it probably was random – or some kind of act of rage. Things like that happen. When I was little one of my mum's boyfriends smashed the windscreen of a car he believed had taken his parking space with a crowbar.

And yet I *was* a slag.

I told myself it was ridiculous to think Dave had seen me on the phone to Richard, and somehow knew. He hadn't been in the bar. He hadn't been following me. The figure I'd seen in the street, skulking under the tree: I'd imagined it.

I tried to drive out my sense of growing dread with domesticity. I tidied the bedrooms and changed the sheets on our bed. I put on a load of washing and made a pile of clothes to take to the dry-cleaners. I cleared out cupboards and scrubbed the kitchen. But images kept coming into my head; Richard's fingers tracing patterns on my stomach, over the lace of my underwear, the tug of his tongue. I rubbed harder, poured on more bleach. I felt almost frenzied with the fear of discovery. What if Jepsom did know? What if he told Marcus? I'd behaved so badly. I'd risked so much. I loved my family; I loved my home. I was so lucky to have both. I had so much to lose.

In the afternoon, Josh slept, and I sat on my bed and opened my laptop. It had been on my mind for a while to involve myself more closely in Marcus's work. I thought it might help us. I began by Googling some of his clients. Maybe if I was a bit better informed and could ask the right questions, he would talk to me more – like he used to.

Tilly Elworthy had provided an insight into her make-up bag for *Stylist* and Citrus Burst was in a taste-comparison grid in the *Observer*. And McCready, the racetrack millionaire, seemed to be in trouble – the MailOnline was enjoying the fact that he'd been caught speeding. Headline: HOLD YOUR HORSES.

On the BBC website I read about Tony Judd's arrest. I had an inkling; I'd overheard snippets over the weekend, but I hadn't realised it was this serious. The accompanying photograph was of Judd being bundled into a car as he left the Ritz-Carlton for the airport, throwing a panicked look at the camera, his face red and pouchy. I hoped Marcus was being cautious. It was as good as a family business and would need careful handling – it would be easy to get it wrong.

My eye was caught by an item below it. A French business-man, Michel Lefevre, 44, had been found dead in his car in Moscow – an apparent heart attack. The journalist, restrained by legalities, seemed keen to layer on the insinuations. Lefevre, 'heavily involved with the Ukrainian pipelines', had recently been seen with the Russian billionaire Dimitri Mikhailov. There was a photograph of the two men shaking hands – the Russian in a dark suit, another man hovering behind, a gun tucked in the back of his trousers.

I hoped Marcus knew about this. And that he was being careful.

I could hear Josh stirring and was about to close the computer when I clicked on Facebook. Dave Jepsom's friend request was still waiting.

My finger hovered for a moment. I clicked on his profile. It was blank, with the strap 'To see posts on Dave's timeline, accept his friend request'.

I pressed 'confirm'.

A line of entries flashed up. I quickly scanned down. It was one of those alarmist streams that some people veer towards: alerts about outrageous scams and name-and-shame notices of people being cruel to animals. He'd reposted an article about a student who'd bullied another child and been protected by rich parents.

Only twenty-five friends, and just three photographs. I looked at them in sequence. They were all taken in Greece. One from a distance was of those two boys playing football, another, posed, was of the girl called Tracey, blowing a kiss, and the third image – I stared – the third image was of us.

It must have been taken just as we were leaving the beach. I was sitting in the boat with Josh on my knee, my mouth grim, while Marcus was bent over, untangling the ropes. It was taken at close range. Jepsom must have held up his phone and pressed the button just after we'd said goodbye.

I felt hot behind my eyes, my mouth dry. I closed the page. He was clearly new to Facebook, so possibly it wasn't odd that all of his photographs were from the holiday. And as Rose said, saving Josh was bound to have been a big moment for him so maybe it was natural to record the experience. It was just one harmless picture, wasn't it? There was nothing sinister about it.

Him

I didn't see much of Tessa that week.

Work continued to be frantic. Not just constant phone calls about Tony Judd and nerves to calm in-house about the 7Nights launch – the chief exec was still unhappy about the guest list. But random things, too. Citrus Burst was upset by an article in the *Daily Telegraph* claiming sales of their soft drink spiked during Ramadan. (Problematic: we'd worked hard to downplay the company's sugar-rush reputation, but to weigh in too hard would be to risk sounding anti-Muslim.) And on Wednesday, we had an unexpected upset from one of our more low-key clients: Jeff's old prep school, Cartingdon Hall.

It wasn't a typical account. The owners had decided a couple of years ago to rebrand the school, become less traditional, more liberal, and as a favour we'd helped redesign the website and draft a new mission statement.

The headmaster rang Jeff to say he'd received an anonymous letter from an ex-pupil, claiming they were the victim of historic sex abuse, and threatening to blow the whole thing open.

We had a tricky discussion in the office over this. There was a strong feeling from some, particularly Mary, that in the current climate it was important to be open, to inform parents about the letter, and to announce an immediate investigation. Jeff disagreed.

The room got heated.

Jeff said, 'Oh for God's sake, calm down everyone, a little buggery never hurt anyone.'

Obviously, he was being flippant. One of his strengths is his ability to steer decisions with a light hand. And in fact we did conclude that it would be better to hold off until something more substantial surfaced. But it wasn't the moment. Allegations like that could close a school if not handled carefully. After the meeting, I told him he had to apologise to everyone present.

As far as I knew he did.

It was an odd period, looking back. Usually, one of our clients was demanding, while the others lay dormant. That week they all seemed to be clucking and twitching at the same time. If I hadn't known better, I'd have thought someone was going through our client list and messing with our heads.

On Thursday Jeff and I had promised to go out on the town with Dimitri and Olaf. I really should have cancelled. I'd worked late on Tuesday and Wednesday; I'd hardly seen Tessa and I was a bit worried about her, after her oddness about the car incident. She'd asked if I could get home early so we could have an evening together. But when I suggested to Jeff we cancel the Russians, he reared backwards in comedy shock. 'Rather you than me,' he said.

I rang Tessa instead and told her I had an unavoidable dinner with clients. Not a complete lie. I'm sure you could get dinner there if you wanted. But it wasn't exactly what they had in mind (Executive Gentlemen's Club, my arse.)

She sounded upset. 'I might go out myself then,' she said.

I didn't ask where.

✶   ✶   ✶

Leather and Lace was in a side street close to Shepherd Market, in the middle of a row of low white stuccoed houses. I rang the bell, on a discreet gold panel, and once the bouncer had consulted his list, descended into the basement. It was all red and black – red and black flocked walls, red and black carpet, red banquettes and black leather stools, slightly too low and small for some of the portly executive gentlemen who sat astride them. The sex industry could do with re-thinking its colour scheme, I thought. They should get Ilse Crawford – she'd do wonders. Enormous chandeliers sent splinters of light across the tables, but otherwise it was gloomy. Weird to remember it was still bright as midday outside. Candles flickered, though closer inspection revealed them to be battery-operated LED. Tacky and fake, as befitted 3.2 stars on Google review.

I scanned the room – a lot of men in suits. Up on the stage, two women with long black hair wearing heels and elaborate lacings of underwear had embarked upon a series of elegant contortions. It's not that I hadn't been to a lap-dancing club before – once with another client, and once, before that, on a stag do – but I'd never felt comfortable with the etiquette. Was it demeaning for all concerned to stare, or not to stare? Once one was actually there, was it in fact *rude* not to ape interest and involvement? Who knew? I certainly didn't.

Spotting Dimitri and Olaf at the front, splayed in a circular VIP-style throne arrangement, I ambled over, a fixed smile on my face. They were with two other men, both bearded, one on his phone, the other gazing ahead at the writhing on stage.

'Ah, our great friend Marcus Nicholson has arrived.' Dimitri got to his feet and beckoned me with little flapping gestures of his hand. He was wearing a white shirt with several buttons gaping to reveal a smooth, bronzed chest. Olaf was in a suit, a triangle of spotted handkerchief sticking out of his jacket pocket. Ignoring their companions – their security detail, I assumed – they kissed me and clapped me on the shoulders, in turn, and made room for me in the middle of the bench before throwing themselves back down. I caught the smell of vodka and the rich musky tang of expensive aftershave.

Olaf leant forward to pour me a shot of vodka and then shoved it across the low table. I put out my palm just in time to stop it spinning onto the floor.

'To get you in the mood,' Olaf said.

I drank it in one. He fetched an open bottle of champagne from a bucket of ice at his feet, and clicked his fingers at a scantily clad waitress, who brought another glass, and then made a performance of pouring it out for me, bending at just the right angle to graze my ear with her breasts.

It was loud – rock music, with a heavy bass. I put my glass down. I had no intention of drinking too much tonight. I might even get home in time to see Tess. Resting my elbows on my knees, mannishly, I tried to engage Dimitri in conversation. How had the speech at the business lunch gone? Had he remembered what I'd said about eye contact? He moved his head from side to side, and up and down, both directions indicating a positive response.

Six poles were occupied now. One woman was unlacing, or pretending to unlace, the bodice of another with her teeth. She was swooping one of her own legs low across the floor at the same time, running her fingers suggestively in the strip of skin between the top of her stocking and her G-string.

I leant forward again, raising my voice. 'Did I ever tell you,' I said, 'about Henry Kissinger's famous press conference opening gambit?'

Dimitri's eyes flickered away to the stage and back. I wasn't sure he had heard, but I persevered. 'It's worth remembering.

A model of its kind. Cheeky but effective. He said, "Does anyone have any questions for my answers?"'

Dimitri smiled politely, and stretched out a hand to pat my arm. 'Yes, yes, my friend. But we are here to relax, to celebrate.' He leant into me as he reached into his back pocket, bringing out a small black wallet, from which he peeled a couple of fifty-pound notes. He clicked his fingers and two women walked over, one blonde, one dark.

Tucking a note into each G-string, he jerked his chin in my direction.

'On me?' he said.

I shifted uncomfortably, and made a not-for-now gesture with my hands, like someone refusing a second helping of pudding. *Fuck.*

He bowed his head and said something to Olaf who smirked.

During their lap dances, I leant as far back as I could. A finer detail of the protocol: was it appropriate to admire a bare arse when it was presented to one as part of another person's private entertainment or avert one's eyes?

Just when I thought I was about to curl up and die, a woman in a tartan bra and kilt weaved towards me.

'Mr Nicholson,' she said. Her accent was Middle European. 'There is a man asking for you.'

'That'll be Jeff,' I said pointlessly to Dimitri. 'He's come from a pitch.' I got to my feet and, unwilling to pass between him or Olaf and either of the girls, stood on the banquette and leapt over the back.

At the top of the red stairs, the bouncer was standing, clipboard in hand.

He jerked his chin towards a figure on the steps just beyond the doorway.

'Marcus. Marcus, my man. He won't let us in.'

His tie undone, his eyelids half closed, fluttering, he wasn't alone, but leaning into a woman for support. No, not a woman, a *girl* with long blonde hair, short skirt, skimpy top, black tights.

'No,' I said, when it hit me. 'Not this, Jeff. No.'

'Marcus, my man!'

'No,' I said again.

'Come on, mate.' He put his arms out for me. 'It's just a bit of fun.'

Jem, released from his weight, took a couple of steps to the side. She pulled the sides of her mouth down in an embarrassed grimace.

'Jem,' I said. 'I'm so sorry, this is awful. Quite awful.' And then to Jeff, 'Have you lost your mind?'

'I lost the pitch,' Jeff said, 'so maybe I've lost my mind, too. I'm good at losing things. I lost my wife, Jem, did I tell you?'

'You did,' Jem said. 'It's really sad.'

He reached out both of his hands for her, pleading, shoulders hunched like the theatrical ham he so often was. 'You want to come in with us, don't you? You're following me. Me and my shadow. It's all part of the job.' He pulled down his chin and began to sing, about strolling and souls and troubles.

Jem giggled, but I was between them now, and managed to untangle his hands and push him away, coaxing him to sit down on the bottom stair.

'Wait there,' I said firmly.

'He can't sit there,' the bouncer said. 'He's blocking the entrance.'

'I'll be one second,' I said.

I led her back onto the road, apologising, holding her with one hand while phoning for a car from Addison Lee – the safest mode of transport I could think of – with the other. Then I waited with her on the corner of the street until it came. She said she was fine, that the pitch at the software provider had been quite interesting, 'not gonna lie', and that Jeff had only 'got weird' in the last half-hour or so. She said, 'His wife isn't dead, is she? I thought that's what he meant, but she just left him, right?' A yawn escaped her. When the car came she scooched along until she was bang in the middle of the back seat, and looked around herself, absorbing every detail, as thrilled as she was anxious to be the sole passenger. I checked the address with the driver – Bromley; well I'd send the bill to Jeff's personal account – and told her not to come in the following day. 'Have a lie-in. We'll see you again fresh as a daisy on Monday.'

Jeff had gone from the step when I got back up to the club. The bouncer gave a non-committal shrug. I found him slouched in the middle of the round sofa, flanked by the Russians. Shot glasses lay discarded on the table and they seemed to have moved on to beer. I re-entered the banquette by the same ungainly route I had exited: hoisting myself over the back of it and slithering down, pushing Jeff out of the way – he pitched sideways like a felled tree – to make space.

Jeff's head lolled back against the velvet. 'What happened with Linda?' he said. 'Lovely Linda. The love of my life. How did I let her slip through my fingers?'

'You fucked her over,' I said.

'Of course I fucked her. She was my wife.'

'I said, "You fucked her over." You fuck.'

'I did, didn't I? Oh God.'

It was a long, lingering 'Oh God', Jeff at his absolute worst: self-pity combined with a desperate desire for drama – the same personality traits that had got him into trouble in the first place.

I felt suddenly conscious of the tension behind my fore-head, of the pressure that had been building for days, weeks, ever since the holiday in fact. I don't know when I had last felt able to relax – long before that moment on the beach when I thought I might be about to. I could feel each stress pulsing; the worries about the business, my son, my marriage. The weight of it was unbearable.

I made a gesture at Dimitri, pointing to the vodka bottle, and he grinned and ceremoniously poured me another shot. He passed me a beer with his other hand. I downed the first and then the second, suddenly very keen for the hit and release of it. I needed to dispel the tension, for a moment to feel it thrum out of my nerve-ends. 'Fuck,' I said under my breath.

'More beer?' Dimitri said. 'Or more champagne?'

'I don't care. Either. Both.'

He grinned again.

'So, my friend.' He ran his forefinger in a line, under his lower lip, all the way along and then back. 'This time will you join me in a little entertainment?'

'I'm a married man,' I said.

'And there I was thinking extreme experience was not something you were averse to.' He gazed at me, a smile play-ing at his lips, a calculating look in his eyes. Then he wrinkled his forehead and turned to Jeff who appeared to be asleep, his lids a livid blue against the pallor of his face. Dimitri said, 'Unlike your partner.' He let a beat pass, and then he said, in a silly voice, 'Not tonight, Josephine.'

I laughed, and then I couldn't stop. Even as I was thinking *no, don't do this, walk away,* a wild angry part of me was wriggling free, eager for the opportunity to be more of a man than Jeff. Somewhere deep down, I was aware that my logic was off, that my definition of a man might be askew, but *everything* was askew: the room had begun to throb, colours coming and going like a pulse, the music clamouring weirdly in my ears. On stage the women were still writhing. On the floor mostly, their legs wide. Flesh and skin and hair; lips, thighs, mouths, tongues. Three of the girls were now topless – their breasts large and bare, their nipples weirdly pink. I downed the drink in my hand. What was it this time? Too fizzy for beer. In a glass, not a bottle. Champagne! And another shot. Down, down, down in one.

A waitress reappeared, holding a large tray of food above her head, which she carefully laid down on the table in front of us. Olaf handed over a fifty-pound tip without looking at her face.

'Wagyu steak with caramelised onion,' he said as he began to cut into it.

'OK,' I said, watching the blood leak beneath his knife onto the china plate.

'Cajun-style fries.'

'Nice.'

'Cherry milkshake.'

'Rather you than me.'

'It's good.'

'Excellent.'

'You want a fry?'

I took one from him and chewed it, beginning to laugh. 'I told my wife I was having dinner with a client!'

'OK.' Dimitri had got to his feet. 'So you have finished your French fry?'

'Cajun fry!'

'So now it is time for the main event. In my country, we take our hospitality very seriously. Tonight you are my guest.' He hooked his hand companionably under my elbow and brought me to a standing position.

'Whoa!' I said, putting my other hand on the back of the sofa for balance. 'Easy, tiger.'

He had clicked his fingers again and the hostess in the tartan bra and skirt returned, there was an exchange of some sort, and then he and I followed her across the room, swaying, weaving past the cheap lads in the cheap suits in the cheap seats – 'Sssh,' Dimitri said – through a door, to a room that was all fur. Fur walls and fur sofas and fur carpet. Big-cat fur. It was soft under my hands. I stroked it up and down and over, and then the women were in too. They weren't wearing fur. In fact, as the music throbbed, and their bodies moved, pretty soon they weren't wearing anything at all.

I could hear Dimitri making guttural noises on the seat opposite me. The woman giving me attention was wearing thick make-up, layers of mascara. As her hair flicked back and forth, it was impossible to make out the true contours of her face. Though that wasn't the point.

'Easy, tiger,' I said again.

My arm was strung across Dimitri's shoulders. Jeff was part-nered with Olaf. 'Two by two,' I sang. 'The animals went in two by two.' Up the red stairs, past the bouncer, out the front door and into the street. I didn't know what time it was. Five in the morning? Nine at night? The sky wasn't yet dark, still a lifeless blue, the air warm and stirring. A siren sounded. Traffic rumbled in the distance. The world was going about its business.

A car engine purred, but it wasn't for us. 'Move along, mate,' the driver said.

Now I looked, I couldn't find Dimitri and Olaf. They'd disappeared. Did I go back into the club? Or perhaps I only tried. I remember the thrust of the bouncer's hands, flat against my chest. Pouf! A push. Almost tumbling down. I remember laughing, rubbing my elbow. I think there was shouting, or singing. Jeff was reeling towards me. We crashed, pulled each other upright, creased.

My shirt buttons were undone. I made an attempt to do them up, and got in a muddle. I couldn't find the right hole. There was lipstick on the breast pocket, and on the collar. I tried to wipe it off, but it wouldn't budge.

I put my arm out for a cab, though there didn't seem to be one. Cars passed. A van, too close – oops – honked. A smooching couple on the opposite pavement stopped what they were doing. 'Are you looking at me?' I said.

Jeff seemed to be trying to put his hand over my mouth.

The couple moved on, and then in the shadow under the blue awning of the shop opposite, between some railings and a door, my eyes snagged on a man in beige chinos and a white T-shirt. I tried to focus, my feet suddenly hot, my head dizzy. I had an image of the beach, a stretch of empty sand, the sea. His arms were inked blue, a rim of barbed wire across the lower bicep. Seaweed, stars, letters, traces. His face was without expression. It was Dave Jepsom and he was looking straight at me.

And then a black cab was vibrating at the kerbside. Jeff was in, and I was in too, and thrown back into the seat, the acceleration like horizontal lines going past me, a vortex. And as I looked back through the rear window, the man grew smaller and then I couldn't be sure.

When I got home later, I climbed the stairs as carefully as I could and undressed in the bathroom. I scrubbed the lipstick off the shirt with soap and then I sat on the edge of the tub and stared at myself in the mirror. Five o'clock shadow. Dark circles under my eyes. Bloodshot corners. Was my hair receding? I stood up and looked more closely, scooping up a handful and scraping it back to inspect the temples. I decided it was. I made a face at my own reflection – somewhere between revulsion and despair. And then I cleaned my teeth and gargled with a capful of mouthwash. It stung my tongue and the corner of my lip. An ulcer, a small cut. I was a mess. I was falling apart.

Was it Dave Jepsom I had seen as I'd been getting into the taxi? No, of course not. It couldn't have been him. Why on earth would he have been outside a strip club in Mayfair? I was going mad.

The tap dripped onto the porcelain, running into the grooves of a calcified stain.

Tessa stirred when I got into bed.

'How was your dinner?' she murmured sleepily.

'Boring,' I whispered back. 'The usual.'

Her

I spent the Wednesday and Thursday of that week in the house. Josh was still feverish, and with every day I began to feel more feverish myself. It shouldn't be so hard, I kept telling myself. I had one child. Rose had a baby as well as a toddler. I didn't know how she coped. All my efforts to be a good nurse-maid failed. The mess seemed to pile up around me; the kitchen was full of dirty plates, the floor littered with toys. Josh was fractious, nothing I did was right – my eggs were runny, the toast was too hard, he didn't want the book I was reading. He wanted Daddy.

When Marcus rang on Thursday to say he wouldn't be home after all, he had 'a client thing', I felt close to tears. I'd been desperate to see him, to see someone.

I could hear the pull in his voice to get off the line, but I wanted him a little longer. 'A client *thing*?' I said. 'Why do you always say "*thing*"? Why aren't you more specific?'

'A dinner. OK? A dinner.'

'It's just I was hoping we could have supper together, talk for once.'

'What about?' He sounded anxious.

'Work? I'd like to know what's going on.'

'Work?' He sighed. 'Listen. Please don't give me a hard time. It's not like I *want* to go.'

I sat staring at the kitchen wall, and the marks made by Josh's dirty fingerprints; at the Lego I hadn't yet tidied up. I didn't *want* to meet Richard. I wanted to work on my marriage.

One more time. What difference would it make?

I texted Richard and found a babysitter: a neighbour's son, tall and gangly with jeans hanging well below his waistband. I showed him the tea and coffee and the emergency numbers pinned to the noticeboard in the kitchen. I explained that Josh, who was already in bed, had been ill, but that he was better. 'Goddit,' he kept saying. I tried to pretend I hadn't noticed the slight smell of weed.

Richard had suggested a Turkish restaurant in Waterloo – he was probably looking to take it over.

It was a large cavernous place, on a main road close to the railway arches, with a jungly courtyard outside and clattery tiles, hard-backed rush-seated chairs and brick walls inside.

He was already seated when I got there, at a table near the back. His eyes followed me as I crossed the room, unsmiling. I bent down to kiss him. Next to us, a large group of glamorous young women, scantily dressed for a Thursday night, were raucously celebrating a birthday. He looked across at them and frowned.

I apologised for having been out of touch. 'Josh has been ill so I've been pretty tied to the house.'

'You mean he's not been at work?'

I considered what he had just said.

'No, Josh. Not Marcus. Josh, my son.'

'Yes of course. Brain freeze.'

I let a beat pass. 'Anyway,' I said. 'I'm here now.'

He was dressed down tonight, in jeans and a black T-shirt, though the fabric was expensive and had a slight shimmer. I felt a flurry of irritation, an intense wish that I hadn't come. It was risky; anyone could see us. I felt foolish, and grubby. I liked him in a suit, generally navy with a crisp white shirt. The business look was somehow integral to the fantasy. In 'casual gear' he seemed older, dandy-ish. There was something feminine about his beautifully pared nails, the sheen of golden tan on his lower arms.

I ordered a gin and tonic, Richard a beer. I was wearing an old tea-dress and plimsolls, to show I didn't care, but I'd left the three top buttons undone. His eyes lingered on my cleavage. Despite everything, the muscles in my stomach tightened.

'Remind me what it is your husband does?' he said.

'He's in comms. You know that. You met him at Ekelund. He's since set up on his own.'

'Of course, of course. I did.' His forehead furrowed. 'What's his company called?'

'Hawick Nicholson.'

'Yes. I did know that. They've just taken on KazNeft, is that right?'

I looked at him cautiously. 'Yes.'

'He should be careful. There are rumours they're connected to some dodgy business: that murder in Moscow the other day? The guy found in the back of his car?'

'It's just media training he's doing,' I said. 'Eye contact, that sort of thing. It's not exactly on the edge. And that bloke – it was a heart attack, wasn't it?'

He shrugged. 'Just a coincidence that Lefevre turned down their business?'

'Well, anyway, Marcus is doing fine; they've just about paid off their starting-up costs. They're finally beginning to make money.' I sounded prickly.

The waiter arrived to take our order. I let Richard choose because I didn't care now whether I ate or not, and when the food came, he studied it carefully: the glistening mound of

135

mashed aubergine, the chunks of charred lamb, the neat moulds of sesame-beaded falafel. When he started eating, he put it away quickly, apparently without judgement. For him the restaurant business was more about concept than flavour – more taste, so to speak, than taste.

'Not hungry?'

I shook my head.

After a moment, I said: 'I was thinking about going back to work. Just part time so I can be there for Josh, but a few hours here and there. Some sort of consultancy.'

He nodded, but I'm not sure he heard.

'When we first met up you said you might have something for me. I wondered if anything had come of that?'

He cupped his hand behind his ear, shook his head. 'Can't hear you,' he said. Under the table, his hand had reached for my knee. He was pushing the dress up and out of the way.

I moved my legs away from him. 'Too many people,' I said.

His eyes didn't move from my face. 'I thought you liked that,' he said, continuing to stroke my thigh. 'I thought public affection was your thing, maybe . . .'

I pushed his hand away and this time he brought it out from under the table and raised it in surrender. 'Perhaps we should find somewhere quieter?' he said.

I didn't want to find somewhere quieter. I wanted to go home, to my husband, and my son. I didn't know what I was doing there, how I had let it come to this.

He popped a last falafel in his mouth and was already getting to his feet, stretching sideways to reach with his other hand for the wallet in the back pocket of his jeans. He gestured to the waiter, made a small mime for the bill, and I pushed back my chair and stood too.

It was only because I was waiting for Richard to deal with

the bill, averting my eyes from the actual embarrassing trans-
action, that I looked away and scanned the room, glancing
over the white-clothed tables and the high-backed chairs, the
rounded shoulders of the other diners, the weaving waiters, to
the far side of the room, and to the terrace.

One person was standing alone over there. The doorway
out to the patio was arched, and he was leaning against one
side of it. Trails of ivy dangled down from a window decoration above his head. Behind him, too, was a blur of green: the
vertical spikes of plants on the patio. He was a tall, broad man
– that I could see from here; casually dressed, the sleeves of
his T-shirt rolled up onto his shoulder, his inked biceps
bulging. I could see the faint fuzz of his hair against the light
behind.

He was looking in this direction, and there was something
about his stance that was unnerving; his jaw jutted forward
and his shoulders were rigid as if he was exerting pressure on
himself in some way, showing some kind of restraint.

I focused then on his face, on his eyes. And I had a sensation as if I had been knocked on the back of the head, my
arms floating, my legs giving way. It was similar to queasi-
ness, as if I were going to be sick, but it was more in my
limbs than my stomach; in my knees, the joints in my shoulders. It was like falling backwards, or collapsing inwards.
The girl on the next table shrieked: 'No, I wanted the lamb
thing! Save me some.'

His eyelashes were pale. I knew that. And his irises were soft
blue. I imagined I could see the pupils contract, the tiny kalei-
doscope patterns around them. I imagined I could see the five
o'clock shadow on his jaw, a muscle twitching on one side of it.

It was Dave Jepsom. There was no question this time. I
wasn't making it up. There was no doubt. The man standing
there was Dave Jepsom.

Richard's arm had snaked around my waist. His breath was on my neck, in my ear. I tried to move away; his fingers pressed against my ribs. Ahead of me, across the room, Jepsom was still watching me. For a moment I felt pinned between the two men, silent points in the raucousness of the room.

'Let's go,' Richard murmured, releasing me, and then I was off, pushing ahead, negotiating a path between the birthday party table and the table next to it, sweeping my way past chairs and legs, stumbling on a jacket that had fallen onto the floor, knocking someone's cutlery. I turned to apologise – it only took a second – but when I got to the front door and was out of it, and had turned between the spiky leaves of the plants on the terrace, he had vanished. I pushed past the smokers and the weekday drinkers, and searched the terrace up and down, checking every face. He wasn't there.

I went back into the restaurant, scanned it again – no sign – and then pushed the main door open and ran out onto the street. Traffic thundered past. A helicopter was spiralling overhead. People from the bar next door were smoking on the pavement. From the terrace next to me rose laughter, the clamour of voices. Black bin bags were piled close to the kerb. A bus was pulling away from a bus stop. A few metres down the road, people were spilling out of a venue.

Richard was across the road now, outside a launderette, talking into his phone. He waved to me, a couple of fingers twirling – just a minute, they said. He was frowning, concentrating, turned his body back to the piles of laundry, the spinning machines. I pushed my way back into the restaurant, desperate to know for sure now – to prove or disprove – and down some stairs, throwing open the door of the gents. The stench of urine, a bin trailing paper towels, a row of empty urinals.

When I got to the top of the stairs, a waiter approached me: 'Have you lost something, madam? Can I help?'

A couple close to me were watching; other people on other tables had turned their heads. 'No, no,' I said. 'No. I'm fine. Sorry.'

I stepped outside. Richard was in the middle of the road, waiting for a line of cars to pass. He jogged over to meet me, slipping his phone back into his pocket. 'Nightmare,' he said. 'Three possible cases of food poisoning at Fish Tales, the Marylebone branch. We've got a new chef there. I don't have to go immediately, but I will have to head off to make some calls quite soon.'

He threaded his hand between my body and my elbow, and wrapped his arm around me. I let him propel me along the road, down a turning and through a network of quiet streets. I didn't notice the route; I was studying each face that came towards us, alert to every sign of movement behind us or across the street, flicking my head if I heard footsteps. Richard didn't seem to notice anything was wrong. If he did, perhaps he thought I was upset. He kept saying how sorry he was to be cutting things short.

I thought we might be going to the station, but we reached the South Bank, where faces and bodies began to stream thickly towards us. His fingers gripping my waist, he marshalled me towards one of the buildings, and I let myself be steered through the big spin doors, and across the vast empty foyer. The performance was still going on, I think. It was subdued; the sound of our footsteps seemed muffled despite the loftiness of the ceiling, the endless stretch of tiled floor. He tried to kiss me at the lift, but I turned my head. A man and a woman were sitting on the wide, shallow steps up to the next level, holding plastic cups. I should have told him I wanted to go home then. I don't know why I didn't. A scurrying desperation, a need to feel something other than fear? His grip on my arm was so firm.

When the lift came, he pushed me inside. It was empty and he pressed the button with one hand, while raising my dress with the other.

The doors opened onto an underground car park, a hot concrete trap with a low ceiling snared with thick round silver-insulated pipes, the ground uneven and stained with oil. 'The Merc's over there,' he said, pointing to a far corner.

We crossed towards it, our feet clicking on the concrete, past rammed rows of cars, ranks of squat white pillars. It was deserted, but it felt creepily as if it might not be. Each seat-back in every car looked like a person, waiting silently, watching. A strip light flickered on and off. There was the sound of dripping water, as if someone were tapping a stick on the ground, and a hum which pulsed, getting softer and then louder again, like breathing.

Richard opened the back door carefully – the pillar next to it was streaked with scrapes of different-coloured paint. Oil pooled on the ground. He beckoned me onto the seat with a mock-courteous flick of his hand, saying, 'After you,' and then he was in on top of me. It was airless, and uncomfortable. We were both in a hurry. He had his food poisoning issues to sort out. I simply wanted to get it over with.

Richard held my wrists above my head against the door handle. My elbow trapped a strand of my own hair. His signet ring pinched my skin. And in that moment, even as I was pinioned, even as I felt the force of him, I began to free myself. It came quickly – a contempt for his shiny shirt, and his body, and his needs, the way his face was twisting, his lack of concern. And I started thinking about the babysitter, and Josh, and whether he had woken up at all while I'd been out and when the earliest was I could get home and—

BANG.

'What? Fuck!'

Richard leapt off me, knocking his head. 'Shit.'

I was cowering, slinking down, hiding my body with crossed arms. 'What is it? What is it?'

The noise had been loud and sudden. The car had shaken under the impact.

He was pulling up his jeans, peering out of the window at the same time, his head at an angle. 'Shit, I can't see.'

Perhaps one of the pipes on the ceiling had become detached and fallen on the roof of the car. No. There was someone out there, behind us, between the boot and the wall. They had their foot on the bumper; it was creaking, the car was vibrating.

Richard had done up his jeans and I slunk downwards along the seat out of the way so he could get to the door. He put his hand on the handle. I whispered, 'Be careful.'

He nodded and turned the handle, then pushed the door open.

A figure loomed up at the rear window, a face with its mouth open, eyes wide staring, tongue protruding. It made a noise like a battle cry, and then reared away. I shrank down. Richard had started shouting, 'Oi! You fuckers. Get lost, go away.'

Cackles of laughter, another body on the other side of the car, against the windscreen, the car shook once more.

Richard shouted again. He was trying to get around the car, but they were getting away. He swore. And then there was the sound of running footsteps.

Richard's face appeared. 'You all right?' he said.

There was a crash of a door, the sound of disappearing laughter.

I was still shaking. 'No.'

'It was kids,' he said.

'Fuck.' I started to cry.

He smiled gently, and slipped in next to me. 'Teenage kicks,' he said. 'Probably just jealous.'

But now I'd started, I couldn't stop.

'I'm sorry. It's just . . .'

It would be a relief, I realised, to put it into words.

'I'm being followed,' I said. 'This guy we met on holiday. I thought that was him.'

'But it wasn't. It was kids. That's all it was. Our fault for being so . . . adventurous.'

He looked at his watch.

'Just listen for a moment. Please.'

'OK.' He put his hands together in his lap, his fingers stroking the dial of his Rolex. He wanted to get going, but he could spare me a few minutes.

It was a relief to tell someone. I told him about Dave Jepsom then, about how he had saved Josh's life and we had bought him lunch, and then how when we were back in London he had turned up at the house and gatecrashed the dinner party. I told him I thought I had seen him on my way back from his flat on Monday, on the very same day that someone keyed the word 'Slag' into the paintwork of my car. I told him I thought I might have seen him in a shop near my house, and how I had definitely just seen him, half an hour before, in the restaurant, and that that was why I had been so scared. I had thought it was this man, Dave Jepsom, who had banged on the roof.

Richard listened. 'But it wasn't,' he said, when I had finished. 'It was just kids.' He rolled his fingers around my knee. 'You're imagining the whole thing. He's probably just got one of those faces, one of those body types that are more common than others. There's a woman on reception, a very attractive girl, and every time I see another blonde of a certain height I think it's her. You're seeing people who look like him, that's all.'

A very attractive girl. Had he really said that? If I hadn't been so upset, I'd have laughed.

'You think?'

'Yes.' He looked at his watch again, and then turned the handle of the car door. 'Now, forget all about it.'

I got home, paid the babysitter and went to bed. When Marcus stumbled into the bedroom shortly afterwards, I pretended to be half-asleep.

I lay there, thinking, into the early hours. My fear at the restaurant seemed frenzied and overwrought. Richard was right; I had imagined seeing Dave. He had saved Josh's life and somehow he had assumed a symbolic importance in my mind. I was summoning him up at moments when I felt the most shame. He was my conscience. That's all it was. He was a hysterical manifestation of my own guilt.

It was clear what I had to do: finish with Richard and he would go away.

Him

I received a text from Dimitri on my way to work on Friday morning: *I am glad to have partied with my new business associate. Magenta seemed very happy too.*

I stared at the words for an instant or two and then closed my eyes. Magenta – was that the name of the girl in the booth? I didn't want to try too hard to remember.

Luckily, the office was quiet. Jeff, when he arrived, looked even worse than I felt: red-rimmed eyes, grey skin. His breath smelt of fags and spearmint mouthwash. We convened in the kitchen and I showed him Dimitri's text. He shuddered, muttering about the evening having been 'a bit of a blur'. We agreed it was best to put it behind us.

There was no sign of Jem but, halfway through the morning, as I walked past Gail, I noticed she was looking up 'florists in Bromley' on her computer. I stopped and stood at her shoulder, feeling uneasy. I couldn't, or didn't, put it into words, but flowers felt off to me, as if they didn't convey quite the right message, or that they created the wrong one. But it was Jeff's call and my anxiety was only vague, shapeless. I went back to my own desk without saying anything.

I did ring my sister Sarah. She works in development at GlaxoSmithKline so I don't usually bother her at the office, particularly if it's 'just for a chat'. Our relationship has always been slightly tense; she carries guilt, I think, for having been our father's favourite. After running through the usual topics – her children's accomplishments, Josh's wellbeing, Dad's health – I asked casually about Jem's 'set-up'. She sounded guarded but she told me they were 'a nice enough family, bit pushy maybe, but who isn't?' and that Jem was in the top stream: 'Bright girl.' I suppose something in those words must have satisfied me because I let it go.

I spent the morning drinking coffee and catching up with emails, including a last-ditch attempt to persuade Yasmeen to come to the 7Nights press launch. My previous appeals had been jokey, and lightly ironic: 'I'm sure you'd really rather pull out teeth . . .' and included references to our shared local experience, 'or spend the evening finger-painting with Miss Jenny from Little Bears'.

This time, emboldened by desperation, I thought harder about what I could offer her. Her columns were usually arch in tone, but she tackled serious subjects, often with a political slant. In the end, I wrote: 'How about a piece on the gentrification of the motorway stopover, how terrorist events abroad combined with the inward-national stance of Brexit, have led to the rise of the staycation?' I was pleased with my little pitch. God, I might even read a piece like that. I kept checking over the course of the morning to see if she'd responded, but she hadn't.

Lunch was a long-standing arrangement with Tilly Elworthy at the Chiltern Firehouse, where she always orders the chia-seed crackers and the spiced Cornish crab and lobster omelette. It was buzzy; that perfect combination of tinkling glasses and fluffed white napkins. A model Tilly knew was sitting at the bar; a Hollywood star at a table in the corner. My stomach still delicate, I studied the menu at arm's length (crab-stuffed donuts: are you kidding me?); in the end ordering a pork chop and some French fries. I felt my mood settle, my body expand into the comfort of the seat and the surroundings.

Tilly could be great company, just the right side of flirtation, and that day she was on top form She was happy with me, and with my company's services; she called me 'Marco', the pet name she gave me when she was in a good mood. The measures Mary had put in place to save her reputation among the younger demographic had included a careers talk under the banner 'Inspirational Woman' at St Paul's Girls' School, which had been 'a blast'. She was delighted she'd been put forward to front the Save the Orang-utan campaign, and was finding life on the cutting edge 'seriously rewarding' (earnest face). Drum roll, she said, she had decided to stop using palm oil altogether, and had been researching coconut oil and shea butter replacements. Bill Hayes, her CEO, was worried about the financial implications, and felt sustainable palm oil was the only way forward for the world as well as the company, but she was digging in her heels. 'You agree, don't you, Marco? It's not just the orangutan, it's forests everywhere.'

Obviously, my role here was to agree wholeheartedly, and the cogs had already started whirring. Hadn't Tessa suggested this in the early stages of the crisis? I should have listened. Sustainability would be a great repositioning opportunity. I nodded enthusiastically.

'I'm so glad because I've got something else to run past you.'

She flicked her hair over one shoulder and leant forward, fixing me with her almond-shaped hazel eyes. 'Marco, you know the girls at St Paul's? They loved me! And you know, I found their spirit, their fire, so inspiring. Ever since then, I've been mulling it over and now I've decided: I'm going to launch a new range for teenage girls. Eco-friendly, natch. But also at a lower price point, with edgier packaging. Make them feel they own the brand. I want Tilly Elworthy to be their go-to make-up for life. What do you say? Are you with me? I have to tell you I'm super-excited!'

I was super-excited too. Of course I was with her. It meant a huge slice of potential new business. The trick with Tilly though was always to pretend to be one step ahead. I nodded wisely. 'You'd have to tread carefully,' I said. 'There are moral issues. You don't want to be promoting ideal versions of beauty. It has to be about diversity, and being happy in your own skin.'

'I knew you'd get it.'

'It might be good to go simple,' I said. 'You could call it TeEn.' I scribbled the letters down on a corner of the menu. 'Keep your initials in the form of the original logo, squeeze the "e" and the "n" alongside.'

'Marco,' she said, leaning across the table to cup my cheeks with her hands. 'I could kiss you.'

In the cab, on the way back to the office, I noticed I had a missed call from Tessa. I wasn't in the mood to ring her back. I was too fired. Seeing Tilly could do that to me. It was so easy to under-estimate her. I did a little drum roll on the side of my thighs. When it came down to it, she and I were the same. We both knew how to build a brand.

There was a voicemail, too, but I didn't listen.

Her

It rained in the night, and in the morning the sky was a peerless blue, puddles glinting. I sat on the step in the garden while Josh was having breakfast and composed a text. I know it would have been better to have done it in person, but I seemed to forget myself when I was with him, and anyway, I wasn't so much a part of Richard's life that leaving him would make an impact.

I wrote: *Dear Richard, I've had a lovely time with you but as I keep trying to tell you, I think we should call it a day. I have a family that needs me. Hope all continues to go well with the business (not too many people ill with the food poisoning!) I mean it this time! Love, Tessa*

He replied almost immediately: *How can I change your mind?* Quick type. *You can't.*

It was an inadequate exchange in many ways. It didn't matter. It was done.

Josh was better today, but I kept him at home to be on the safe side. I had a sort of high restless energy, a desperate urge to be with him that felt almost like alarm; a frenzied combination of relief and love and fear. It was over, I tried to tell myself. No one had found out. I had got away with it. And yet it seemed extraordinary that I should have betrayed my husband and my son, that I should have come so close to destroying everything I had fought so hard to get, and that there should be no consequences. 'You get what you deserve,' my mother used to say. I had a fear that someone out there knew I deserved nothing.

I had never loved Richard. I hadn't even particularly *liked* him. I'd risked everything. In Greece, I'd even risked my own child's life. Jepsom was right to hold me in contempt; I wasn't to be trusted.

It was warm and sunny, though, and Josh's spirits were high. I contrived to think of something different we could do together, to squeeze the most out of our time together.

Marcus was supposed to be in charge of the garden. He knew what to do. He'd pruned and propagated at his mother's knee. We hadn't even had window-boxes at the flat where I grew up; my mother used to say why bother spending money on something that will only die? But Marcus seemed to have let things slide out here recently, and there was no reason I couldn't learn. It wasn't too late. The Fiat had been delivered back that morning and so Josh and I drove to the garden centre. I was aware of emanating a prickling alertness, but Josh ran up and down the aisles grabbing things at random and I pushed the big metal-cage trolley behind him, saying, 'Yes, good idea, let's go for those.' To his motley collection I added some terracotta pots, a trowel, a pair of gardening gloves, and, at the suggestion of the woman at the till, a bag of compost.

Back at home we set to work, arduously and clumsily transporting the plants into either the flower beds, or the new pots. It was so much messier than I'd anticipated. Out of their plastic containers, the plants seemed to vanish down to nothing! We needed so many more! The compost went everywhere!

We were enjoying ourselves though. You didn't have to be good at things, I realised, to have fun. So it was a disaster; who cared? I was wearing shorts, a grubby T-shirt and a pair of gardening gloves and I didn't bother taking them off when I heard the doorbell.

A blob of soil from one glove attached itself to the metal as I turned the latch. I pulled the other glove off with my teeth.

Did I already suspect? I don't see how I could have done, and yet when I remember the details, the earth against the paint, the roughness of the glove on the inside of my upper lip, they are already coloured with dread.

It was Dave Jepsom. On the doorstep. Dave Jepsom – not an imaginary projection, but a real person, blood and bone. I'd imagined him so often since our last encounter that he seemed shockingly familiar, imbued with dark significance.

Josh charged up behind me and pushed his head through my legs, so that I was toppled sideways. I was already unbalanced, my hand reaching to stop myself from falling as I pulled the door towards me.

What is happening? It was the only complete thing in my head. The rest was fragments. How? What? *Fuck.*

'Hello, Josh,' he said, leaning forward. He was wearing a faded green utilitarian boiler suit.

'We're planting a garden,' Josh replied.

Crouching down, leaning one elbow on his bent leg, Jepsom pulled out a hexagonal tube from his top, brandishing it like a magic wand.

'Smarties!' Josh tunnelled forward, grabbed the packet and immediately ran back into the house, like a dog with a stolen bone.

Jepsom stood up and for the first time met my eye, with a sideways glance. The faintest blush came to his face. I realised he was embarrassed; shy, even. 'Kids, eh?' he said. 'They'll do anything for a sweetie.'

'Yes.' I swallowed, and took a breath. 'Nice to see you again.'

I had managed to stretch my mouth into a smile. He wasn't a threat. He wasn't a stalker. There was nothing malicious about him. It was all in my imagination. And yet I couldn't bring myself to move from the step.

'I expect you're wondering what I'm doing here,' he said. 'It's nice to be connected on Facebook, by the way. Did you see my pictures?'

'Yes,' I said faintly.

'So, yeah, I was thinking about you and the little lad, and I thought I know what, I'll pop in, do them a favour.' He picked up a big black bag that was slumped at his feet. It said DeWalt in orange writing. 'I thought I could mend your dripping tap. The one in the en-suite?'

I stared at him. How did he know we had an en-suite?

'What dripping tap?' I said.

He lowered his chin into his chest, as if to say, *Come on.* 'I discussed it with Marcus. It's probably a washer.'

'Marcus didn't mention it.' I looked over my shoulder into the house, and then back at him. He cocked his head expectantly.

'Do you want me to mend it?' he said slowly. 'I'm here now. It's no trouble.'

I felt a sense of vertigo, a confusion that was physical. I let the moments tick dangerously past. And then, like retribution for my rudeness, came a thump inside the house and a loud cry.

In the sitting room Josh was still lying where he had fallen, on the floor, at the base of the sofa, his head against the hard polished wood. I felt hysteria begin to rise. It was my fault. It was what I'd been dreading. I'd been fatally distracted. I'd brought disaster down on us.

Dave pushed past me and was there first. He lifted Josh into his arms and carried him over to a chair, where he checked him over, lifted his eyelids, felt his skull. 'He's OK. He's OK,' he said. 'No damage.' He stood up, making a noise of relief from between his lips. 'Nasty moment.'

I was kneeling down myself now, but Josh had stopped crying, astounded by the attention, and was struggling to get down to collect the Smarties he had scattered.

'You can't take your eye off them,' Dave said, with little vibrating shakes of his head.

'Yes, I know,' I snapped.

His expression was sombre, judgemental. 'It's just . . .' he began. 'Anything can happen.'

'I know,' I said again.

We looked at each other.

'I'll go up then, shall I?' he said after a moment.

'Yes.' I felt suddenly depleted. Once more he had got to Josh before me. 'Yes. Thank you.'

He went ahead up the stairs and I followed; the fabric of his boiler suit rustling as he moved his legs. Josh trundled up behind. We reached the first landing, and he pushed open the door of the bedroom. I was suddenly acutely aware of the mess – the intimacy of the unmade bed, the squashed pillows, snagged sheets. I kicked a tangle of dirty clothes, underwear, under the chair.

In the bathroom, he unzipped the bag. Inside it were pliers, Stanley knives, cutters – stainless steel, sharp points, sharp edges, hefty handles. He cracked his knuckles and brought out a large metal wrench, which he tapped a couple of times in the inside of his palm.

Josh made a lunge for it. I pulled him back, tried to keep him close to my side. He struggled to get free.

Dave smiled. 'You like what you see, do you?' He rootled around and drew out a series of instruments. 'Your pipe-cutter. Your ball-peen hammer. Hacksaw. Needle-nose pliers. Everything a man needs.'

He was talking to Josh, but he looked at me then.

'Women too,' I said also to Josh. 'Everything a woman needs.'

Jepsom laughed. 'Women's libber, are you? I thought you were a mum.'

He was still holding the red-handled pliers. The ends were tight and pointed.

'I'm both,' I said. 'It's possible to be both.'

He turned his head to the tap. 'I see.'

I swallowed. 'OK, we'll leave you to it, thank you.'

I tried to draw Josh out of the room with me. He fought back. 'I want to help. I want to help.'

He continued to cry out as I battled to get him down the stairs and into the kitchen. I warded his small blows off with my knees while I pushed the door shut, standing there with my legs and arms out, pressing against it to form a barrier, and fumbled with my phone. The call went straight to voice-mail and I left Marcus a message. Josh threw himself to the floor, beating the tiles with his fists and feet. Within the walls of the house, rattling noises, cranking, the impact of heavy objects on hard surfaces. I put the phone back in my pocket, moved away from the door and sat down at a kitchen chair. Josh raised his head and looked at me, gave another half-hearted wail, but didn't get up. He lay his head back down and was still for a moment, the cool of the tile against his cheek.

Just because he was actually in the house now didn't make any difference – did it? – to the imaginary sightings. It didn't make them suddenly real again? No. This was real and those weren't; there was no correlation between the two. I should take comfort in that. I should re-tune my instincts. He did judge me. He suspected I was an unfit parent. But he'd done nothing to lead me to believe he knew about Richard, or that he'd seen me make that call. This was normal, cordial behaviour. I'd opened communications by accepting his friend request. Turning up was over-familiar perhaps, but nothing about it was intrinsically odd.

Ten minutes or so later, I heard his footsteps on the stairs and he pushed the door of the kitchen and peered round it.

He talked to me, then, like any builder or odd-jobber, with the self-conscious air of one talking down to an imbecile: what he'd done, what he'd liked to have done if he'd had more time or if the pipes hadn't been so badly plumbed in in the first place. 'Polish, were they, your builders?' he said. 'Like your friend's?'

I said I wasn't sure.

Anyway, moving on, he had some advice about the shower attachment – the head was too heavy, he said, to hang above a clawfoot bath; if it fell it could do 'serious damage'. It might be worth replacing it. He could get one like it for me, if I wanted. Where did we get it?

'C.P. Hart,' I said. 'I don't know anything about it, but Marcus seemed to think they were the best.'

'Oh, he did, did he?' He gave me an odd look, a small smile playing in the corners of his mouth, as if we were in collusion against Marcus's middle-class demands. 'Yes, I expect he would.'

He was standing by the wall calendar, and he took a step towards it. Marcus's mother had given it to us for Christmas. Each month was illustrated with a different picture of Josh. For 'July' he was wearing a sunhat and Marcus's Ray-Bans.

He studied it for a moment, our life in grid-form: dentist appointments and playdates, our holiday blocked out: 'SUFFOLK'. And in smaller letters beneath: 'Seagull Cottage, Thorford'.

'Another trip?' he said.

'Yes.'

'Nice,' he said. 'To get away, I mean.'

'We're lucky.'

He leant against the sink. 'You certainly are.'

'I didn't have many holidays when I was growing up.' I wanted him to know I hadn't always been this fortunate.

'No?' The look again, as if I didn't need to tell him anything he didn't know, that he saw through the accent, the clothes.

Josh had been playing in the corner with the fire engine, and he now began pushing it across the floor. Jepsom followed its movement with his eyes.

'He works hard, doesn't he, Marcus? Long hours. Not much time for the family.'

I made a non-committal bob of the head, somewhere between a nod and a shake. I tried not to sound defensive. 'Not much.'

The fire engine was wonky, missing a wheel. The plastic widget that attached the hose to the side had snapped so the hose dangled and stopped the remaining wheels from turning properly, and part of the bumper had fallen off. It was an indictment of our parenting, I realised. We hadn't looked after it.

Dave stared at it a moment longer, his eyes narrowed; his jaw jutted an inch forward. Then he picked up his tool-bag, turned abruptly and walked up the stairs and into the hall.

I followed him, watching as he squatted down and fiddled with his bag, rearranging a tool, to make it easier to close the side pocket.

'How's your brood?' I said. 'Your baby's how old now?'

He was still struggling with the zip, and he used both hands to tug at it. It hissed shut. 'There, done.' He stood, hurling the bag over one shoulder. 'What baby?'

'The baby? Poppy, is it?'

'Poppy. Yes. She's bonny.'

'And the boys? Back to school OK?'

'Er, yup.'

'Oh, good.' I was looking at him carefully now. 'And Sherry completely recovered from her food poisoning?'

He took a step towards the door and, with his back to me, tugged at his trousers, bending to lift the hems.

A moment passed before he answered. 'Yes,' he said. 'No problems there.'

He turned and I reached for my handbag, which was hanging on the back of the buggy, and delved into it for my wallet.

'How much do I owe you?' I said.

He took a step back, his brow furrowed, his face screwed up in disgust. 'I don't want payment. It's a favour.'

'No. Please. I don't . . . I'd feel uncomfortable not giving you anything for your time.'

'I don't want your *money*.' He sounded repulsed.

'No, of course not.' I spoke too quickly, plunged into embarrassment. 'I'm sorry. I just—'

'What do you two think I'm here for?'

'I'm sorry. Thank you.'

Josh had come up with us and was pressing himself against my legs. Jepsom now bent and, without speaking, lifted his chin, surveying his temples and running his hands over his head.

'You look after him,' he said, rising up again. Something had soured. The crude power of my insult, the offer of money, expressed itself slowly like a burn.

'I will.'

'You have to keep your eye on them the whole time at this age. You answer your phone and before you know it . . .'

I felt the heat rush into my face. So he *had* seen me talking to Richard.

'Before you know it, something fatal has happened. You've got a dead kid on your hands.'

'Yes, I understand.'

He took a step out, and another onto the path. I held my breath, tense for the moment I could finally close the door. I was already anticipating the sound of it, the crunch, the *confirmation* of it.

But he turned at the pavement. 'I meant to say: it was unnecessary of Marcus to send me the shoes.' Lifting one foot to show me, he spoke carefully as if he knew he were spilling a little venom. 'But I appreciate the gesture. Pass on my thanks if you could.'

Him

My hangover, temporarily diverted by the excitements of lunch with Tilly Elworthy, returned with a vengeance on the commute home. My head thumped, and I had regular spasms of nausea, which were worsened by the lurch of the train.

As I crossed the patch of common that separated the station from the main road, I took my phone out of my pocket, and listened to my voicemails. Bill Hayes, Tilly's CEO, had rung asking if we could have a meeting (he wanted to elicit my support for palm oil, I suspected), and there was a bum-call from Jeff; lots of rustling and clanking. And then Tessa. Josh was screaming in the background, so it was hard to hear what she was saying. Did I hear the name Dave Jepsom? 'Dave Jepsom's here'? Was that it? No. Maybe I misheard.

I cupped my hand over my ear and listened again. 'Where are you?' she said, followed by a rant about me never answering my phone and then, 'Your friend Dave Jepsom's here' and something about a tap. She told me to ring her and then she hung up.

I stopped walking and leant against a tree. Dave Jepsom had been there that day. In our house. From the haze of last night, I remembered something I'd forgotten. *I thought I saw him outside Leather and Lace.*

Images came to me in flashes: the naked woman in the private booth; the ruched velvet on the ceiling; the lipstick on my shirt. How far had I gone with that dancer? Magenta, I assumed her name was. I'd been suppressing the question all day. There was a loud buzzing in my head. Had Dave seen me? Had he gone round to the house to talk to me about it? He'd have known I would be at work. Had he gone round to tell *her*? Would he do that? Is that the sort of thing anyone would do? It would if he felt somehow responsible for us, or for Josh, and the weird thing is I felt that perhaps he did. I pushed away from the tree, suppressing a desire to get back on a train and go back to the office, to busy myself with other people's crises.

My head was pounding, my mouth dry as I let myself into the house. I could hear footsteps coming to the door, and I tensed.

'Car's here I see,' I said, with fake cheeriness. 'Did they drop it back this morning?'

Her hands were flicking the air, and her mouth was twisted into an odd shape. 'So you're home,' she said. 'Did you get my message?'

I scanned her face. She was unreadable, that was the problem. She always was. Unknowable. She was nothing like the girls I'd grown up with, or the women I'd dated at uni. It was what had drawn me to her when I'd seen her across the office. The ground around her was always uneven.

I shrugged off my bag. 'Yeah,' I said casually. My hands were shaking slightly. 'You said Dave Jepsom came round?'

'Yes. To mend a tap. Did you know about it? Did he mention to you that he might come?'

'Yeah,' I said, pretending to flick through the letters, the junk mail, on the hall shelf. 'Actually, that does ring a bell. He noticed when he was round here the other night.'

159

'How did he notice?'

'He used the loo.' I shrugged to imply this was obvious

'The one in our bedroom?' Her eyes were bright. She was biting one of her fingernails.

Where was she going with this? I raised a shoulder. 'He got lost, I think. I don't know. But it was kind of him to follow up on it, wasn't it? He's a decent chap.'

She took her finger away, chewed the side of her lip instead, kept it skewed under her teeth. 'I didn't like him knowing his way around our house.'

'Does it matter?'

'He thinks he's our friend now, that he's in our life, that he can say anything he likes to us.'

I looked up at her again quickly, needing to know what he had said to her. But Josh bounded up then, wanting to tell me about some flowers. I bent down and let him lead me through to the kitchen and out to the garden. I pretended to admire the impatiens they'd put in the flower beds, and the terracotta urns they had planted up with a combination of lavender and stocks and cacti (lavender and stocks and cacti! She had no idea). Tessa was leaning against the bi-fold doors, adding the occasional comment: 'We'll buy more next time, won't we, Josh? We didn't realise how little they would look once they were in the earth.'

The lavender was floppy; I gently dug around at the base to release the roots into the soil. I was feeling defensive – I hadn't had time to do anything out here this year. But when I looked up, I realised she wasn't resentful. Her expression was anxious as if she were waiting for my approval. 'Is it all right?' she said, with a hopeful smile. 'There was so much. We didn't know what to choose.'

I remembered a story about the mustard and cress she'd been given at school to take home and grow; only she'd kept it inside her desk and tried to care for it there, taking it out to water it at break, because she knew if she took it back to the flat her mother would throw it away.

'The plants are great,' I said. 'You've done brilliantly.'

Her shoulders dropped, and she let out a small sigh.

Nothing else was said, and I put Josh to bed. The weight lifted, eased. She didn't know about the strip club. Dave Jepsom had not been there. I'd imagined him. Nothing awful had happened. Nothing awful was going to happen. Later that evening, she and I sat out in the garden as the light began to go. She had made a rich pasta dish which I had just managed to get down. I was longing to go to bed, to feel the pillow against my throbbing head, when she said: 'So you really don't think it was odd him turning up like that?'

I felt a rush of irritation, almost anger. I'd thought we were finished with this. 'No. Let's try and forget all about him, shall we?'

She stared at me hard. 'You really think it is OK?'

I was aware that earlier I hadn't separated my personal paranoia from the more general implications of his visit. I pretended to consider her question for a moment. 'Yes. It is OK,' I said. 'Over-friendly, but that's all.'

She glanced at me, and away again, wrinkling her nose. 'There's something about him that gives me the creeps. He's weirdly judgemental. And it's odd. As he was leaving I asked him about his kids – you know, the baby, and the boys, Carl and Mikey. And I got this sense that he didn't know who I was talking about. He said the new term had started, but we're past the middle of term. He was just so vague. I don't know . . . It just occurred to me, that maybe they weren't his kids. But if so, why didn't he come out and say it?'

A breeze shook through the bushes. I said, 'I assumed he was married to that woman we didn't meet, the one who had food poisoning.'

'We assumed a lot, though, didn't we?' She looked up at the house, at the window to Josh's bedroom. 'We don't really know anything about him. He knows his way around our house. He spent a long time looking at our calendar. I feel as if he's checking us out.'

'What? You think he might be casing the joint? Come on, Tess, he's not like one of your mother's dodgy boyfriends.'

I regretted it as soon as the words were out of my mouth. Her cheeks reddened. 'Maybe I'm being more realistic than you. You want everyone to be your friend. Well, great. The truth is a couple of times I've thought he might be following me. I'm probably imagining it, but I've seen a man like him in odd places. Last night, for example . . .'

The hairs on my arms rose.

A motorbike in the street at the front of the house revved loudly. A few gardens down, a dog started barking.

'What happened last night?' I said.

'I thought I saw him at the restaurant – the one I went to with Ruby.'

'Which was where? Which restaurant? Where?'

'I can't remember the name. It was in Waterloo.'

I'd been holding my breath and I let it go. 'I thought I saw him last night, too, at my client dinner. But I was in Mayfair so we can't both have seen him.'

Her face loosened. She said: 'Possibly he's just one of those men who looks like other people.'

'Yeah. He's definitely a certain type.' I pushed my chair back. 'I think I might hit the sack.'

I stood up and started stacking the plates. I was aware that she hadn't moved. I could feel her eyes on me.

'So when he came today,' she said. 'He told me something else.'

I put the plates back down and pressed the fingers of both hands against my temples. 'Oh yes?'

'You think you got away with it, that I wouldn't find out, but I have.'

I reached for the new lavender and pinched one of the fronds, hard, snapping it off between my fingers. A sharp pain under my ribcage. This was it then. He had seen. Maybe he'd even been inside the club. He'd know everything. This was where it blew apart. I had a sudden inexplicable urge to sweep the plates onto the ground, to hear them smash. I managed to cock my head as if I wanted to hear what she had to say.

'You idiot. Nearly three hundred quid for a pair of trainers. I can understand the gesture, but it might be one reason why he won't leave us alone.'

I felt a surge of emotion twinned with a spasm at the top of my spine. My vision cleared. 'Yes, I should have said I did send them in the end. It was the least I thought we could do.'

I did pick up the plates then, and shortly after found myself in bed. Crisis over, I told myself. She didn't know. He hadn't seen.

I don't know why it didn't feel like relief.

Her

I had the dream again that night. The sea was a pock-marked gun-metal grey, the sand the dead colour of wet concrete. Josh was a long way from me, at the end of the jetty; I was on the far side of the bay. My feet were deep in the sand and I couldn't move them. I could only watch as Josh toddled to the edge, about to fall. I couldn't get there in time. The beach was deserted. No saviour, no hero.

And then, I was back at home and everyone was saying to me what a relief it is, that it's over, that everything is all right. Aren't we lucky. And I couldn't get anyone to listen, to understand that it's not OK, that the terrible thing has yet to happen.

It had been several weeks since we'd visited Marcus's parents, and as soon as Marcus was awake that Saturday morning, I suggested we see if they could make lunch. I was desperate to get out of London. The dream had unsettled me; I had an overwhelming sense of doom and paranoia. Jepsom knew I'd been on the phone as my son almost drowned, and he'd guessed about Richard. My body language, the flush in my cheeks, the twist of my body had given me away. I'd offended him, too, by offering him money. What if he came back and told Marcus?

It's a cliché that a daughter-in-law puts a wedge between a son and his parents. In my experience it's the son who makes his own wedge. Marcus was resistant; he had phone calls to make, he wasn't sure he was up for the drive, etc. I persuaded him; it would do us both good, I said. And I meant it. I'd always taken comfort from the solid conventionality of Marcus's upbringing, its dogs and Aga and piano lessons, so different from my own. And it helped, too, when we weren't getting on well, to remind myself of the small suburban battles so many men conduct with their fathers, or the expectations of those fathers, that make them what they become.

We spent the morning in separate rooms. He made his calls, Josh watched TV, and I stayed in the kitchen. I opened my laptop and went on Facebook. I called up Jepsom's home page and ran my eyes down his short list of friends: none of the people we'd met in Greece were on it. No Mikey or Carl, though I realised they'd be too young. But also no Sherry. No Tracey. No Maureen. Did it mean anything? Not necessarily: plenty of people weren't on social media, and many who were didn't use it to connect with their own families. But still – not a single one of them? That was odd.

The friends he did have were all male, most of them with a generic profile picture.

I closed the page, and put his name into Google. A list of results flashed up.

Dave Jepsom Profiles | Facebook

Dave Jepsom | Professional Profile – LinkedIn

I began scrolling down.

'Shall we go then?'

Marcus had poked his head around the door.

'Yes. I'm ready,' I said.

I closed the laptop without looking any further.

FOURTH

Him

My parents lived in a village in Surrey: picture perfect, cottage gardens frothing with climbing roses and sweet peas, a gently sloping green that lacked only sheep. There was a pub, The Three Crows, but no shops, though the names of several houses hinted at the bustling community it had once been: The Old Forge, The Old Bakery, The Old Dairy. Mum and Dad tended to buy everything on the outskirts of Guildford in what they described as The New Waitrose, though it had been there for twenty years.

It might take a while, if you met my father for the first time, to notice anything was amiss, but it was painfully obvious to me. He was thinner and very slightly more dishevelled: his hair was combed oddly, and he had missed a swathe of bristles on one side of his cheek. Formerly head of maths at the local grammar, he was a well-read, argumentative man, who had contempt for a lot of things – including television. He was in the front room when we arrived, watching QVC.

It was a glorious day, proper bees-in-the-bushes, sun-on-the-back-of-your-head *warm*, and we laid the table in the garden. Mum had made salmon en croute because family legend says it is Tessa's favourite and my mother always wants to feed her up. The dogs – two elderly dachshunds – lay at our feet, and we talked about their neighbours (Margot at the Old

Post Office was going on a cruise) and the rest of the family: how well my sister Sarah's eldest daughter was doing at veterinary college; how the youngest wanted to study English. My father had been quiet during much of the conversation. 'Of course Sarah studied English, though I think she regretted it,' he said now. 'She should have done sciences. I told her but she wouldn't listen.'

'No, that was me,' I said. 'Sarah did do sciences. Biochemistry. It's why she works in global healthcare. It was your son, me, who wouldn't listen to you and threw everything away by studying English.'

I tried not to sound irritated.

'Sarah wanted to be a writer, a novelist. We soon put a stop to that. No money in writing. Told her in no uncertain terms to train to be a lawyer.'

'No, Dad. That was me too.'

He made a face, as if he was comically astounded that I was making it all up, being contrary to confuse him. 'Are you pulling my leg?' he said. It was one of his new phrases, along with 'I don't mind telling you' and 'I've just about reached my limit'. He'd repeat them like someone stuck, flailing, halfway down a cliff might reach for a rope.

'It didn't work out, Dad,' I said. 'I hated it.'

He looked at me with sudden clarity. 'Oh yes – you dropped out, wasted all that money, all that potential.'

'But it's OK now. It all worked out fine in the end.'

Tessa, who was clearing the plates, was just behind the old man's seat and she paused to look at me. With her spare hand, she stroked a tuft of his hair back into place and then planted a kiss on the top of his head. He's a product of his upbringing too, she used to say. As, of course, was she. I was aware again of the chasm that had opened up between us, that I'd neglected her. With intense pain, like a needle being stabbed in the centre of my chest, I remembered that I loved her: not *how much* I loved her, just the irrefutable, immutable fact of it.

After lunch, I tried to make my mother sit and rest while I made the coffee, but when I came out, she was in and out of the garage, pulling out the paddling pool and then searching under old oil cans and jump leads, with a lot of frustrated groaning, for the pump. Tessa was helping her and it took the three of us to clean the pool, and inflate, and then fill it.

In the old days, my father would have been master of operations, telling us what we were doing wrong, but today he sat smiling blandly in a deckchair under the tree, doing a Sudoku. I went over to join him, reaching over to choose a section from the newspapers at his feet. I watched for a moment, and then realised he was putting numbers in at random.

I turned back to the paper so he wouldn't see me look. I'd picked the *Sunday Telegraph*, which I usually only flicked through at work.

Not much in it, I was thinking idly, but then I turned the page and the article leapt out at me.

The writer had used a pseudonym but the school was described in detail – from its Palladian frontage to the fireplace in the headmaster's office. The narrator recounted returning to the school on a recent show-round and how 'the everyday cruelty of his life there' came back to him in 'the give of a floorboard in a corridor, the sunlight through a window'. He described the whippings from one teacher – but also the 'tugging' on his penis from another; he talked about the effects the systematic abuse there had had on his adult life, and how he hadn't yet gone to the police, 'to add to their files', but that he thought about doing so daily.

The more I read, the more it was clear the writer was describing Cartingdon Hall: a 'feeder for Marlborough'; an 'alma mater of politicians and actors' which 'nestled in the Quantocks'.

I felt for my phone; no missed calls but no signal either.

It was better out the front of the house, and standing out on the gravel by the main road, I got through to Jeff straight away. He'd already spoken to the headmaster, and had already drafted a letter to the 'stakeholders' (which in this case was every existing, former and prospective parent), expressing 'concern' and giving assurances that everything was being done to look into the issue, but that the school was 'a different place' now, etc, etc.

Jeff and I agreed – though he hadn't shared this with the headmaster – that the tone of the article was as worrying. It was erudite, referring in places to 'baroque cruelty', 'symptom-ology', 'attachment fracture' and 'hyper-arousal and hypo-arousal'. Words can be the most damaging things of all in business, and this guy seemed to know how to use them.

I returned to the house after this, recharged, reinvigorated. 'Sorry,' I said, my shoulders sagging in mock exasperation. 'God. Bloody office.'

I didn't mean a word of it. I love it when work interrupts my home life. It doesn't bother me at all. It speeds up moments that might otherwise drag, providing an extra dimension, an *escape*. There, I've said it. The Cartingdon crisis was a gift. It distracted me not just from the problems in my marriage, but from the disintegration of my father and his disappointment in me – apparently one of the last things to go. Who wouldn't want that?

Tessa was quiet on the way home, fiddling with her phone.

'Sorry about speaking so long to Jeff,' I said. 'I'm sorry if you felt dumped in it.'

She was looking out of her window, as the A3 trees dashed past, so she might not have heard.

Her

Arthur's dementia – which Marcus couldn't bear to put a name to – had progressed since April. Ann looked tired and strained. When we were alone in the garage, she told me she'd taken him to the pub the day before and he'd insisted on wearing his winter coat and hat, despite the heat of the day. He'd disappeared at one point and she'd found him on a chair outside the kitchen, looking confused.

I hugged her as we left, apologising for not having been more help, promising to come down more. I'd been feeling messy swirls of guilt all day. I had avoided them for the last couple of months – I felt as if I'd been unfaithful to them, too – and now I suddenly couldn't bear how long we had left it.

She held me out at arm's length and said, 'You're a good girl. I know you didn't have much of a role model, but you're doing bloody well. My son's not easy.'

I made a face.

She shook her head: 'He's not. He has his demons. But you're keeping it together. You're a damn good mother. There.' I felt tears pricking at the corners of my eyes, and she picked up my chin. 'You look after yourself. I'm glad he has you.'

When I met Marcus's parents, my mother was still alive, and the contrast between the chaos of her life and their calm, quotidian existence would feel like a pressing in my chest.

Their house was like a sanctuary, but after leaving, I would often become agitated. I'd feel ashamed. I'd realise my palms had become cold and sweaty. Sometimes I might pick an argument with Marcus, just to push him, to test things out. I had the impression that, without their ballast, I might spin out of control.

I hadn't felt it for years, but that same sense of panic, of loss, came over me again as we left that evening. I *had* lost control. And it seemed so very hard to get it back. The idea that Jepsom knew, and that he might tell Marcus, had become a persistent worry. I had had a text from Richard earlier (*I'll miss you!*), which I hadn't answered, and as we drove into our street, I got a follow up: *Need to talk. Flat tomorrow?* I pressed my head against the window, breathless with a sense of unfinished business, the realisation that it was more complicated than I'd realised, still grubby and incomplete.

A car was parked across our drive. Marcus pulled up alongside it, and we waited for a few minutes. He sounded the horn. No one emerged.

He became suddenly, explosively impatient. Leant his arm on the horn again, for longer.

Josh woke up and started crying, and, with a loud, enraged groan, Marcus threw the car into gear and drove on down the road and round the corner where he found a space. His movements as he parked were aggressive and fast. He yanked up the handbrake and, even before taking off his seat-belt, he was reaching into his pocket for his phone.

I got out of the passenger door, pulled back the chair and managed to undo Josh from his restraints. Marcus was making a call now, so I left him to it and walked slowly back round to the house.

The car, a black Jeep, was still parked outside. It had smoked windows so you couldn't see in, but as I pushed through the gate, I had the sensation again of being watched, a heat at the back of my head. I fumbled for the key and, with Josh on my hip, let myself into the house. I switched on the lights in the sitting room and was closing the blinds when the car revved into life and drove off.

The weather held and we woke to another of those blue and acid green days you hope for all summer. It should have been perfect. I tried to pretend it was. We got up and out early and spent the morning in the park, our ears full of birdsong, the squeak of grass, the distant pock of cricket balls.

At the playground, we bumped into Rose and Pete and bought takeaway coffees, which we drank on a rug on the grass. Josh and Chloe were playing with some sticks under the tree, and Marcus and Pete were speculating about Miss Jenny's sex life (all the fathers were obsessed by it) when my phone buzzed.

I covered it with my hand to cast it in the shade. The message read: *Aren't you supposed to chuck a man in person?*

I quickly typed out a reply: *No.*

I returned it to my pocket.

Rose was looking at me enquiringly. I smiled and shook my head. 'Nothing important.'

A few seconds later my phone buzzed again. I didn't take it out until after Rose and Pete had left. Marcus lay back on his hands, his elbows folded, and closed his eyes. Josh had wandered closer to the playground, and had found a couple of small boys to play with.

I took my phone out again and read: *Let's meet. Today? The flat?*

Marcus let out a gentle snore, his lips blown slightly apart by the pressure of it.

I can't, I replied.

Almost immediately it rang. I scrabbled to reject the call, but at the last minute changed my mind.

'Hey, have lunch with me,' he said. His tone was light, amused. 'You owe me that.'

'It's over, I told you. I can't see you. I'm sorry.'

'Go on, please come. Just as friends. Colleagues. I've got a work proposition. Something to run by you.'

'I'm sorry. Bye, Richard.' I hung up.

I wouldn't go. I couldn't. But the idea rested in my head, expanded. What did he mean, a work proposition? Perhaps he had something proper and concrete to offer me. We'd had a professional relationship before; one that had worked well. It was always me he'd wanted, on every account, every launch. 'No one has your way with a press release,' he'd say. We could return to that, maybe, place our friendship on a more formal, non-adulterous footing. I felt a spasm of longing for the woman I'd been. He could be offering me the perfect part-time job; something I could do at home, around Josh. I should see him. And then I decided I wouldn't. It was too dangerous. And then, with a kind of agitated dismay, I swung back. Perhaps after everything that had happened between us, I had a duty to.

Him

On Sunday morning, we ran into Rose and Pete at the playground. It was busy, I remember that, scooters criss-crossing alongside the railings, dogs barking, a bunfight for the climbing frame. We sat on a rug under a tree in the end, drinking takeaway coffee, and God knows what we talked about. Clients of Pete's. Their holiday plans. Whether Miss Jenny at nursery had a boyfriend. After Rose and Pete left, I fell asleep on the rug, Tessa's voice drifting in and out of my consciousness. I woke, my hand squashed against my cheek, my mouth half open, a line of dribble trailing out. I was staring up at the sky. Clouds were moving behind trees, and for a moment I felt as if they were motionless, and I was the one who was moving. I forced myself upright, pins and needles numbing one side of my body, in a muddled panic. Where was I? What was happening?

All seemed well. I was in dappled shade. The common was where it had been. Josh was playing football with another boy. And Tessa was still next to me, sitting stiffly, her elbows on her knees, staring off into the distance.

On the way home, she told me she had forgotten she had agreed to meet an old friend, from the temp agency; it had gone out of her head, how stupid she was, how lucky she'd remembered. 'You don't mind, do you?' It was years, she said, since she'd seen her. She seemed brittle and nervous, and I wish now that I'd persuaded her not to go. Something was off. But I didn't want to pry, or even to think too hard about it. It was important to me that I trusted her. I didn't want to ask too many questions, or at least behave like the kind of husband who might think of doing so.

Josh started to whinge the moment she left. He was bored and over-tired; we'd got back late from my parents the night before. The day, which had started out so blue and bright, was disappointing. High mackerel clouds had appeared, the scales slowly spreading to blot out the sun. The world looked flat.

I persuaded Josh to play with the fire engine Dave Jepsom had given him while I read through the draft Cartingdon letter, and sent a couple of emails. I was reading the newspaper when the fire engine lost its novelty. I could tell by the way he kept cracking it aggressively into the legs of the sofa. When he hurtled it into the back of the page I was reading, so the paper crumpled in on itself and the fire engine came close to taking out my eye, I let out an oath. I tried reading to him instead, but he wriggled out of my arms, rolling his head back and making inarticulate noises between gritted teeth.

At one point I lay on the floor with my eyes closed while he clambered onto me and tried to prise open the lids. 'Daddy, Daddy,' he intoned.

In the normal way of things, had Tessa been there, I'd have drifted upstairs with my laptop. I'd have drummed up some work even if nothing had been pressing. I love my son, but when he behaved badly I tended to make myself scarce.

'OK,' I said, sitting up. 'What do you want to do?'

'I want to go to a playground.'

'I don't want to go to a playground. We've been to a playground already today. What else?'

'I want to wash the car.'

I took a deep breath. 'OK. Fine.'

At first it went well. I positioned him in front of the bonnet with a J-cloth, a bucket of water and the bottle of detergent. He squirted and rubbed, and I poured water over his efforts. But I was distracted, and didn't notice he was squeezing all of the Fairy liquid out of the bottle in one go. I tried to prise it out of his hand and we had a small fight, during which I managed to stay calm, and then I went back into the kitchen for another bucket of water in order to clean it up. This time, his face scrunched up with determination, he tried to take the water off me, but I was concentrating this time and wouldn't let go, and in the ensuing struggle, he managed to tip it not on the car, but over me.

'Fuck!' I shouted. 'Stupid boy.'

His face went still and then slowly began to crease at the edges. The corners of his mouth went down; tears gathered in his eyes.

I wrapped him in my arms. 'I'm sorry, I'm sorry,' I said. 'Don't cry. Don't cry.'

Half an hour later, we were in a playground in Battersea Park: not just an ordinary playground but an adventure playground, with wooden struts to climb, and ladders, and rope bridges. We clambered and explored and I chased him along the wobbly walkways and he squealed with fear and pleasure, and we ate ice creams and watched the bigger boys play football, and walked back to the car hand in hand. It was 5 p.m. when we drove back. I was feeling stronger, a better father. I had put work out of my mind and retrieved the day.

I had the door key halfway to the lock when I realised the door was already ajar. I called for Tessa. She must be back, I thought. But there was a draught pulling through the hall. The Diptyque candle, which had been on the shelf next to the post, was on the floor, its glass case cracked open like a coconut. A smear of prints ran along the floor, interlaced, in different directions, like the tracings children make of leaves. A rank odour rose: sweat and stale garlic, and yes, even down here, shit.

Josh was clinging on to the bottom of my shorts. I said a few reassuring things, oh dear, and what a mess we made with our car-washing, what will Mummy say? And he repeated everything back to me as if he needed convincing. In the sitting room, books had been pulled off the shelves, and photographs, including our wedding photo and a picture of Josh as a baby, were on the floor, frames splintered. Josh's face had been obliterated, as though someone had repeatedly ground it under their shoe. The iPad had gone, but the TV was still there, too big to steal perhaps and, thank God, my laptop was under the sofa where I'd tucked it out of Josh's way earlier.

I settled Josh there on a corner of the sofa, watching CBeebies, while I inspected the rest of the house.

In the kitchen, the fridge had been emptied onto the floor: a gloopy mess of broken eggs, spilt milk, cracked pots of mustard and chutney, a naked chicken, its wrapping ripped, a bag of mixed lettuce leaves ripped open and scattered. A bottle of wine had been smashed. The back door was wide open and beyond it pots had been knocked over, the lavender and the cacti and the impatiens, chosen so carefully and so randomly by Tess and Josh, trampled; the bag of compost had been kicked over. Earth spilt.

I switched off the hot tap, which had been left running, and then sat at the table to ring the emergency services. I asked for the police, and was told someone would be round shortly. And then I tried Tessa. The call went straight to voicemail. I didn't leave a message. Better for her to find out when she was home.

Upstairs, in our bedroom, the cupboards and drawers had been ransacked. Tessa's underwear was strewn over the floor.

Delicate pieces of lingerie, which I hadn't even known she still had, was laid out on the bed like a votive offering. It was horrible, taunting. I wanted to gather up the little pieces of lace and put them out of sight, but managed to stop myself. The police needed to see it.

I knew I was going to find something disgusting in the bathroom. I smelt it before I saw it, the stench of their violation. They'd chosen the tub, the bastards.

Back downstairs, I sat on the bottom step. I could hear the cheerful theme tune to Gigglebiz in the front room. But I didn't want to go in. I didn't want to move. It didn't feel like my house; everything was ruined. My hands were clammy. I had to fight not to be sick. I wished the police would come. The intruder or intruders had made such a mess, and yet what had he or they made off with? An iPad and a couple of chargers; some jewellery, maybe. It seemed so pointless, so *personal*. And the shit in the bath. It was a miniature act of terrorism. How could someone you'd never met hate you so much? Why us? All the clichés ran through my head: all true. And then another one: *who would do such a thing?*

I started to study a footprint closest to where I was sitting. It was almost complete. The tread was distinctive: not heavily grooved like so many trainers, but flat, with a clear single outline and within it a tiny criss-cross pattern, smudged.

Did I recognise it? I began to think that I did.

I took my phone out of my pocket and Googled. An American website was the first to come up. I swiped down several styles, all black, until I found it. Burberry. They came in black or white. There were three photographs, showing different angles of the shoe, and I zoomed in on the final image. The Retford sole: flat, no ridges, a tiny criss-cross pattern.

What had I said to Tessa? *You think he might be casing the joint?* I'd been sarcastic. I hadn't taken her anxieties seriously.

And yet, who was he? We knew so little about him; we had simply made assumptions. And we were rich pickings. I'd flashed my money around in Greece, buying everyone lunch, stumping up for one round of drinks after another. I'd sent him a pair of expensive trainers. He'd seen us having dinner with our rich friends, planning one holiday after another. We must have looked like a sure thing.

Is that why he turned up that night and why he went upstairs for so long? Had he been getting a feel for the place? My laptop had been on the bed that night. Had he been searching the drawers looking for that? And then turning up to 'mend the dripping tap'; what if Tessa had been right about him all along?

A car had pulled up outside the house. A door opened. There was the sound of police radio, heavy footsteps, voices at the door.

'Mr Nicholson?'

'Yes.' I leapt to my feet.

There were two officers standing there, a tall young man with a receding hairline and a shorter round-faced woman, both in uniform.

They stepped into the hall and introduced themselves, showing their ID: PC Arnold and PC Garcia. Arnold was the senior officer; her handshake was firm and to the point. She asked if I was alone, and when I gestured to Josh watching TV, she suggested we went through to the kitchen. The three of us sat at the table while she took a statement, writing my answers down in a notebook. She wanted to know what time I had discovered the burglary, and at what time I had vacated the house earlier in the afternoon. 'Is anyone else resident?' she said.

'My wife but she's seeing a friend.'

She wrote that down too.

'Have you spoken to her since returning to the house?'

'I've tried but I haven't got through. She's not answering.'

'Any idea yet what might be missing?' she asked.

I mentioned the iPad and Tessa's jewellery and she wrote that down, too. She wanted an estimation of value, but I said I wasn't sure.

'OK,' she said. 'We'll have a little look around. Get a sense of the layout of the property.'

'We've lived here five years and we've never been burgled,' I said.

'There's a first time for everything.'

They told me it was OK to clean the kitchen so I did that while they went upstairs. I chucked the ruined food in bin bags, swept up the glass and cleared up the floor, the whole time aware of them in the house, of doors opening and closing, creaking floorboards, the echo of their voices in the bathroom, the crackle of the radio. When PC Arnold came back down she was talking into her receiver: 'Dwelling burglary. No sign of forced entry. A few missing items. Some damage. Yup, yup.'

'SOCO will be round,' she said, raising her mouth. 'There are some footprints out there that might be worth taking a look at. In case they match with anything else in our database.'

I blurted: 'I think I have a suspicion who might have done this.'

'You do?' she said.

'You might think this sounds a bit ridiculous, but there's this bloke we've met recently, and I'm wondering whether it might be him. Look . . .' I fiddled clumsily for my phone. 'Look.'

She craned forward.

'You see – the sole is a match for the footprints. And the man I'm talking about has the same shoes.' I was feeling flustered. My fingers fumbled.

'And you're sure about that?'

'Yes. I am sure about that,' I continued more calmly, 'because I bought them for him.'

'You bought them for him.' She turned back to the phone, noticed the price tag and drew her chin into her neck. 'And after that he wants to burgle you?'

'It's complicated,' I said.

'Well, we can look into it. Though I have to say, um, Mr Nicholson, that there's a lot of burglary in this area. It's a crime hotspot. And most of it is opportunistic . . . I notice all the doors and windows are intact. No breakages. Could you perhaps have left the front door open?'

A vein throbbed in my temple. 'No. I definitely didn't. But the man I've mentioned, he has been in the house recently. He was here only on Friday. He could easily have taken a key.'

'Would you be able to check?' The younger policeman spoke for the first time.

I fetched the pot of keys that we keep on the shelf in the hall and tipped it out onto the table: a hairbrush, a used Zipcard, a half-eaten Penguin biscuit, a motley collection of keys. I rummaged through the mess. 'It's hard to tell. One might be missing.' I looked up at the male police officer. He was tapping the spine of his notebook on the table. 'We're a bit disorganised,' I said.

'Best not to have too many spare keys,' he said.

I scooped everything up and put it all back in the pot. I felt deflated. 'It feels so personal.'

'It always does.' PC Arnold nodded a few times as if she completely understood. 'It's the sense of violation, isn't it?'

'It's more than that. My wife's underwear drawer – why?'

'First place they look. It's where people keep their valuables. Honestly.'

'And the mess? Breaking our photographs? Shitting in our bath?'

'It's the release of stress. These criminals – kids usually – they're often drunk, no control. They have raised heartbeats. They lose control of their bowels. And they're clumsy. They're either high or wired and once they're in, they lose mental concentration. That's why they knock stuff over, break stuff.' She scratched the side of her head. 'It's hard not to take it personally, but few of us,' she laughed, 'know anyone who hates us that much. Take it from me, ninety-nine per cent of the time it's *not* personal. It's anything but.'

'Do you think I'm over-reacting? I mean, I've got no proof. It's just a gut reaction.' I shrugged.

She looked at me carefully, and then flipped open her notebook again. 'Most burglars operate within their own neighbourhood. They don't have much imagination. But of course I will take it seriously. So why don't you give me this bloke's name and address and we'll go and talk to him? Get to the bottom of it once and for all.'

I felt my insides cave. I swallowed. Was this the right thing to do? If Jepsom wasn't responsible, it would be awful to send the police to his door. And yet, if he *were* responsible, if he *had* done this, he should know I was on to him. You can't treat people like that. Who knew what other vulnerable people he might prey on next. He shouldn't get away with it.

'Yes, OK,' I said. 'I've got his work address. Give me a minute and I'll get it.'

'Great. We'll run through the witness statement. Carlos, can you get an MG11 from the car? And then we'll get out of your hair.'

Her

This time he met me at the lift. He was smiling broadly, his arms outstretched.

I dodged them. 'It's over. You do understand that?' I said. 'I'm married. I have a child. I've come to hear what you have to say.'

He was not laughing now. 'Those facts had not escaped me.'

'I'm not staying.'

'Sweetie.' He cupped my chin with his hands, looked into my eyes. Lavender and sandalwood. I felt a stirring, butterflies in my stomach. 'You can go home whenever you like. No one is stopping you.'

He'd had lunch delivered from Ottolenghi. It was laid out on the terrace. A bottle of Pol Roger on ice. He let me think I was in control. He was light, not at all intense. We exchanged small talk. He enquired after Josh, and his illness, and the holiday in Suffolk that was fast approaching. He asked where we were staying, and had advice about restaurants. 'I'm unlikely to get out for a nice supper,' I said. I rolled my eyes. 'Not that kind of holiday.' He told me I needed a break: he was worried about me, after my tears on Thursday.

'You made me feel better,' I said. 'I'd got it all out of proportion. Though weirdly, the man I was talking about turned up at the house the very next day. A bit of a coincidence.'

'Maybe he can't tear himself away from you.' He let his eyes linger on my mouth. 'I know how he feels.'

'Don't,' I said, as a warning. I changed the subject, admired his pots and asked him what flowers they were. 'God knows,' he says. 'The gardener does it.'

'How's Marcus?' he said, after that.

'He's fine.' I looked across at him. 'So?'

'I wanted to ask you something. I might need some new comms advice.'

I smiled, and leant forward. I tucked my hair behind my ears. 'Yes,' I said, waiting.

'That thing with Sushi! I'm not sure Ekelund handled it particularly well. It went a bit nuts on Twitter at the weekend. They could have shut it down faster than they did.' He took a sip of champagne. 'Plus I'm keen to open the new Greek place somewhere a bit edgier. Wouldn't mind some focus input on up-and-coming areas in London for future expansion.'

He asked me how far I would travel for a locally sourced, heritage tomato and Persian lamb kebab. Willesden Junction? Woolwich? Dalston? We bartered neighbourhoods like City dealers. I congratulated myself on how well it was going. I was still employable. I could do it. I could feel the cogs slotting into place, the neurons firing. Brick walls, I was thinking, marble plates, an open kitchen.

'So – it's just his connection with the Russians I'm not sure about,' he said.

'Whose?'

'Marcus's. If I'm going to jump ship I want to make sure I'm going to a company that's solid. It's a symbiotic relation-ship. You know that, too.'

'You're thinking of going to Hawick Nicholson?'

Of course he was.

I took a sip of my drink. Humiliation, embarrassment seeped through me. I managed to smile. 'Don't go to Hawick Nicholson! I'll do it. come to me!'

'I always want to come to you.'

I drew back, still smiling. I felt wretched, foolish, sick, 'Is it appropriate.' I said. 'You know, working with my husband?'

'I never mix business and pleasure,' he said.

It was still warm, but it had clouded over, cumulus gathering, upwardly swelling. Storm flies were milling; spots of rain polka-dotted the terrace. A woman high up at the window of the next-door building was looking down on us. He suggested we took our drinks inside. I told him I had to leave. We sat on the sofa. The cushions were soft beneath my neck. He touched his Sonos remote and k.d. lang filled the room.

Helpless. Helpless. Helpless.

It just about summed it up.

One last time.

He started to kiss me, his hands tugging at my clothes, and for a few moments I let him. I gave in to it – it's all I was good for – and then I was kicking him off me, my palms pressing against his breast-bone, my feet scrabbling at his legs. It was ungainly and awkward, and for an instant or two, he carried on as if it was part of the game, his hands grabbing my wrists and pressing them down, his mouth so hard against mine I tasted blood. And then, realising I was serious, finally he rolled away, with a laugh.

'I misunderstood that,' he said.

On the Tube, I stood even though there was a free seat. I closed my eyes and let the nausea wring through me. My strap-hanging arm ached. The leather at the back of the sandal had given me a blister on my heel. I deserved it all. When we got to Balham, I thought about not getting off. I imagined staying on until the end of the line. Going up and down for eternity. The Northern Line: my penance.

I kept thinking about my mother in her low-cut tasselled shirt and her push-up bra, the blood at the back of her heels, the lipstick on the rim of her glass.

When I turned the corner, saw the police car parked outside our house, I began to run.

An officer was standing at the open door. My shoulders heaved. I couldn't speak for the dread of it.

'Are you the wife?' she said.

Pounding in my ears. 'Yes.'

Her hand touched my arm. 'There's nothing to worry about,' but there was screaming in my head and I thought she means the opposite of that; she's going to ask me to sit down. I thought in that moment about the beach, the blinding sun, Josh's floating armband. And I thought about the dream.

'Where's Josh?' I said.

'He's fine. He's watching TV.'

My hand went to my neck. I thought my heart was about to break out of my chest. 'And Marcus.'

'He's fine. He's fine. You've had a break-in, that's all. Everyone is safe.'

I felt the panic shunt.

'Your husband did try to reach you,' she said. 'He was keen to let you know.'

Her eyes slanted off my face, down to my sandals, my bare legs.

I managed to say, 'My phone has been off.'

'Well, you're here now,' she said. 'And as I say it's all under control. Your husband's filling in the witness statement. Actually, it's quite lucky you've come. I know it's a bit of a shock, but it would be useful if we could go through a few things now. Saves us coming back. I'm PC Arnold, by the way.'

No one was hurt. It was not my fault.

She looked at me closely, checking I was all right, and she led me into the house. The floor was muddy; there was a strong smell of alcohol and spoiled food, of someone else's dirty clothes. I gave Josh a hug, and then spoke briefly to Marcus, who was sitting at the kitchen table next to a man in police uniform, reading through a document. 'I'm all right,' he said, nodding. 'Everything is OK. Don't worry.' And then PC Arnold asked if we could go upstairs to our bedroom.

'Yes, of course,' I said, wondering whether she meant to sound so cautious.

I stood in the doorway and stared. My tops and tights had been riffled through, and thrown onto the floor. Hangers lay muddled at the bottom of the wardrobe, our shirts and dresses crumpled up with our shoes. All our possessions had been touched. My skin crawled as if a stranger's hands were on me, scratching against my skin.

PC Arnold was already in the room. 'You all right?' she said. 'It can be a bit of a shock.'

'Yes, I'm OK.' I took a step.

She said, 'I'm assuming that you didn't leave it like this.'

I didn't know how she could possibly think so. 'No. Of course not.'

'I meant that.' She pointed. 'Specifically.'

My underwear drawer had been tipped out onto the bed. There was a shape by the pillow, like an elongated body. I took a step closer. My fanciest lingerie – a diaphanous black bra, a matching thong and a suspender belt, things I'd worn to see Richard – had been laid out neatly, one above the other, in line with the body's anatomy. A pair of seamed stockings were attached to the suspender belt, draped down the side of the mattress in a creepily realistic imitation of legs.

I put my hand to my mouth.

'Aren't people weird?' she said. 'It never fails to amaze me.'

'It's just horrible. Can I?'

She nodded, and I bundled it all up and put it in the bin. 'I don't blame you,' she said. 'The thought of their dirty fingers.'

'I know.'

I sat on the bed for a moment while she asked about my jewellery. My husband had said some was missing. Would it be all right if I checked, so they could complete the form? I said that I would, and I checked the box: the two precious things – a necklace Marcus had given me when we first met, and the plastic bracelet they'd put on newborn Josh in hospital – were still there. But I told her a couple of silver chains were missing, and maybe five pairs of earrings, approximate value £150.

We went back down to the kitchen and she added the jewellery to the witness statement, which I read. It ran through Marcus's movements and described the layout of our house, and listed the missing items. It included the detail: 'I noticed on the hall floor a muddy footprint, which had not been there when I left the house. I recognise the print belonging to a pair of shoes of a person of my acquaintance. I did not invite that person into my house today.'

It ended: 'Nobody had permission to enter into my house or take any of my belongings. I fully support police action.'

Marcus signed it and they told us the scenes of crime officer would be round in the next few hours. We should also expect a call from victim support over the ensuing days. They told us to improve our security – 'kids, more often than not, see their chance and take it'. Then they got in their car, radios crackling, minds already on another call, and left.

In the hall, I put my arms around Marcus. I breathed in the familiar smell of him – his skin, his hair, his breath. I closed my eyes, imagined the feel of his hands on my back, under my clothes. 'I'm sorry you had to come back to that.'

He shuddered. 'I'd better sort out the shit in the bath. Turns out it's not an urban myth.'

'Ugh. It's so horrible. The thought of them in our house. Some vile stranger.'

'Yeah.' His eyes moved quickly from side to side. He bit his lip. 'If it was a stranger.'

'What do you mean?' I remembered the detail in the statement. 'And what was that about a person of our acquaintance?'

He bit his lip. 'I think I might owe you an apology,' he said.

He made me crouch down to inspect the footprint. And then he showed me the website on his phone.

'Those shoes I sent Jepsom. It's the same tread. I'm wondering whether you were right. Maybe he was casing the joint.'

'You think it was him? But you thought I was being hysterical.' I felt my pulse begin to race. I thought about the lingerie on the bed, the sexual nature of it. Had Dave Jepsom touched my things? Had he laid them out like that, in a taunting display? The thought was like a wave engulfing my chest. 'You really think it might have been him?' I said again.

He looked more doubtful. 'I don't know. Maybe you put the thought in my head. Anyway.' He shrugged, and raised one hand. 'I mentioned it to the police.'

I felt the creeping presence of doubt. 'What will Jepsom do if they talk to him?' I said. 'He'll deny it, won't he? How will we be able to prove it was him?'

'I don't see how I couldn't have told them. Not after everything.'

'What if he didn't do it? What then?'

'So now you're saying you think he *hasn't* been behaving suspiciously?'

'I don't know. He might have. I don't know.'

'Don't we?'

We cleaned the house late that night, scrubbing away every trace of the burglar. I slept badly. Even in clean sheets the bed felt soiled. Turning my head on the pillow, I thought I caught the scent of someone else's sweat.

Him

The burglary had been traumatic, and the suspicions we
harboured towards Dave Jepsom deeply unpleasant and yet,
on Monday morning, I left both to Tessa and the police, and
returned to the office.

Jeff was away for a few days – he'd taken his kids to a
Mark Warner in Portugal – so I was even busier than
usual. The Cartingdon headmaster was on the phone first
thing, obsessed by some of the details in the *Telegraph*
article: the marble fireplace, for example – he'd been to
every room in the building and couldn't find one that
matched. He had been shown a memoir, published only
last year, about life in the seventies at Ashton Park School
in Yorkshire, which contained similar details to those in
the letter and the article. He started reading from his
notes: 'the give of a floorboard in a corridor', 'sunlight
through a window'.

'It's too much of a coincidence. It *has* to be a hoax. Some
kid who's left and got it in for me.'

I told him I'd ring him back and called Mary into the
conference room. She was unimpressed by his so-called
revelations. 'The tragedy, Marcus, is the details *are* the same,
in boarding schools, and – as we now know – in youth clubs
and football clubs, in hospitals and church confessionals. All

these poor kids were victim to the same kind of abuse, except that of course each individual case was a personal apocalypse.'

'Yeah, you're right.'

'It's almost irrelevant if it's a hoax or not. The letter needs to accept blame, to apologise unreservedly, and to talk about moving on. Sometimes you just have to say sorry.'

'You're right.'

Sometimes it's just perspective we offer. *That's* why their money is well spent. *That's* where our time goes.

Jem was back in that Monday, seemingly unscathed by Thursday night. I decided to make no reference to it, which in retrospect was a mistake. She looked bored. I'd forgotten how the presence of a work experience person seeps into the atmosphere. You're embarrassed by how uninspired they are, and feel responsible and guilty, and then you start seeing the office through their eyes, and before long you're locked in a spiral of inadequacy.

In the end, I suggested she help Gail arrange the last-minute details of the 7Nights relaunch, and I heard her ordering bunting and fairy lights over the phone, looking animated for the first time since she'd arrived.

We had made some headway with the guest list by then. The usual ragbag of journalists was signed up: two local papers, a couple of trade mags, an intern from *Accountancy Age* and the travel editor of *Busy Woman*. Mary had also managed to rope in a contact at the *Mail*, an editor on Femail, who had pitched a piece to Health, comparing the 7Nights experience with an organic service station in Gloucestershire. The list was perfectly acceptable but I sent one last plea to Yasmeen, just in case. Subject: *You know you want to.*

There was also a whisper of new business that morning: the restaurateur Richard Taylor, an old connection from Ekelund, rang to see if we could meet up. He had plans for a new project and was wondering whether it was a good opportunity to move agencies. The deal, if it came off, could be extremely lucrative, and I put a meeting in the diary as early as I could.

I had just walked away from Gail's desk when the name Yasmeen O'Shea flashed on my phone.

'Well hello,' I said.

'Have you literally been waiting for my call?' she said.

'You found me out. I've been moping! Have I begged enough?'

The moment I heard her say yes, I pushed back my chair and put my feet on my desk. I'd known from her tone it was good news – a little bit flirtatious, a little bit business-like. Hah!

'Did you like my angle?' I said. And when she didn't answer immediately: 'You know, the staycation idea?'

'Yes!' she said. 'You'll be there, won't you?'

I made a snap decision. 'Yeah, absolutely,' I said. 'I wouldn't miss it for the world.'

It was the middle of the afternoon and I had just sent Jem out to buy me something from Pret when PC Arnold rang.

'It turns out yours wasn't the only burglary in your area on Saturday,' she said. 'Summer – it's a dangerous period. Windows are left open, doors unlocked. A property that backs on to yours was also broken into – quite a bit of jewellery, and a couple of laptops went missing there. I'd say you got off lightly compared to them. Most likely the intruder accessed your neighbour's property from your garden. It explains your trampled plants. So . . .' She paused. 'So – I think you can rest assured it wasn't personal.'

'Are you sure?' I said. 'What about the footprint?'

'Identical footprints in their kitchen. It turns out they're a match for several other less expensive casual shoes, including a trainer regularly sold in Primark.'

'Oh.' I felt a loosening in my neck. 'So it was just some random person going to the toilet in my bath. I suppose that makes me feel better. OK. Good.' I hadn't realised how relieved I'd be. 'Phew. Well, thank you. I suppose I'm glad you haven't had to bother Dave Jepsom. It would have been very awkward now I think of it. God. Yes. That's good at least.'

Jem came back into the office with my superfood salad, and I was distracted, mouthing my thanks and removing the plastic carton from the paper bag, pulling back the wrapper, sorting out the fiddly pot of lemon dressing.

'Actually, we did bother Mr Jepsom.'

'Sorry?' I stopped tipping the dressing.

'Myself and one of my fellow officers went to see him this morning and he can confirm – hang on . . .' Her voice changed, became more monotonous, as she began to read. 'That Mr Jepsom was with his mother in Chelmsford. He arrived about lunchtime and was home at about 9 p.m. Cameras on the A12 have confirmed the presence of his van, and his mother has also corroborated his story. So,' she had clearly put her notebook down, or closed the file on the computer. 'I think we can quite safely eliminate him from our enquiries.'

'Did you tell him why you were asking?'

'We wanted to know if he had been in your area on Sunday and I would be lying to you if I said he didn't then mention you and your wife by name. It is fair to say that he became a little agitated. Listen,' she changed gear, 'my advice to you would be to make things right with Mr Jepsom. I can see a misunderstanding has arisen between you and in our experience these events are usually best sorted out sooner rather than later.'

I pushed the salad away. I'd lost my appetite.

'Don't let it fester,' she said.

Her

The house still smelt on Monday: dank and ripe. After dropping Josh off, I cleaned the floors again and had another go at the bathroom, and then I sat at the kitchen table and tried to get my thoughts in order. I felt scared and on edge. I knew I was responsible; because of me, unknown forces were playing out. I had exposed us to this. I had put my family in danger.

If Marcus was right and Dave Jepsom was behind it, then I had more to fear even than I had anticipated. The way he'd laid down the underwear felt like a message: sneering, ridiculing, telling me that he knew. Was I being blackmailed? Tell the police and I'll tell Marcus. Too late if so.

And yet, even as I worked it out, I felt my certainty waver. The burglary could have been random. Jepsom might have had nothing to do with it.

I didn't know what was worse, to be right that he *had* broken in, or to be wrong, and to have accused him of doing something he hadn't.

He was so unknown to us, that was the problem. Maybe he was the family man we'd assumed, but that didn't explain his oddness, his detachment, when I'd asked about his children. Who was he? When I tried to concentrate my mind, I found I couldn't remember what he looked like. I couldn't bring him into focus. I couldn't work out why he had summoned such strong responses in me, or in both of us.

I opened my laptop and Googled his name again.

The same list appeared.

Dave Jepsom Profiles | Facebook

Dave Jepsom | Professional Profile – LinkedIn

dave jepsom (@davejeps) | Twitter

And then at the bottom of the page:

'Man given restraining order . . . Enfield Advertiser.'

My finger hovered over it as I took the words in, and then I clicked to open the story.

It was short, and lacking detail, from a local news site.

In 2015, a Dave Jepsom had been put under a restraining order at Tottenham Magistrates' Court, preventing him from making contact with his ex-wife. There was a photograph, but it was grainy, and the subject was wearing a hooded raincoat and had turned his face from the camera so only a cheek and one eye was in shot.

Was it *our* Dave Jepsom? Was it him? The man looked too slight and thin. And Tottenham was a long way from Catford.

And yet, it rang true. It made sense. A restraining order. A wife and son he was prevented from seeing. It would explain so much; not the break-in, but the character of the man, his over-familiarity with us, his claustrophobic interest in our family.

I put a different subject into the search engine – 'Dave Jepsom restraining order' – but the same story appeared, several times over, in the same words, syndicated in other local newspapers and websites.

I felt an intense curiosity then. Fear but also sympathy, the stirrings of pity. I wondered whether he wasn't just lonely, drawn to us because of that, broody without having the self-knowledge to recognise it: he was a man, after all, with little subtlety. Maybe he was a little jealous of our life, hoping to become part of it? Or was I being mad? I remembered the way he had tousled the heads of those small boys, his teasing relationship with the teenage girl.

If only I knew for certain.

I wished there was someone who knew him that I could ask. Those people in Greece: we didn't even know their full names. Sherry – whoever she was – and Tracey, and Maureen.

And then into my head dropped the memory of Maureen's Eatwell wheel. She said she worked in a primary school in Orpington. I racked my brain. Something to do with wood. Oak . . . Ash . . . Ashburton. No. Ashburnam. That was it. She worked at Ashburnam Primary in Orpington.

I Googled the school and found the number on the website. I rang the office and asked to speak to Maureen.

'Maureen David?'

I pretended to sound confident. 'Yes, that's it.'

'She's on break duty at the moment. Can I leave her a message?'

I left my number and asked for her to call me back.

At pick-up, Rose made a bee-line for me. 'Are you all right?' she said. 'You rushed off this morning before I could say hello.'

I filled her in on the burglary. She looked concerned and offered to give us lunch.

I sat in her kitchen, envious of her set-up: the bunting above the door, her daughters' names in large gold letters up on the wall, the enamel pots that hung so confidently from hooks. Even her scented candle, 'vine tomato', came in a Kilner jar with a lid. It was all so natural and unself-conscious.

The children were in the garden eating a picnic and Rose put a cafetière down on the table. I was about to ask her where she had bought the candle, when she sat down next to me and said: 'Listen, I know something is up with you. I wish you would tell me what it was.'

I was pouring out the coffee and I spilt a drop. The blood rushed into my face. I mopped it with the edge of my sleeve. 'What do you mean?'

'The last few weeks you've been distracted, and yesterday in the park, your phone . . .' She shrugged, and tipped her head to one side. 'You're not ill, are you?'

'No.'

'Good.'

Something rippled in the air between us. The silence grew taut.

She got up to fetch the kitchen roll. 'Well, if you don't want to tell me you don't want to tell me.'

'Nothing is up,' I said, burying my face in my cup.

When Marcus came home, he seemed at first to have put the burglary, the fear of Jepsom, behind him. His walls were back up, his barriers already reconfigured. Not for the first time, I marvelled at the certainties forged by his privileges – the grammar school, the university – how confidently he occupied his place in the world, how robust his sense of self.

He was cock-a-hoop because Yasmeen had agreed to go on his 7Nights launch. 'I feel like I've caught a big fish,' he said, jumping up to sit on the kitchen counter. 'Like I've won the pools. Did she say anything to you at nursery?'

'I didn't see her,' I said. 'I was in too much of a rush. I've cleaned the house again, by the way.'

'Good job,' he said. And then he got down from the counter and came close to me.

He said, his mouth twisted awkwardly: 'I've got something to tell you. The police rang.'

'And?'

'It wasn't Jepsom.'

'It wasn't Jepsom?'

'He has an alibi. He was with his mother.'

'His mother? Is that Maureen?'

He wrinkled his face. 'I assume so. Does she live in Colchester?'

'She works in Orpington. Is that close to Colchester?'

I reached for my phone and began looking the two places up on Google Maps. 'No. She can't live in Colchester. It's miles away. So Maureen isn't his mother – though of course she could be his mother-in-law. And listen, Marcus, today I found a Dave Jepsom online who is on a restraining order against his ex-wife.'

'Whatever.' The information seemed to be glancing off him. 'The important thing is the police went round to ask him and he didn't burgle our house.'

I felt the implications of what he had just said. 'The police went round and asked him?'

'Yuh.' He winced. The bluster when he came in had just been a front. He was sheepish, mortified by what we had done.

I felt only a moment of relief, followed by a thud of horror. We'd accused the man who'd rescued our son of burgling our house. It was unspeakable. My stomach clenched. I had an image of Jepsom opening the door, the expression on his face, the dawning comprehension, when he realised what the police were there for, the jut of his jaw. He would be bewildered, angry, bitterly aggrieved. And who knew what form his revenge might take?

Him

No further word from the police on Tuesday and Wednesday. Our file had clearly gone onto a tottering pile of break-ins in our area. I left Tessa to deal with the insurance company and expected to hear nothing more about it.

It was quiet at work, too, that week. I was usually tense when Jeff was away, waiting to be shown up, but I managed forty-eight hours of relative peace. No major dramas. No mistakes on my part. It was Thursday morning, the day of the launch, and I had not only steered the ship, but secured the attendance of a *Sunday Times* journalist. A night in Bicester had begun to seem less of a chore and more of a treat.

I was on the phone to Tilly when I realised Gail was trying to get my attention. A hugely successful teenage retail company had expressed an interest in stocking Tilly's new TeEn range, and I'd been congratulating her. The name, half the secret of these things, had been my idea, so I was feeling smug. 'Oh, top news,' I said, my legs resting on the overnight bag I'd packed for Bicester, and then 'Laters' or something equally complacent.

Gail laid her phone carefully down on her desk, as if trying not to make a sound that would disturb the person on the other end. 'There's a man asking to see you downstairs,' she said. 'He won't give his name. There's nothing in the diary. He sounds a bit . . .' She was picking the word cautiously. 'Insistent. Do you know anything about it? No? Do you want me to go and find out who he is?'

'Perhaps you'd better.'

I heard the lift doors open and close. The murmur of voices as Basty and a couple of tech guys in suits headed into the meeting room. Jem, next to me, was swinging her chair back and forth. Every time it knocked the edge of the desk, the pile of documents on it shifted slightly. I had more calls to make, but I just sat there for a moment, biting my thumbnail between my front teeth.

It's two floors down, reception.

She was gone three minutes.

When she came back, walking crisply across the space, her heels clacked on the floor. Her forehead was furrowed. She said, 'He says his name is Dave Jepsom and you will know what it's about.'

'FUCK.'

Jem stopped her spinning. The tech boys beyond the meeting-room glass looked up.

'Shit.' Deep in my psyche, buried as far down as I could, I had been expecting this.

Gail flicked her wrist over to look at her watch. 'I'll get rid of him, shall I? Say you're in a meeting?'

'No. If I know him, he'll wait.'

My eyes fell on my overnight bag.

'Tell him I've already gone to the 7Nights launch,' I said.

She looked like she might be about to ask a question, then thought better of it. 'OK.'

She didn't say anything when she returned the second time, just slipped back onto her chair and started tapping on her computer.

'That work OK then?' I said.

She nodded. 'Yeah. It seemed to.'

I didn't ring Tessa to tell her about Jepsom's visit. She was obsessed enough about him as it was. She was still going on about this violent Dave Jepsom she'd found online, convinced it was him. I shouldn't have let her paranoia affect me. It was important to keep perspective. We had embarrassed ourselves by sending the police round about the footprints. He had every reason to be annoyed, to want to confront us. I'd deal with it. With him. After the launch maybe. Just not now.

Mary had given the journalists the option of a rented car, a choice of SUV or soft-top, to make the journey itself part of the thing, but those of us who were heading up to Bicester from the office took the train from Paddington. It was quite a band in the end: myself, Mary, Basty, Gail and Jem, whom I'd invited along at the last minute. Basty interrogated me a little about Dimitri and Olaf: was it true they were Russian mafia? Had they really ordered a hit on that oil executive in Moscow? 'Almost definitely Russian mafia, but I think we're safe,' I joshed. And then added, 'Hold your nose and think of the money.'

We took a taxi to the motel and in the foyer met Chris Longridge, the 7Nights CEO, a lugubrious Mancunian with a steely handshake. Maggie Thornton, his in-house PR, insisted we took a final tour and so we shuffled, in an awkward funnel, around the building, checking out all the bedrooms. Mine was one of the smallest but still pleasant enough, all cream and beige and pale grey, with red scatter cushions and a rug providing splashes of primary colour. The bathroom was white, with miniature bottles of Molton Brown shampoo and shower-gel provided free of charge.

I dumped my stuff and met the others downstairs, where money and attention had been spent in order to distinguish

7Nights from its cheaper rivals. The lounge or 'The Pit Stop', where guests would be able to drink Nespresso coffee and Twinings tea next to a real-effect gas fireplace, was bolder and less functional than your average motel lounge: dark reds and purples, with comfy chairs, squishy sofas and kilim-style printed rugs. The whole look was colonial without the dead animal heads: sort of Raj Lite.

The motel had views at the rear – a field with a stream running through it, and woods beyond. Due to the noise from the road at the front, the view could only really be appreciated from behind reinforced glass, so a soundproofed conservatory, signposted 'The Fuelling Station', had been built across the entire back of the building. The furniture was wicker, and the room contained several unusual decorative items such as stone-effect urns containing bare tree stems, and rustic-looking ladders. Gail had brought the fairy lights and bunting Jem had ordered, and spent a lot of time sourcing an extension lead. Basty and Maggie supervised the laying of a long table.

At 6 p.m., the journalists began arriving in dribs and drabs; a tatty middle-aged man from the *Bicester Times*, a young lad from *Accountancy Age*, Maura Peabody, beheeled and spiky-haired, from the *Mail*. Yasmeen was one of the last to arrive – she'd opted for the most expensive of the hire cars on offer, a Range Rover Evoque Convertible from Hertz's Dream collection – and she walked into the room, all long limbs and liquid silk. Longridge turned away from Mike Bostridge of *Motor Lodges Today*, a shambolic man who had been writing shorthand in a spiral-topped notebook, and broke his first smile of the evening. As Yasmeen rested her hands lightly on his arm, her red nails glinting, Mary smiled at me across the room. I made a little fanning gesture in relief. Client happy: job done.

We'd advised Longridge to get his talk over quickly; it's a painful necessity. You could easily do without a presentation, but the client won't listen: all CEOs like the sound of their own voice. He had a PowerPoint and a few boring anecdotes, but in a nutshell, he explained how they had basically nicked the idea from the easyJet model: aiming to attract a wider demographic with a cheap, accessible, tasteful experience, using trusted brands for instant taste and kudos (see Nespresso, Molton Brown).

Nothing helps a speech slip down as easily as circulating trays of cocktails and by 8 p.m., when we had finally taken our seats at the long table, the evening felt as if it might be a success. The editor from *Busy Woman* was chatting happily with a man from the *Oxford News*, Mike from *MLT* showing an avuncular interest in Jem's A-level choices. Yasmeen had been carefully seated next to Longridge. I could hear her from the other end of the table, trying to persuade him to open a 7Nights on the M20, to break her route from south London to Deal. 'It would just be perfect,' she said. 'My friends and I would *literally* live there.'

The food, Charlie Bigham's Chicken Kievs with SunBlush tomatoes, French Fries and Fresh Garden Salad, was being efficiently picked at, if not devoured, and the empty bottles of Jacob's Creek were beginning to stack up. I remember sitting back in my chair, feeling we had done a good job.

Was it then that it happened, or was it a few minutes later that my life began to unravel?

I heard the commotion first. I had my back to the entrance and I turned my head.

At the time it sounded like a sudden explosion, but when I remember the scene, as I do often, particularly at night, I am unable to do it in anything but slow motion. It was at the other side of the room from us, about 20 feet away, just this side of the doorway. He was a big man – I know I've mentioned that before – and he had tripped on Gail's extension lead, throwing his hand out to save himself and knocking into one of the ladders, which tipped sideways; the pots of cacti and the battery-operated wax candles, which had rested on its rungs, sliding to the floor. He fell onto his knees and must have pressed his palm on the spines of a cactus, as he frowned and rubbed hard on it, bringing his hand to his mouth as if to suck on it.

A receptionist in uniform rushed from the foyer, and across the lounge area to the doorway. 'You all right, sir? Can I assist you in any way, sir?' She helped him to his feet. 'If you want to come this way, sir.' She tried to pull him away with her. 'There's a private function on in here.'

Not everyone had noticed. Only Maura Peabody turned her head, made an expression of concern, and then resumed her conversation.

Dave Jepsom looked down at the receptionist's hand with a frown. She removed it from his arm. And then he looked over at us. I was frozen to my chair, my legs paralysed. He was wearing navy trousers and a white shirt; part of a tattoo was visible on his neck. Even at this distance I was acutely conscious of the gold in the back of his teeth, the pugnacious shape of his shaved head.

I felt the shudder of a passing juggernaut.

Seconds passed. His head moved fractionally as his eyes scanned the faces along the table, from Longridge, one face after another, until finally they rested on me. A faint flush rose below the wingspan of his cheeks, and his mouth twitched, as if perhaps he might smile. Was I imagining the relief in his eyes, almost a welcome? But then the smile went.

I managed to get to my feet. 'Excuse me,' I said to the editor from *Busy Woman*, and I heard the scrape of my chair, and a rattle as it settled on its feet, and I walked as calmly as I could across the room towards him. Each step was careful but I had the sensation of being on the rugby pitch at school; as if I were running, head down, as if my intention was to tackle him to the ground.

'Dave,' I said, my voice sounding oddly dry and crackly. 'Can I help you?'

'I want a word if that's all right.'

'Of course.' I put my hand on his arm to steer him towards the foyer, towards the receptionist who was returning with a dustpan and brush to sweep up the earth and bits of pot at our feet.

But there was resistance. He pulled back against me. 'You won't answer my calls.'

'I didn't realise you'd rung.'

'And when I called to see you at your office this morning your secretary said I could find you here.'

'OK.' I was still speaking almost under my breath. I noticed Longridge look over at us. 'Shall we go and sit down?' I pointed in the direction of the largest sofa in the other room.

His feet were firmly planted, spaced apart, his weight evenly spread. He took a step back towards the door and reached his arms out on either side of him to touch the frame, the muscles in his back pulling at his shirt, as if he were stretching after exercise.

'I don't want to sit down. I want to have it out here and now. It's why I've come all this way.'

'I can see you're upset.' I raised my voice without meaning to.

'Too right I'm upset.' His voice had risen too. He dropped his hands from the doorframe and took a step forward. 'You sent the police to my place of work.' He took another chess-move forward. 'How could I not be upset?'

'I'm sorry. It was a misunderstanding.'

'What kind of a misunderstanding? That's what I want to know.' He closed his mouth, sticking his tongue into his cheek so that it bulged. 'You accuse me of breaking in, twenty-four hours after I have been in your house, mending your tap, chatting with your wife. I mean what kind of a world do you live in where people behave like that?'

I closed my eyes, shaking my head, to try and convey penitence. 'I'm sorry. I've had a lot on.'

'A lot on.' He narrowed his eyes and pushed his head towards me. 'A lot on.'

He leant into the wall, as if he needed support to deal with this, against a photograph that was hanging there. It was of a woman and a man in 1950s bathing suits sheltering behind a windbreak on a beach. He had jogged it so they were askew, smiling out sideways. 'A lot on,' he said again.

'I'm sorry,' I repeated. I was aware of the sound of my own voice – thin, weak. 'We responded badly to the break-in, but it's not entirely our fault.'

Behind me the conversation had lulled, and when I turned my head very quickly it was obvious several of the guests were interested now in what was going on. The man from *Accountancy Age* was tapping on his phone. Longridge cleared his throat and caught my eye, and then took his napkin off his lap and pushed his chair a few inches back from the table, though he didn't get up. It was a signal. Whoever this man was, I should get rid of him. Fast. Jepsom was everything the new 7Nights wasn't. Worse. He was what they *had* been. He was what this long, complicated, expensive exercise, from the original idea to the relaunch, had been about distancing themselves *from*. He was what I was being paid to *get rid of*.

'Come on,' I said again. 'Let's talk about it over there.' I tried again to usher him out of the dining room. 'Or I tell you what. I'll get you a room for the night. We can talk about it in the morning.'

'I don't want a room for the night.' Prominent lines were carved on either side of his mouth, but I noticed another line on one side, a sort of tributary, equally deep. I wondered how the lines had formed. His face so rarely moved. 'I've come here, tonight, to hear you explain.'

I put my hand on his right shoulder, tried firmly to push him now, to turn him round. He took a deep breath and there was a sense of energy restrained when he pumped his right arm, brought it slowly up, and flicked my hand away.

I jerked my elbow back up. 'Perhaps you need to change your own behaviour a bit. You know? Maybe you give out threatening signals. Great you mended our tap. It doesn't leak any more. Thank you. We're grateful, but I didn't *ask* you to mend it. Of course it was kind of you – as I say, thank you – but you didn't *have* to do it. I shouldn't feel in your debt because of one leaking tap.'

He lifted his chin and narrowed his eyes. 'What did you just say?' he said. 'One leaking tap?'

I became aware that behind me the table had gone quiet. His eyes had never left mine and I wondered now if he was going to knock me flying, one clean punch sending me backwards into the dining table in an explosion of cutlery and breaking glass and scattering journalists as a slack-jawed Chris Longridge of 7Nights Motels looked on in horror. The blood sang in my ears and my jaw twitched in anticipation of the imminent contact from Jepsom's meaty fist.

Instead, though, Jepsom took a step from the wall. Behind him, the picture he had dislodged fell to the floor. He flipped it over with his foot, causing the broken glass to patter onto the floor, and when he looked up, his expression wasn't angry so much as puzzled.

'He would have drowned,' he said. 'You know that, do you?'

'Yes,' I said quietly. 'I know that.'

He took another step back, and considered me. 'In Chinese culture, if you save someone's life you are responsible for that person forever. Japanese warriors would think twice for that reason – it's a hell of a burden. A *lifetime*.'

'Japanese or Chinese?' I tried to laugh.

'It's not a laughing matter.' His face was suddenly close. Sweat had pearled on his upper lip. I smelt the musky mineral tang of his aftershave. He spat saliva. 'You're not worthy to be Josh's father. He deserves better. One day someone will take that child away from you.'

'Everything all right? Marcus?'

Mary had left the table and was standing a few safe steps away.

'Contempt,' said Dave, still looking at me. 'He holds me in contempt.'

And then Basty was beside me. 'OK, that's enough,' I heard him say and he put an arm around Dave's shoulders and began to propel him out of the room. Dave's eyes stayed on me the whole way and he was in the foyer, almost at the entrance, when he twisted his body around and called back into the waiting silence, 'You'll be sorry.'

I heard the doors slide open, a rush of traffic noise, and then the sound of the doors sliding shut and it was quiet again.

Her

Marcus was away for the night, at the press launch of his new-look motel chain in Oxfordshire. It was a warm evening and, after I had put Josh to bed, I sat out in the garden with a glass of rosé and a cigarette from the secret packet of Silk Cut I kept hidden at the back of the larder. The fag was a bit stale – that's the problem with occasional smoking – but the wine was cold and, on an empty stomach, I quickly felt the hit of both.

I was feeling calmer. There had been no contact from Dave Jepsom and I had begun to think maybe I had let my imagination run away with me. He hadn't seen me on the phone; he didn't know about Richard; he wasn't going to tell Marcus. He would hate us, obviously: who wouldn't after what we had done? But maybe that was a good thing; he would leave us alone.

The sky was a pale violet; the air felt like bath water. Swallows were swooping from the roofs and laughter drifted from a garden further along the street, a murmur of talk and the clink of cutlery, the occasional excited shriek of a child someone had forgotten to put to bed.

The house phone was ringing but I didn't answer it. It had rung a lot this week; each time I picked it up it was silent. Cold calls from India, I assumed.

I finished my glass of wine, stubbed out my cigarette, and was about to go up to bed when my mobile rang, too. It wasn't a number I recognised.

I answered with a cautious hello.

'You left a message for me to ring?' said a voice. 'Maureen David here. Is it about the ad in Sainsbury's? Car's gone if so.'

For a second I couldn't think who Maureen David was. I turned the name over in my head and when I remembered, it came with a small dig of embarrassment, a measure of shame. I wondered whether to pretend I had rung about the car.

'Maureen,' I said, because in pausing I'd left it too late. 'It's Tessa here. From the holiday?'

'Tessa?' She sounded baffled.

'The woman whose son almost drowned.'

'Oh. Yes. Hello.' She sounded no less confused.

'You're probably wondering why I rang. It's a little bit delicate.'

She gave a sharp intake of breath. 'Don't tell me something's happened again to the little boy?'

'No. No, of course not.' I frowned. Did she think I couldn't take care of him? 'I tracked you down because I had a question about Dave Jepsom.'

'Dave Jepsom?'

'Yes, um . . .' I wanted to get it over with now, and off the phone. It had begun to feel intrusive, ludicrous even. 'We've bumped into him a couple of times, and I just wondered . . . We should have showed more interest at the time, and I feel bad that I don't know, when I'm chatting to him – is he your son-in-law?'

'No.' She laughed. 'He's not my son-in-law. Did you think he was with Sherry? He's not her type.'

'And you're not his mother?'

'Excuse me! How old do you think I am?'

'I'm sorry. No, so . . .' I tried to think how to phrase my question. 'Sorry, this is difficult . . . so how do you guys fit together?'

'We don't, love. We met him out there, day before we met you. He sort of attached himself to us. Couldn't shake him off. But no, we don't fit together as you put it.'

A breeze was stirring in the wisteria; a bough tapped the window where Josh was sleeping. I felt a shiver down my arm.

'Your Dave Jepsom,' she said. 'I don't know him from Adam.'

I took a while to get to sleep, and it felt like almost immediately I was awake again. I was hot. The under sheet was damp; the top sheet tangled on the floor where I'd kicked it off. The bedroom window was open and from the street rose overloud voices, stumbling footsteps, a drunken shriek, laughter: closing time at the pub.

That wasn't what had disturbed me.

From downstairs, a small noise had punctured my sleep. I strained to listen.

Silence.

I raised my head off the pillow.

Nothing.

I waited a minute and laid my head down again. I must have imagined it.

And then I was bolt upright again.

It was unmistakeable this time. A quiet rattle, as if a drawer was being opened slowly, jerkily, as if someone was trying to muffle the sound. The drag of a chair, the vibration of a footstep, a creak.

I reached for a T-shirt on the floor, made a tunnel of it, and eased it carefully over my head. Josh was asleep in his bed, half a floor up. I lifted my legs out of the bed, lowered myself to the floor, and took four steps to the door, bent double with the effort to be quiet.

More footsteps, beneath me, across the sitting-room floor. My breathing was fast and too loud; I cuffed my hand over my mouth and nose to muffle it. There was pounding in my ears, a pulse at the back of my neck. I needed a weapon. I scanned the room: a scented candle, an armchair, a pile of paperback books. The matching Best & Lloyd reading lights on either side of the bed mocked me with their fragility. The bathroom? I could think of nothing, and then yes – the stainless-steel shower head, 'heavy enough to do serious damage'. A creaking board lay between me and the door. I'd have to unscrew it when I got there. Could I be quick, and quiet? I wasn't sure, but I had begun to imagine it now, the weight of it in my hand.

I took a step towards the bathroom door, and the board gave beneath my right foot, groaned. I froze. Whoever it was, did they think the house was empty? Had they heard me?

Nothing for a moment and then a low twang, the spring giving in the armchair, followed by a scrape – the door raking against the wooden floor. And then a human sound, like a small cough or a catch dislodged in a throat, followed by silence.

Someone was standing still, below there in the hall, listening.

Dave Jepsom was in my head immediately. Maureen's information had confirmed my fears – he was a sinister stranger, whose motives were unknown to us. But it was usually kids who burgled in London – the police had told us that. No, it wasn't him. Whoever it was would grab my laptop and my iPhone from the kitchen and scarper. Why would they come up? Why would they want to hurt me or Josh? They would leave in a minute. They wouldn't take care to be quiet, once they'd got what they needed. They'd thud out the back, crash over the fence, maybe they'd blast out the front door.

Downstairs there was just silence.

A heavy footstep on the lowest stair.

An object colliding with a bannister.

Silence.

A slow, snagging rattle, like a zip.

It was the same rasping sound I'd heard when Jepsom unzipped his bag.

Another creak.

He was taking the stairs one at a time, pausing to listen between each tread.

My breath was shallow now; my forehead beaded with sweat. Josh in his bed. My phone downstairs.

My hands empty. Nothing. The shower head, still screwed to the hose.

He was on the landing outside my bedroom now. A shadow crossed the crack at the jamb of the door. I braced for it to open, for his body to loom, for his face.

But the door didn't move. The footsteps paused and then continued; the weight of him balanced on the first stair to the next floor; another pause; a second step.

My stomach seemed to fall in on itself, my arms to collapse forward. The intruder was heading towards Josh.

Blind with anger and panic, I thrust out of the door.

I released a cry, a blood-curdling yell of fury and fear. The door cracked against the wall. My hands were clawed. I was ready to tear out his eyes.

Turning round, he leapt back down the stairs, taking them in one. He took me by the shoulders and I was still making small roaring sounds when I collapsed into him.

'You fucker,' I sobbed. 'What the fuck are you doing, creeping about the house? What the fuck are you doing here?'

'I'm sorry. I'm sorry.' He held me out to look into my face. 'I was on my way to the upstairs bathroom. I didn't want to wake you. I'm sorry I scared you.'

'Why aren't you at your thing?'

Marcus sank down on the step. He was shaking and pale, with dark shadows under his eyes. At his feet was his overnight bag; in his hand he clasped, like a miniature weapon, a toothbrush.

FIFTH

Him

I didn't want to go to work on Friday, to leave Josh and Tessa alone, but she said I had to show my face.

It didn't make much difference either way.

He knew where I lived. He knew where I worked.

From the station, I took a different route to the office, fighting my way along the back streets past the cathedral, keeping my eyes peeled. It was a hot day, tourists cheek by jowl with men and women in suits, schoolkids. The market was bustling, stinking of sausage and leather. Every other person was carrying a smoothie. I crossed back and forth, walking in zig-zags to case as much of the area as I could.

The foyer was empty, CNN silently showing footage of the America's Cup, and then I patched myself through and I was in the lift, and up.

The office was half dead, the 7Nights team not yet back. I nodded at Sam and Emma, who were flirting quietly in a corner, wondering if they'd already heard of my disgrace from the others, and then I sat at my desk and tried to think straight.

Tessa and I had hardly slept. We'd talked about Jepsom half the night. She was horrified to learn he'd turned up in Bicester. She asked me again and again what exactly he had said. I couldn't remember the details, just the feeling I had that he wanted to break my life open, that he was obsessed with her, with Josh. The thing about feeling responsible for him – I couldn't get that out of my head. *One day someone will take that child away from you.* I didn't tell her about that. But she was right, I admitted: he must be the Dave Jepsom she'd found online, the one who was banned from coming within 300 feet of his ex-wife. What had he done? What kind of danger did that sort of person pose to the general public? It was terrifying. Plus, Tessa had heard from Maureen, the woman from the beach on holiday, and Tessa's hunch was correct. He wasn't related to any of those people. He'd latched on to them, just as he'd latched on to us. Who the hell was he? And what did he want with us?

I put my head in my hands. I'd made things so much worse in Bicester. I'd enraged Jepsom. And I'd displayed such lack of character, dithering and swearing – in front of my colleagues, clients, journalists. And then I had run from the room, like a coward, a shivering wreck of a man.

I rearranged a pile of pens, laying them out neatly, lids aligned. One thing was sure: he wouldn't get the better of me again.

It was a long wait until the 7Nights team returned. For posture reasons, Emma had started using a Swiss Exercise Ball as a chair, and every time he passed Sam tried to push it from under her. The room smelt of meat pie; one of them had used the microwave. I rang Mary twice. Her phone went to voicemail the first time, and the second, she asked crisply if she could ring me back. Normal work stuff was pressing in – I had a message to ring Dimitri – but I was incapable of concentrating. I paced, occasionally standing to stare out of the window. It was hard to see down – there's a thick ledge that blocks your eyeline – and I found myself gazing across into an almost empty white room in the building opposite. A man in a suit was lying on a single bed.

When the lift finally pinged, I walked towards it, hoping for some bear hugs, or high fives, some sense at least that my actions had not been being held against me. Basty, the first to amble out, nodded and said, 'Marcus, glad to see you got back safely.' Gail and Mary followed, clip-clopping in their sandals, and I bobbed across the office floor behind them, asking whether they wanted anything. Sandwiches? Coffee? I was repentant, buoyant, desperate to discover we were still good, that I was still the man.

Mary had some phone calls to make and I pretended to be busy. At last she came over to my desk. 'Shall we have a quick chat now?' she said.

I nodded and followed her into the meeting room, as if I were the subordinate. She closed the door behind me.

She was upbeat when we first sat down; sensitive, I realised afterwards, to my mood. The pudding – Heston Blumenthal chocolate fondants – had been a success. Most of the guests had gone to bed early, not long after my departure. But Yasmeen, Longridge and the guy from *Bicester Times* had stayed up drinking until well past 2 a.m. At breakfast, every-one professed to have slept well, appreciative of the 250 thread count Egyptian cotton sheets. The editor from *Busy Woman* thought the mattress topper was the best she had ever slept on.

'And no one thought it weird that I left like that?'

'I told them you had gone to check . . . that man . . . what was his name again?'

'Dave Jepsom.'

'I said you had a personal issue that you needed to sort out.'

'And Longridge is OK? We're not about to be fired from the account?'

'I think he's looking forward to the piece in the *Mail* and hoping for a big plug from Yasmeen. Fingers crossed she delivers the goods.'

'Yes.'

'And he said to tell you how impressed he was with Basty.'

I stroked the round edge of the table. 'It didn't just look pathetic when I left?'

'No.' Her eyes slid away from mine. I stood up to leave, but she didn't move. Her legs were crossed, her hands clasped between her knees. 'So what was it about, Marcus? What on earth did you do to upset him? He was behaving like you'd slept with his wife.'

I waved my hands vaguely in the air. 'It was nothing like that. He's someone we met on holiday. He's taken umbrage at something I've done. Now he won't leave us alone.'

'Oh, OK.' Seemingly satisfied, she stood up then, and peeled open the door.

As she was about to step out, she added, 'Poor man.'

I must have misheard. 'What did you say?'

'I said, poor man. I felt sorry for him. He looked pretty harmless.'

'Harmless?' I stepped between her and the door so she couldn't get by. 'He said that thing about taking my son away from me. He was violent. He was going to attack me.'

'Hm. You were the one who pushed him. You were the one who swore.'

'Mary. He *threatened* me.'

'He didn't threaten you, Marcus!'

'Yes he did. He said, "You'll be sorry."'

'That's not what I heard.' She used her hand, tapping on my shoulder a few times, to make me move out of the way. It felt like a small physical reproof, but she was smiling. 'He said, "You *should* be sorry."'

★　　★　　★

I stayed later than everyone else that night, counting them out one by one. 'Night Sam . . . Night Ems . . . Basty see ya tomorrow.' I was pretending to be in control. The phone messages and emails had piled up all day. I had done exactly nothing. What a fake I was, what a jerk.

At last Mary had typed up her report and put on her coat, and I was alone in the office. I gave her a few minutes, stood up and was finally about to creep home myself when the lights on Gail's phone flashed.

'Hawick Nicholson,' I said.

'Marcus. Just who I want to speak to. Glad I caught you. It's Maura Peabody from the *Mail*.'

'Oh, hi. How are you? I'm sorry not to have had a chance—'

She cut me off. 'Just got a couple of follow-up questions if you've got time to answer them.'

'Great.' I perched on the edge of Gail's desk. This was more like it. 'It's a terrific place, isn't it? Big improvement on the old 7Nights motel. Fire away.'

'Yes, so I wanted to ask about Jemima Wallace.'

The name was familiar, but I couldn't immediately place it. 'Jemima Wallace? Remind me?'

She made a noise, somewhere between a huh and a snort. 'Your "intern"?'

'Oh, Jem.' I stood up to scan the office – pointlessly; there was no one here but me. Had she been in at all that day? No. The last time I'd seen her had been at the motel.

'Jem isn't really an intern. She's more of a work experience girl.'

'A girl?'

'Student then. Work experience student. A shadowing student.' I could feel the heat rising up my neck. 'We don't really have a policy. It's more casual than that. She came in as a favour to my sister – Jem's at school with my niece. Why do you want to know?' I tried levity. 'Have you got a child who fancies coming in?'

'I just wondered if you had any statement to make regarding her presence at the 7Nights motel last night?'

I sat down properly on the chair. I chose my words carefully. 'I thought it would be fun for her, that's all.'

'Were you concerned about taking a fifteen-year-old away to a hotel without a chaperone?'

I paused, took a breath. 'She wanted to get a feel for the business. It seemed a good idea to make her experience as varied as possible.'

'As varied as possible.' She repeated my words slowly as if she was writing them down. 'And afterwards, did you check on her welfare? Did you check she got home all right.'

'Not personally, no. I was a little preoccupied but Mary, my colleague, she—'

Peabody interrupted. 'So not personally? Despite the fact Jemima was under your supervision?'

'Listen, what is this about? I thought you were writing about cotton sheets and organic vegetables?'

I heard a rustle as if she was turning a page. 'Is it true you also tried to take her – in the interests presumably of providing "as varied an experience as possible" – to a strip club?'

I had been fiddling with a pen on Gail's desk, inverting and releasing the button at the end of it, feeling the pressure on the ball of my thumb. 'An executive gentlemen's club.'

'Leather and Lace in Mayfair, no?'

I threw the pen down on the desk so hard it splintered. 'Listen. I'm the good guy here. I stopped her going in. It didn't happen. It's not a story.'

'But if it had been left to Jeff Hawick, your partner, she would have gone in?'

'Yes. No. Look, between you and me, he had a bad day and had too much to drink and he wasn't thinking straight. I think he just forgot she wasn't a junior employee.'

When she didn't say anything, I added, 'She looks older than fifteen, you know?'

There was a long pause. 'And you felt, despite those circumstances, he was a good person to mentor Jemima?'

'Yes. Ordinarily. He's had a lot of experience; he's good with young people. Listen,' I was trying to suppress my rage, to sound as reasonable as I could, 'I mean, what's this about? What piece are you writing?'

'It's just background for a column I'm working on.'

'So it's not on the record?'

'Would you like it to be?'

I tried to think back over what I'd said. It seemed better to stay on the safe side. 'No.'

'Right. OK then. What about Mr Hawick – is he available to comment on this?'

'He's on holiday, and I really don't think he'd have anything fruitful to add anyway.'

'If you're sure.'

I unclenched my teeth, feeling the headache that had been circling all day land. 'I am genuinely sorry about this. Have you spoken to her? Is she all right? Jem, I mean?'

'Yes, yes she is.' It sounded as if she were talking from between her lips, her mouth pursed. Her tone was irritatingly sanctimonious. 'No thanks to you.'

I went for a run when I got home to try and calm down. I felt panic, but also rage at the injustice of it. I'd tried to do someone a favour, to give that girl a chance. I didn't know why everyone was against me. Halfway across the common, at the railway bridge, I came upon Yasmeen also in Lycra. I managed to manufacture a sheepish laugh while apologising for not having 'stayed the distance' at the motel. I pulled my foot up to my thigh and stretched it out, to give a cover for my grimace. I hoped she'd had a better time than I had. 'Quite a character, Chris Longridge, isn't he?'

She nodded, seemingly rather amused. She bounced gently on the spot, tapping the balls of her feet, keeping her calves pumping.

Had she talked to Jem, I asked casually. 'She was shadowing, um, Mary. Terribly bright girl.'

No, she hadn't.

She didn't suggest doing the circuit with me as she had done the last time we'd met out here. Yes, she'd let me know if there was any more information she needed for the article. No, she wasn't sure when it would appear in the paper, possibly Sunday. She left me with a wave: 'Give my love to Tess.'

I was awake most of that night. Work, all-consuming, had once again driven the other worries out of my mind. I got up several times to check the *Daily Mail* website, but nothing had appeared by the time I finally fell asleep to birdsong around 4 a.m.

I heard the newspapers drop onto the doorstep just after 7 a.m., followed by the sound of a car pulling away. I lay there for a moment, not moving, until Tessa said: 'Do you want me to go?'

I nodded.

She slipped out of bed and I watched her walk to the bedroom door. My eyes felt scratchy, my head hollow with lack of sleep. Dread clenched in the pit of my stomach, but I still felt a stir of arousal. It wasn't inspired by her actual body – not much of it was showing: she had put a dressing gown on over the T-shirts she had started wearing at night. It was more the reach it took to *imagine* her body beneath all those layers, the realisation that it was becoming unknown to me. All my emotions were heightened, I suppose, and I felt lost for a moment, drowning in a desperate need for her physically, combined with a sense of dread that I was losing her. I had been preoccupied; boorish; she was everything to me, and yet I'd forgotten she existed.

She brought the papers up, laid the weight of them down at the end of the bed, and handed me the *Daily Mail*. I turned straight to Maura Peabody's column and scoured it. When I'd finished reading, I lay my head back on the pillow.

'So? How is it?'

'It's not too awful. It really isn't. It's just her last item – a few sentences about interns being exploited, a reference to "a young girl" of her "acquaintance". Nothing in there to identify Hawick Nicholson.'

I feel sick, when I remember what I said next.

'I think we got away with it.'

Her

I had the sensation over those few days of having entered a state of suppressed terror; that a blade was poised above my head.

I was one wrong word, one misplaced encounter from being found out.

Marcus thought Jepsom's appearance at the press launch had been a professional disaster. He had no idea how close it had been to a personal one, too. Jepsom had mentioned me, Marcus said. He'd got the impression he 'wanted to say more'. It was only Basty's intervention, getting him out of the room, that stopped him. It was unfinished business. Any day, any hour, any minute he could be back. I braced myself for it; I was waiting for the blade to fall.

It's hard to separate guilt from fear of discovery; the double-headed Janus of adultery. I churned with both; mortified, unable to speak naturally; one minute longing to throw my arms around my husband and child, the next needing to hide my face for fear of what they might see there. I loved them both so much; the thought of losing either was unbearable. That weekend, as events began to press, I began to imagine the reality of it.

Marcus's brow was furrowed when he came through the door on Friday, his jaw rigid. Josh was tugging at his jacket, trying to get his attention, and he yanked the cloth away. 'Fucksake, Josh,' he said. 'Not now.'

Later I said, 'You took a fifteen-year-old away for the night?'

'So? Is that so heinous a crime?'

I didn't dare say anything else. His expression when he looked at me was dark. I wondered how he would look at me if he *knew*. He was panicked, I knew, angry with the journalist and with himself, but it felt as if his anger was already directed at me.

The world was still sleeping when, barefoot, I unlatched the door early Saturday morning. I bent to pick up the bundle of papers, clutching my dressing gown at my neck, and realised there was a plastic bundle leaning against the side of the house.

I took a step out, my toes curling in cold, and reached for it. It was a bunch of flowers, or sort of a bunch – some lilies, and spiky greenery, some yellow roses. But within their cellophane packet, they disintegrated beneath my fingers, the stems still attached in a pink bow, but the blooms falling and crunching against the wrapper. Each individual head was snapped off.

I looked up. Next door's bin was still out, with its lid on the pavement; a fox slid quietly across the road.

The broken bouquet dangled in my hands. I couldn't think what they were or how they had got there. Could they be from Richard? He was the only person I could think of who might have sent flowers – back at the height of the affair maybe. Perhaps they had been leaning against the wall out of sight for a while, and been bashed by the bin yesterday? It was plaus-ible. Or maybe they had blown in off the street. Somebody else's rubbish.

I stuffed them in our bin before taking the papers upstairs.

Released from the clutches of anxiety – the article not that bad – Marcus slipped his hand beneath my dressing gown, his fingers wrinkling up my T-shirt, reaching for my skin. I leant into him. In that instant, Marcus wanted me. It could still be all right. But a few minutes later, Josh was awake, bouncing on the bed, scattering the sections, demanding horse-play, and we drew apart. Maybe later, I thought. Maybe later we could begin to make this right.

We went out for breakfast instead – to the cafe at the far end of the common, next to the bowling green, with its emerald shot of lawn and its manicured summer borders. We sat on the terrace outside, in a bolt of shade. A helicopter was circling and aeroplane lines ran like scratches across the sky. On the other side of the cricket pitch, the Royal Patriotic building towered above the sycamores.

Josh got down to try and stroke a small dog, who was nosing about for crumbs, and Marcus swivelled round on the bench to keep a closer eye.

I wasn't thinking about Jepsom, or my infidelity; I was thinking of nothing but my family. But then, in the peace of that moment, a woman with short, dark hair in a flowery summer dress walked towards us; a smiling missile.

She was holding a takeaway cup out to one side. 'Hi!' she said. 'You're Tess, aren't you? I thought I recognised you.'

Two lanky boys, on the cusp of adolescence, were standing by their bikes, waiting for her.

'Hi!' I said.

'India. We met at Rose's for dinner that time.'

'Yeah, hi. How are you?'

We exchanged pleasantries for a few moments – how nice this part of the common was, how hard it was to get a good coffee. Marcus nodded and smiled like I did, but then got down to follow Josh, who had hared off after the dog towards the tennis courts. I watched him catch him from behind, lift him under his arms, and swing him from side to side as he brought him back.

India was looking down at me, her pert little face inches from mine. She said, 'Did Rose tell you I saw you in Drip the other day?'

'Drip?' I felt panic like a tiny battering in my chest.

Josh's laughter was getting closer.

'I was about to come and say hello but you got up and left before I managed to get to the front of the queue. It's always so busy in there, isn't it?'

'Where?' I said.

'Drip. The new cafe in Dulwich.' She gestured to the boys. 'It's where the boys are at school. They're supposed to get the bus but they're always missing it. I was meeting a friend for a coffee after dropping them off. I mentioned seeing you to Rose – she couldn't think what you were doing all that way over there.'

My cheeks were burning, my heart beating so loudly I imagined they could see the pulse through my shirt. 'Are you sure it was me?' I said.

Marcus was standing next to me.

'Yeah, definitely.' She smiled, showing her gums. 'You were with that restaurant guy, deep in conversation, the one who's always in the papers. Ah, God, what's his name?'

Marcus sat down on the rim of the seat.

'Oh God, my memory . . . *you* know: sushi . . . pizza . . . the Noodle Palace. He was a judge on *Masterchef*?'

'Richard Taylor.' Marcus had said his name out loud.

My vision blurred. I found I was unable to speak. In my ears, the consonants buzzed, the vowels echoed.

The helicopter continued to whirr overhead.

'Or maybe I was mistaken,' she said.

'Remind me who she is?' Marcus said as we walked home.

235

'Rose's friend. The dermatologist.'

'Oh yes.'

'We met her at dinner, do you remember?'

I took a couple more steps. My mouth was dry, my hands thrust into my pockets so he wouldn't see them shaking.

'Were you having coffee with Richard Taylor?' he said. 'You didn't mention it if so.'

One foot in front of the other. 'Josh – don't run ahead too far. Maybe. Yonks ago perhaps.'

His eyes were on Josh's back too. His voice sounded thoughtful. 'Oh right.'

I added, 'I try to keep up with clients if I can. You never know when I might get back in the game.'

'It's a funny coincidence, her mentioning him, that's all,' he said. 'Richard Taylor has been on my radar for various reasons, too.'

A hammering had started up at the side of my head. 'Really?'

'He got in touch last week. We've got a meeting in the diary.'

'When?'

'I can't remember. This week, I think.'

'What does he want?'

He stopped and looked at me, hands outstretched. His brow was furrowed. 'What do you think he wants? Am I so much of a failure in your eyes that I can't take on new business?'

He didn't suspect me; it was all about him. 'Of course not,' I said.

We walked the rest of the way in silence.

As soon as we got home, I left the house on an excuse to buy milk, and rang Richard from the end of the road. His phone went to voicemail. So he had approached Hawick Nicholson, with no thought of how it might make me feel – my husband working with my former lover. Nothing had consequences in his world. It was all a game to him. I leant against the shop window to leave a message, the cold against my cheek.

On Sunday, Marcus was sitting in the kitchen, eating a piece of toast, when he thrust the newspaper towards me, pointing with his finger.

As I read, he pressed the palm of his hand against his forehead.

The 7Nights item, under the headline DRIVE ON!, was at the bottom of her column, beneath the main feature (a withering attack on a sixty-five-year-old television chef who had just left his wife for a woman half his age). The budget motel chain, she argued, had lost the plot. The victim of its own aspirations, it had alienated its loyal customer-base – the truck drivers and commercial travellers – in the vain hope of attracting the Cornwall-going middle class. 'What concerns me is not that their sheets have a 250 thread count, it's that the management believe (or worse, pretend to believe) that 250 – 250, girls! – is something to shout about.' The item ended with the sentence: '7 Nights? I wouldn't pay to spend one!'

Marcus was in the garden on the phone. He came back in and paced the kitchen, his face twisted with frustration: 'Mary actually interrogated me. She wanted to know how long I'd known Yasmeen, why I hadn't sounded her out. She wanted to know if I had "mistaken my own enthusiasm at the staycation idea for hers". She's already bloody spoken to Longridge to appease him. That's my job. I'm *her* boss, for God's sake. I own the fucking company.'

His phone began to ring. He studied the screen and then pressed the button to switch it off. 'Fuck it. Let's see how you all do without me.'

He stood still, his arms drooping by his sides. He was barefoot and his toes were curled as if it was the only way he could keep steady.

I put my hand on his shoulder: 'It's not your fault. You can't be blamed for a defective business model. You've done your best by them. Don't lose perspective. It's one client, one job. One silly column. It's all publicity when it comes to it.'

He didn't seem to hear me. 'You know what? This is Jepsom's fault too. He's the one who ruined the launch. He's the one who poisoned Yasmeen's mind against me. Everything that's gone wrong: he's behind it.'

'One client. One job,' I repeated. 'Don't take it personally. That way madness lies.'

He pushed my hand away. His answer sounded like a premonition: 'For Christ's sake, Tess. Don't you turn on me too.'

Him

Jeff was already in the conference room when I got to work on Monday morning. He'd had an early-morning flight and I hadn't expected to see him until later. Mary and Basty were with him, and a man in a suit with his head bowed who I quickly realised was Neil Jones, the hedge fund manager who had helped with the initial start-up, still our main backer. Emma and Shreya were frantically typing. Sam, who was on the phone, raised his hand in greeting at me, and grimaced.

'What's going on?' I said to Gail.

She was mopping spilt coffee from her desk. 'You were supposed to be here at 8 a.m. Didn't you get the message? Why haven't you been answering your phone?' She put her hand to her brow, fingers splayed, like someone only just keeping control.

'I switched it off.'

'Why did you switch it off? Jeff's been going mad trying to get in touch with you.'

'I just did, OK? Why's Neil here? And Jeff? What's going on? Tell me this isn't about the Yasmeen O'Shea column?'

She stared at me. 'You haven't seen today's papers?'

I shook my head.

She picked up a copy of the *Mail* from the floor, and thrust it into my stomach. 'It's on page fifteen. You'd better read it.

239

And then' – she nudged her head towards the meeting room – 'I'd recommend getting yourself in there as quickly as you can.'

The article was headlined CONFESSIONS OF AN 'INTERN': MY WEEK AT TOP LONDON PUBLIC RELATIONS FIRM. Two photographs – one of Jem in a purple and grey uniform in the street outside our office, and a smaller, drop-in pic of a 7Nights motel. Across the top of the page, the strap read: 'Schoolgirl Jemima Wallace lifts the lid on the sexism and loose morals rife in the company of former PM advisor.'

I had gone into the kitchen to read it and found myself sliding down onto the floor, my back against the skirting board.

Jemima Wallace was thrilled when, after finishing her GCSEs at St Barnabas School for Girls, she was selected for a prestigious position as a work experience intern at Hawick Nicholson. She had dreamt of a career in communications but she quickly became disillusioned. Not only was she unpaid, and used as 'a skivvy', the atmosphere was extremely intimidating. Her two bosses, Marcus Nicholson and Jeff Hawick, regularly swore at their colleagues. 'You get used to the language,' one employee said. 'But you need a strong stomach.'

Hawick, who advised the former prime minister on the investigation into child abuse in the West Midlands, also told her that, 'a bit of buggery never hurt anyone'.

'I don't think someone in his position should say things like that,' Jemima told our reporter. 'It really upset me.'

Even more shocking is the information that twice-divorced Hawick took 15-year-old Jemima to a strip club – which he described to her as 'part of the job'. It was only the actions of a quick-witted bouncer that prevented her being admitted to the Mayfair venue.

Sam had come to the door of the kitchen, carrying an empty coffee cup. I raised my hand and carried on reading; was aware of him walking off.

Married father Marcus Nicholson, meanwhile, insisted Jemima accompany him on an overnight stay at the 7Nights motel in Oxfordshire, where she was plied with alcohol and subjected to sexual advances from a fellow guest.

'Mr Nicholson abandoned me when it got rough. I wanted to go home, but I didn't know how to get out of the situation. It was frightening.'

While Mr Hawick courted schoolgirl Jemima with deliveries of flowers, Mr Nicholson seemed to have made 'Jem', as he named her, something of an unwilling confidante. He shared his concerns with her about some new clients, 'Russian mafia types', whom he found uncouth. Dealing with them, he said, 'You hold your nose and think of the money.' He told Jemima the company had many secrets. It would be 'scary', he said, if they got out.

'I felt very uncomfortable. Jeff Hawick and Marcus Nicholson made me feel cheap.'

Does she still want to work in PR?

'No, I do not.'

Jeff Hawick and Marcus Nicholson declined to comment.

I kicked the floor. Bloody hell. What did they mean: 'thrilled to be selected'? It was one fucking phone call from my sister. I'd only ever tried to be kind. Yes, I knew Jeff had behaved like an idiot – that buggery comment was ill-advised, I'd said it at the time, and then taking her to the strip club . . . Fuck. Shit, of course Jeff shouldn't have sent those flowers. But the photo they'd used, well, it looked nothing like the young woman who'd hung around our office. Maybe he never even knew her

age. Maybe he assumed she was older. They'd twisted everything. What arseholes they were. Anyway, *fuck*.

Also, what was wrong with swearing in the comfort of one's
own office? What stone would one have to live under in which
that was worth commenting upon? What ninny would find
that 'upsetting'?

Fuck, fuck, fuck.

I bent my face, took a gulp of water from the tap, straightened my jacket, threw the newspaper back down onto Gail's
desk and entered the meeting.

You'd never have known Jeff had been on the red-eye.
Freshly shaved, he was wearing a crisp white shirt and sombre
grey suit. He looked sharp and pulled together. When he's
bored, his whole body is affected, becomes loose and languid.
It's moments of crisis that bring out the best in him. As I
slipped with an apology into a chair, he was putting forward a
rescue strategy: phone calls, followed up by letters, to individual clients. He didn't catch my eye. He was on a roll. 'I
don't suppose we will be seeing much new business in the
immediate term. But we will do everything to reassure and
protect those we already represent. One thing we never do at
Hawick Nicholson is accept the status quo. We move forward,
we evolve.' He can be impressive, Jeff. It's easy to forget day to
day how good he can be. Mary too. It seemed she had already
put out a press release, and updated the website. Lawyers had
been consulted. It's a tough one, whether to confront the
tabloids – usually one advises clients to be careful. But, Jeff
insisted, we had nothing to lose and everything to gain.

Neil Jones, our bankroller, shook our hands before he left.
We were to keep him abreast of developments. It was hard to
tell from his expression whether he had bought Jeff's line.
Jones was a decent man. He took no prisoners, but like the
rest of us he knew the power of the press to present

unsubstantiated gossip as solid fact. He knew the truth or otherwise was not up for discussion. In public relations, it's a cardinal rule: never become the story yourself. Us comms guys, we're ghosts – slippery, see-through creatures who move silently and invisibly. We're stage managers who have left before the curtain rises. As soon as the lights are on us – hello Max Clifford, good day Andy Coulson – we're in trouble. Appearances are what counts. And we were too young and fragile an outfit to withstand this assault.

I tried not to read too much into his expression. We'd find out if he wanted his money back soon enough.

Jeff, who still hadn't met my eye, called a meeting of the entire staff. Sam and Shreya looked shifty. Their CVs were almost certainly winging their way to Ekelund. When the chips are down you find out where loyalties lie. Mary was trying to keep spirits up. 'It's just tomorrow's chip paper,' she kept saying, though we all knew it would have done its damage by then. 'This is your chance,' Jeff said, 'to get things off your chest. Anyone have anything to say?'

Shreya was keen 'to discuss' a couple of issues raised by the article, viz 'the culture of bad language'. Jeff promised to hold it in – to, as she put it, 'show more respect'. Emma wanted to thrash out once and for all the buggery comment. Jeff apologised again. 'I was joking,' he said. 'Well, sort of. It was a sort of meta-joke. I was taking a pop at a politically correct world in which to say something like that is shocking.'

'In the context of what we know is widespread child abuse in this country, after the discoveries of Operation Yewtree, would you care to revise your opinion of whether it was actually funny?' Emma asked.

'Yes,' he said, nodding. 'Duly noted. I apologise unreservedly.'

'Well done,' Mary whispered to him as we filed out.

No one had yet spoken directly to me; I had sat there in silence. Yes, Jemima had come into the office through me. Yes, she was technically my intern. But it was Jeff who had made the most heinous mistakes. Why was I in the doghouse?

I didn't really need to ask. 'You'll never amount to anything,' my father used to say. 'You're a waste of space.'

In our business, as in life, it is not the crisis that makes or breaks you, it's how you respond. It was simple: they'd already risen to the challenge, and I hadn't.

Her

The world was full of obstacles and traps. Richard. Jepsom. India. Then, on Monday morning, like a spider, Yasmeen was waiting for me at the nursery gate.

She was chatting to Rose and another mother but drew apart to greet me. Her smile was studiously sympathetic. 'How's Marcus?'

What should I do? Brush it off? Pretend her silly column was so inconsequential to us we hadn't even read it? Or shovel on the guilt, make her feel really bad?

'Oh, he's OK.'

She nodded a few times. The corners of her mouth were turned up, but her eyes were cold. 'Good. I'm glad. These things blow over. I hope he isn't taking it too personally.'

'I think maybe as you are a friend, you've had dinner at our house, he was a little disappointed you didn't warn him.'

'Oh God.' She laughed, darted a look at the other two women. 'You're talking about my column. I'd have thought that would have paled into insignificance.'

The ground felt suddenly unstable. 'What do you mean?'

'The article in the *Mail*?'

'On Saturday? That was fine in the end. He was dreading it,

but . . .' I caught her expression. 'You're not talking about the item on Saturday, are you?'

She shook her head.

'Which article, then?'

Rose stepped forward. 'I've got to get home and feed Nell. Walk with me?'

'Which article?' I said again.

Yasmeen said, 'Don't worry. It's not so much about Marcus. He gets off surprisingly lightly. It's more about the agency. But I'll be honest: it's not going to do him, or them, any favours.'

I turned to Rose. 'What does it say?'

'I don't know.' She shook her head and shrugged, trying to tell me it was trivial. 'I haven't read it.'

'You should probably dig it out,' Yasmeen said. 'Today's *Mail*. He might need a nice supper to cheer him up when he gets in tonight.'

I bought the newspaper from the corner shop on the way back to the house, and read it at the kitchen table.

The article was entitled 'Confessions of an "intern": my week at top London public relations firm'.

It took me less than a minute to read, though I got the general gist the second I saw it.

I closed the paper and thought for a few moments. It was damaging. That was obvious. No PR company wants to be 'the story'. Jeff was an idiot. I could just *hear* him saying the thing about the buggery. He would have said it to shock, for humour. But taking the girl to the strip club – what was *that* about? It was insane. I was irritated that Marcus hadn't told me any of this. And the 7Nights thing was a typical tabloid semi-fabrication. Marcus hadn't stayed the night. He'd been in such a state about Dave turning up. He'd come home to me. And how lucky it was that he had or this might have really worried me. But the truth was facts didn't really matter.

Appearances counted. Reputations were built on them. And this was potentially ruinous.

I looked at the Hawick Nicholson website. They'd put up a statement but it was too prominent. They needed to get it off the home page and onto a click-through. I hoped Marcus had remembered it wasn't just the clients who needed nurturing but each and every stakeholder. I hoped he was including the whole staff. It would be easy for someone to feel isolated.

I tried to ring Marcus on his mobile. The call went straight to voicemail. Back at Ekelund we had a checklist of the 'six ws': not just the usual five – who, what, where, why and when – but another who: *who's* going to take the fall?

I rang the main number for the company and spoke to Gail. Marcus was in a meeting, she told me.

'Is it bad?' I said.

'It's not great.'

'Who's going to take the fall?'

She half laughed, but didn't answer.

'Ask him to call me if he has time.'

'I will.'

I took Josh to Peter Jones that afternoon – to get out of the house. Marcus hadn't rung back, and I was too on edge to settle.

A motorbike was parked illegally on the pavement. The driver was sitting on it, leaning forwards in his leathers, the black visor of his helmet down, like he was waiting for someone or something.

As we stepped through the gate the motorbike revved and then roared forwards, growled to the end of the road, then indicated and swerved to the left. I could hear it for a minute or two as it turned again at the main road and then was gone.

Instinctively I had pulled Josh back from the noise, and the exhaust. I was still clutching his hand when my phone rang.

I let his hand go to answer, hoping it was Marcus.

'You called?' Richard said. There was a rumble of traffic; I could hear from the breaks in his breathing that he was walking, too. 'Fancy hooking up? I've got a spare hour or two. That cafe in Dulwich? My flat? Or somewhere closer to you?'

'Please don't. It's not funny. Did you get my message? Please don't take your business to Marcus.'

Josh had run ahead down the road, and I sped up to catch him.

'Tessa, I don't understand. Why wouldn't I want to do business with Marcus? Despite what one reads in the papers, he's good at his job.'

I was running now. 'Please don't.'

'I might even get him cheap now.'

Josh had stopped to look at a cat in a doorway, and I got to him before he moved off. 'Richard, please.'

He made a noise, a tuneful tut. I realised he was laughing at me. 'Meet me. I might be persuaded that way.'

'I can't.' I took Josh's hand again, and lowered my voice. 'I'm with my little boy. I have stuff to do. Boring domestic chores. The things my life is made of. Bus stops. Kids' armbands. Peter Jones.'

'Oh, the excitement.'

I suppressed the desire to scream. As calmly as I could, I said, 'Please leave Marcus alone.'

We sat in the front seat on the top deck. Josh wanted to know who I thought would fly fastest round the world, Superman or Batman? Older kids, a few rows behind, were messing about – smoking, throwing food. An empty can of Coke rolled under the seats. Josh kept turning round to look. The kids got louder,

more sweary. 'You fucking eejit.' But then – 'Aw, look. He's so
sweet,' one of the teenage girls said, noticing Josh. She held
him in her stare. Her eyes were heavily kohled. A ring pinched
her eyebrow. I didn't wait for the next stop. I bustled him onto
the stairs to go to the lower floor. There was a bottleneck.
'Bitch,' I heard her say, as we waited. 'What does she think I'm
gonna do? Steal him?'

Richard's persistence, his playful refusal to grasp how
serious I was, had renewed my panic. I had put everything at
risk. Something or somebody would give me away. In the
department store, we took the escalator up to the third floor,
increasingly vertiginous, scaling the atrium. A woman had
fallen over the side recently; I'd read about it in the paper.
Four floors down. Dead on impact. Suicide, they'd said. The
sides were high. You couldn't just fall. My fingers dug into
Josh's hand.

The children and baby department was thronging with
people. A queue had built up at the school uniform section
and there was an officious-looking woman behind a podium
writing people's names on a waiting list. Josh wanted to look
at the displays of grey trousers, the carousels of navy jump-
ers, the surly looking twelve-year-olds forced to wait by the
aertex shirts. He spotted a rack of mini suits, complete with
waistcoats, and I had to drag him away. In the swimwear
section, I found some Zoggs roll-up armbands. The passing
assistant I managed to persuade to attend to us said they
were the best on the market, but I still insisted he take them
out of the packet so we could try them out. I tugged to check
they wouldn't come off. Josh yelped. Yes, they would do.
Definitely tougher and tighter than the ones we'd lost in
Greece. I also bought a rubber ring and a swimsuit with a
buoyancy aid built in. And a 'Micro Scootersaurus Safety
Helmet' in blue.

I'd promised Josh he could look at the toys and we made our way through a rabble of small children to a shelf of plastic farm equipment. He found a red tractor, which he played with on the grey carpet while I leant against a display of VTech Push & Play Animal Spinning Tops. It was noisy. A small toddler was having a tantrum, beating his heels and fists on the floor. A baby in a pram was letting out a relentless hiccupping cry. If you closed your eyes, which I did briefly, it sounded like the inside of a swimming pool. My head ached. I felt a sort of seeping despair.

My poor husband; everything was going wrong for him at work, while at home his own wife was lying to him, pretending their life was something it wasn't.

The holiday was a chance for breathing space, a new start for us. And yet it was based on a lie. How could we ever move forward if I didn't tell him the truth?

Josh had hurtled towards a display on the other side of the end of the row and grabbed a Bob the Builder tool belt; he started dismantling it. 'I want this. I want this,' he said. 'I'm going to be a plumber. I want to mend the bath.'

'I can't buy you that,' I said.

He continued pulling out the tools and I took a step towards him to take the belt away, and in doing so had a sudden clear view, past the large square pillar that had blocked it, of the lift area.

He was standing, looking over at me. His head was tipped backwards, the surfaces of his face flat under the shop lights. His legs were apart, a concave gap between his thighs, as if braced. He rubbed one large hand up and down his upper arm; the muscle bulged beneath the cap of his sleeve. I couldn't see his expression, or his eyes.

The room seemed to shiver. The edges of my vision turned monochrome. My legs weakened and I put one hand out to steady myself.

A lift behind him pinged and the man turned his head. I took a step towards him. But a woman stepped in front of me, a young mother herding two young children, twins, while soothing a baby in a sling. I stood to one side to let her pass, and in that fraction of an instant, the door of the lift was slowly closing and the man had disappeared.

This was it. Jepsom was here. I wasn't imagining it. Not this time. I looked over to children's clothes, through the ranks of little girls' party dresses, to the tills, back to the toys. I darted to the back stairs, swung open the doors and looked up and down. It was quiet, empty.

Another lift in the bank of four opened, and more people got out.

Was I going mad? Had I lost touch with reality?

I walked slowly back to the aisle where I had left Josh.

I couldn't find him.

He wasn't with the Bob the Builder belts. He wasn't with the diggers or the tractors. Not at the Playmobil stand. Or the Meccano. Or the Lego. I checked the dolls, and the Sylvanians. I called his name quietly from aisle to aisle, conscious of my own voice, not wanting to embarrass myself, any minute expecting to see him. And then I was slightly less quiet and then I became loud. My breath was ragged. I lost all inhibition. My fists were clenched. 'I've lost my son!' I yelled. 'Have you seen a boy? My boy. JOSH!!' An assistant came towards me, a young woman in a black trouser suit, with a badge telling me her name was Sharon. 'I've lost my son!' I screamed. 'He's been taken.'

I was explosive with heat, my whole body shaking. The heaving noise I could hear was my own breath. I ran back to the lift. 'A man's taken my son,' I said to the people getting out. 'He's three. Have you seen a man with tattoos and a little boy?' I didn't care what anyone thought of me. I was beyond that. I knew I needed to be in control of myself but I had no control. No control at all.

They took me to one side, and tried to make me calm down. They put me in a chair. 'Dave Jepsom,' I was screaming. 'That's his name. That's the man who's taken him. You've got to stop him.' Another woman arrived. She was older, hair in a bun, pink lipstick, in a black skirt and jacket. Her badge read 'Sally'. She didn't want to know about Dave Jepsom. She just wanted to know about Josh. She took a description. She wanted to know what my son was wearing. She wanted to know when I had last seen him, how old he was, where he had been standing. I managed to stutter out answers and she wrote them down and then got on the phone. I could hear her repeating my words, in a coherent order. 'Aged three. Last seen by the pre-school toys. Shoulder-length brown hair. Green eyes. Navy blue knee-length shorts. A blue and white striped T-shirt.' She put her hand on my arm when she had hung up. The shop floor was being searched, she told me. I was not to worry. He'll have wandered off. It happened all the time. *All the time.* Had I been on my phone? People usually were when it happened. They would find him. They always did.

'I saw someone I know,' I said. 'I think he might have gone with him.' My voice began to rise; my eyes felt like pinpricks.

'Come on now,' she said. She gave me a glass of water, but I couldn't get it to my mouth. 'Take a deep breath. Stay calm. We need you to be calm. You don't want your son to see you upset, do you?'

The young woman with the baby and the twins came over, and the manager stood up to talk to her. A clip was hanging out of her hair at the front, which she swiped vaguely out of her sight line. Her children were standing meekly by her. The baby had stopped crying.

Muttering to myself, I fumbled for my phone in my bag and found the number in my contacts. It went straight to voicemail, a generic message. 'The number you are calling . . .' When the beep had finished: 'Dave. Have you got Josh? I know we've got to talk. But bring him back. Please bring him back.'

Sally, the manager, slipped back onto the chair next to me. 'It's only been ten minutes. I promise you this happens all the time.'

'Has it been ten minutes?' It felt less or much more. Seconds, or an hour, two hours, an eternity.

People were standing around, watching. They were in the middle of their shopping and they were just staring. Heads turned. Their expressions were blank. I was the freak at the circus. I was naked. I wanted to scream. I wanted to bang my head against the wall. Maybe I did.

I stood up and opened my lungs. I shouted. 'JOSH! JOSH! WHERE ARE YOU?'

I can't remember the exact order of the next few minutes. The store detective was there, young in jeans and Nike trainers and a button-down shirt. Huddled conversations. Expressions more serious. Everything went up a gear.

And then, across the shop floor, a change, a ruffle, like wind across a field of long grass. Heads turned. And towards me came the woman with the baby and the dangling clip, though it wasn't dangling any more, and right next to her, right up close, holding her hand, was Josh.

Later, I would say how nice everyone had been. And they had been: they were all so nice. Someone found my shopping, which I'd abandoned in the toys. Someone else gave me a glass of water, and a tissue because once I had him back in my arms, when I thought I'd never let him go, the tears just fell.

No one told me I'd been foolish, or told me off for wasting time. No one asked me any more about Jepsom.

They told me Josh had been hiding in the children's changing rooms, hunkered down, laughing – or maybe sheepish, not knowing how to extricate himself from his own little prank. Or maybe he didn't feel embarrassment. Maybe he was just playing with the Bob the Builder tool belt he'd taken from the shelves, too absorbed in his game to hear us.

Or too interested in the bar of chocolate he had been eating.

No one seemed to care that I hadn't given him chocolate, that someone else must have put it in his hand, that a stranger might have coaxed him there. They kept trying to reassure me; he'd have picked it up, they said. Another child must have dropped it.

And I let them; I nodded. It's funny how quickly your social conditioning can clamour to be reinstated. Minutes before, it had been stripped away. I'd been reduced to pure fear, and panic: animal instincts. I'd been blood and bone. Sinew. I had no surface. Now I was racked with mortification, doubled up with gratitude, riven with smiles. I must have said, 'thank you,' a hundred times. 'Bless you. Thank you. I'm so sorry. What an idiot . . . *God.*'

Sally led us back to the bank of lifts and patted me on the arm when she said goodbye. I pressed the button, holding Josh's hand, watching the lights move above each door.

It's moments when you relax that are the most perilous. When you think the danger has passed, that's when you're at your most unsafe.

I felt his hands, softly, around my waist; felt the cool of his breath on my neck, inhaled the smell of sandalwood.

'Boo,' he said.

My elbows were digging into his chest, my feet braced as I tried to push him off. I was gripping my son's hand, but my ex-lover's arms were still around me, his lips buried in my hair, when the lift in front of me slid open, and out stepped Rose.

Him

I got back too late to speak to Tessa on Monday night, and left for work before she woke up on Tuesday. I felt a twinge of guilt – she'd tried to get through to me several times the day before – but I dismissed it. I had too much on my mind to worry about her, too. Our week in Suffolk was coming up. Another nightmare looming: we'd probably have to cancel.

It was obvious we would lose clients, and on Tuesday they began to fall. Citrus Burst were the first, the bastards, citing a young demographic. The decision from Chris Longridge from the 7Nights group was also inevitable. The reference to my night of shame might have been buried in the piece, but the photograph – actually of the Sheffield city centre branch, but at this stage who cared? – was too damning. The email came through at lunchtime. They would be putting the job to tender. We were welcome to re-pitch. In the meantime they would like every reference to 7Nights removed from our website. We all knew what that meant. They wouldn't touch us again with a barge pole.

Later, Jeff came to find me in the kitchen. His hands were shaking slightly as he poured a cup of coffee from the percolator. 'We lost Cartingdon Hall,' he said, mopping up the spillage with some kitchen roll. 'The veiled accusations of child abuse, directed at both you and myself, have – and I quote

256

– "rendered the relationship untenable". Under the circumstances, it would have been impossible for them to have kept us on.' He took a swig. 'Sad to lose the alma mater. I find it hard not to take that one personally – particularly as they didn't even pay us.'

'It's just not fair,' I said. 'None of it is true. If Dave Jepsom hadn't turned up at the launch none of this would have happened. I wouldn't have left. I could have kept Jem away from Maura, protected her.'

He put his coffee cup down. 'Would you, though?' he said.

It was the next call that really stung.

We went back so far, that was the thing. If you'd asked me the week before I'd have said ours was a relationship based on loyalty, trust, shared experience. I'd have said we had grown up together. I'd have argued our alliance had long, deep roots. But hey. Mutual respect? History? Affection? They stand for nothing in business.

'Marco, sweetie – you do understand, don't you? Not when I've worked so hard to get over the Indonesian problems, and with TeEn in its early stages. I'm a poster girl for young women now, a role model.'

'I'm the one who made you that poster girl! It was down to me!'

'Come on now, Marco. You might have helped, but I have done all this on my own.'

'Couldn't we continue handling the adult range?' I wheedled. I sounded desperate. I *was* desperate.

'I can't be associated with anything that will damage the brand, particularly since the TeEn Brandy Melville deal. It's too risky.'

'But it's lies. We're suing the arse off them.'

'I don't need you to explain or justify. I know *these things happen*. Please don't take it personally. You're a pro – I know you'd do the same in my shoes. I still love ya. We'll still be friends.'

I didn't answer – I couldn't; I felt too weak, as if all the blood in my body had leaked down into my feet.

'We'll have lunch!' she said, before hanging up.

The atmosphere in the office was tense and subdued, the worst combination. The air-con appeared to have packed up too – typical – and the swelling heat seemed to reach every corner. Jeff was locked in the meeting room with Mary most of the day, working on a second statement. They hadn't asked me to join them. I had three messages to ring Dimitri, but I ignored them. At one point, I came across Emma and Sam in the kitchen, sniggering over her phone. It was a gif on Instagram. Probably set up by that tosser from *Accountancy Age*.

The video clip on repeat was of Jepsom saying: 'Contempt. He holds me in contempt.' Because of the perspective my face was tiny and seemed perched on his shoulder, like the disembodied face of a ventriloquist puppet. Over and over, as he whirled round to confront me, my face squashed tight and my mouth dropped open, closed, open, closed in a silly little circle.

Caption: 'PR man shows true feelings.'

The night in Bicester seemed a long time ago. I hadn't thought about Jepsom much since. I'd hardly had time. Concerns I had tried to bury, nasty, stabbing thoughts, threatened to re-surface. I damped them down.

I kept noticing huddled groups, at the water cooler, or the photocopier, which would disperse when I got near. I had a horrible suspicion halfway through the afternoon that I had lost the confidence of my own staff.

I called Gail over to my desk under the pretence of asking her to witness a signature, and when she had lowered her head, hissed into her ear: 'No one thinks it's true, do they, that I slept with Jem?'

She straightened up. 'No, of course not.'

'Promise?'

'Yes.'

'Really?'

'*Yes.*'

You should never ask. With every reassurance, I felt a little less reassured. She wasn't looking at me. She was chewing her lip.

'It's just I'm beginning to think it's sabotage, that someone is fucking with me. McCready's speeding offence? Someone could have leaked that to the press. And Judd? Who started the gossip about his unsavoury business practices? And Tilly – how did those sixth-formers find out about the palm-oil connection? And that letter – *that letter* – to Cartingdon Hall: the headmaster is convinced it's a hoax.'

I could feel rising hysteria.

'Marcus,' she said. 'These things happen. It's no different to usual. The Judd thing will have been leaked by any number of his business rivals, probably ExCav Industries; they wanted that project as much as he did. Who sold the McCready story to the press? My guess: the copper that nicked him. It's a funny story: the man who owns a race track going too fast himself. In his position, *I'd* have sold it. You know as well as I do –' She reached her hand out towards me, as if trying to remind me 'Sometimes crises come spread out, sometimes they come in a huddle. It's the nature of the job. And no, I don't think anything in the article was accurate. But Jemima *was* in your care, her parents were trusting you with her, and maybe you shouldn't have fobbed her off on Jeff. We all know what he's like.'

'So it's all my fault?' As I spat the words out, a tiny drop of saliva landed on her hand.

She looked at it, and then turned away. When she sat back at her desk, she lifted her face, said, 'Don't forget to ring

Dimitri Mikhailov,' and then used her ankles as hooks to pull her chair in sharply.

I rang my sister who said, 'Last time I do anyone at school a favour.'

'Does Izzy call her Jem?'

'I don't think so.'

She told me that now she thought about it, Jemima was very bright and was often bored as a result. 'She's a trouble-maker,' she said.

'You could have told me earlier.'

'You could have behaved more responsibly.'

I hung up.

Her

Rose was waiting for me at the cafe facing the common. She had already ordered when I got there. Two cappuccinos were lined up on the table. A jug of water. A plate of brownies. Items laid out like weapons.

It was a warm morning, busy with the post-school drop-off crowd. A large group of women with prams – an NCT meet-up – were discussing colic and blocked milk ducts at the next table. Dogs barked. Cars idled. White clouds tufted over a mid-blue sky. Half a croissant lay curled under her chair, left over from a toddler's breakfast.

'So?' Rose said. She poured a glass of water and handed it to me. 'He's the man India saw you with, isn't he?'

I nodded.

'Do you want to tell me what's been going on?'

'It was nothing,' I said.

'It didn't look like nothing.'

She had her GP face on: affectedly kind, understanding, sanctimonious. I felt the distance gape between us. She was my friend, and yet my heart was unknown to her.

I opened my mouth and told her everything. It had been a fling, I said, no strings attached. I'd been lost, searching for meaning, for something I was good at. I told her that despite what she had seen the day before, it was over. He had wanted nothing; I had wanted nothing back. It had been a brief meaningless episode for both of us.

'It didn't look like it was meaningless to him,' she said.

'He wants what he can't have.'

'He looked like he wanted to eat you.'

'He's a big one for public displays of affection.'

She took a sip of water; her mouth twisted at one side, in an expression of doubt. 'Why was he there if you'd stopped seeing each other?'

I tried to smile, shook my head slightly to express my own confusion. 'It was a misunderstanding. He thought when I'd told him where I was going, I was suggesting he joined me. He had told me he was at a loose end and . . .' I frowned, and shook my head again. 'Anyway, he knows it's over now.' I couldn't bear her not to believe me. 'I told him I never wanted to see him again. This time I think he understood.'

'Who else knows?'

'No one but you.' My eyes slanted away; Dave Jepsom, I thought. He knows. But I didn't say it.

She was watching me carefully. 'And Marcus?'

I shook my head.

She ran her finger over her glass, releasing a small, high-pitched hum. 'And are you going to tell him?'

I'd known all along that it was coming to this, all week, all month, all year. I couldn't keep it secret, not if my marriage meant anything to me. The usual clichés were at play about honour and openness, the betrayal that bleeds out from pretence. I felt the truth of them, like a bruise blooming in my chest. But I also knew I had no choice. I had to tell him because somehow – through Richard, or Rose, or even Josh – I was going to be found out.

I paused, and in that moment I saw her expression harden. I could feel my friendship with her ebb away.

'If you don't tell him,' she said, 'I will.'

Him

In the hotel suite, the Russian was sitting at a full-sized mahogany dining table, looking through some papers. He'd asked to see me alone, but I'd made Jeff come too. Without him, I was gutless, incapable of action.

Dimitri was wearing the hotel's white towelling dressing gown, his bare, muscular legs outstretched. The sinews in his neck flexed as he nodded his greeting. He didn't stand up. I'd been led to expect both men, but there was no sign of Olaf. Dimitri didn't ask us to sit down. We stood there, with a bodyguard on either side of us. He said: 'Marcus, is it true? That you resorted to an embarrassing cliché and called us "Russian mafia types"?'

'It was taken out of context,' I stammered.

'And you think I am uncouth?' He reached beneath the cellophane into the fruit bowl and removed a satsuma, which he began to peel. His nails were perfectly manicured moons. He picked around the edges for the loose threads of pith. 'You hold your nose when you deal with me. Interesting, interesting. I, as you know, am not a married man. An unmarried man – well, certain behaviours are forgiven in a bachelor, like me, that in a married man are considered, to use your word, uncouth.' He wrinkled his nose. 'A prostitute? Really. What would your wife think?'

I began to stutter – apologies, explanations, denials – but he interrupted. 'In my country, I told you we take hospitality very seriously, but we are also gravely affected by disloyalty.' In front of him on the table was a brown envelope, which he tapped with one hand.

'I'm afraid, Marcus, it is natural to seek redress in business. There is always retribution. I am sorry,' he said, putting a segment of orange into his mouth. 'We no longer request your media advice.' He dabbed at his lips with a thick white napkin. 'Maybe *I* should be giving media advice to *you.*'

Jeff said, 'Listen, please forgive us, we're—'

'No, I have heard enough.' He pointed at me. 'You insulted my business. You insulted my partner and me personally. You insulted my country. You need to be taught a lesson.'

'He was joking,' Jeff said in the lift down.

I didn't find it funny. I didn't like the envelope; he had tapped it so pointedly. Or the glimpse I had caught of Olaf, listening in the other room.

Her

Rose agreed to take Josh at lunchtime so I could have the afternoon to think. I'd rung Marcus and he'd promised to come home in good time. I told him we had to talk, and he agreed quickly. 'Yes, I know,' he said. 'I know.'

He didn't know anything. The innocence of his not knowing was like an open wound in my side.

I spent the afternoon unable to settle. I tried to run through what I would say. I sat in different rooms, trying out words. There was no combination that worked, none that didn't blast a hole through the walls of our life.

I lay on the bed and stared at the ceiling; I sat in the bathroom, studying the calcified stain, like a teardrop, where the tap had dripped. I walked into the sitting room and picked up the broken photo frames lying on their sides now in a pile on the mantelpiece. I should buy new ones. I held the picture of Josh to my cheek, rubbed it across my mouth.

At the top of my ribcage was an acute pain; a tight squeezing.

My phone rang. I fumbled for it. An unknown number. There was only silence at the other end when I answered. I pressed to disconnect. It rang again. The same thing.

I started rubbing my left wrist with my right hand, twisting the skin, bruising the vein with my thumb. I knew with sudden certainty that it was Jepsom who had rung. He didn't need to threaten us with silent calls. I was tired of watching and waiting for his next move. The quiet, the silence was worse than words. There was nothing he could say to hurt me or Marcus now.

The pain in my chest spread; it expanded into my stomach, permeated my limbs.

I stood at the window, looking out into the road, and without giving myself permission first, I dialled the number.

A gruff hello that made me want to slam down the phone.

I kept my nerve. 'Dave,' I said. 'It's Tessa. I feel we need to have a few things out. I'm partly ringing to apologise for some of the things we've done, and partly to—'

'Tessa.' I heard a small sound as he caught his breath, a wet clink as he opened his mouth. His voice sounded echoey, as if he were in an empty room. 'Tessa,' he said again.

My heart had begun to hammer. Perhaps this had been a mistake. I walked away from the window, and into the hall.

'Did you just ring me and hang up?' I said.

'What are you talking about?'

'Is it you who's behind these silent calls I keep getting?'

'Silent calls? Why would I be, Tessa?' His voice was quietly calm.

'I can understand why you might be annoyed with us. I realise we shouldn't have accused you of breaking into the house, and yesterday when I rang . . . I'm sorry I was upset. I'd lost Josh and—'

'That was you? That woman burbling? That was you?'

I felt sheepish now. He sounded so baffled, so hurt. Once again, I felt the ground shift, and the same anxiety that we had got it all wrong. 'Yes it was. Was it you in Peter Jones? Maybe not. Maybe it's all a misunderstanding.'

'I thought we could be friends.'

His voice was flat. He sounded too tired to be bitter.

I began cautiously, as if stepping into quicksand. 'I feel that perhaps we have behaved badly towards you and I should say sorry.'

He didn't answer at first. When he did, he sounded slightly warmer: 'I was feeling, yeah, puzzled by it all. Hurt. I tried to get Marcus to explain, but . . . he's not that easy to talk to. Whereas you and me, I feel we've got a connection.'

I was in the kitchen now and I leant against the sink, looking out into the garden. A crow was standing on the wooden table, picking at a piece of leftover food, tossing it from side to side. 'I think we panicked,' I said, after a moment. 'We thought you were with those people on holiday and then we discovered that you weren't, and it threw us. Clearly, we misunderstood, but for a while there we thought you'd lied to us – about having kids. I don't know what difference it should make but you always seem so concerned about Josh.'

'I did have a kid.'

The way he said it, the way his words seemed to reverberate in a cavernous space. I felt the force of it in my chest.

'Yeah. I did have a kid, a little boy. He died.' His voice was even gruffer now.

'I'm so sorry, Dave. I had no idea.'

'It was an accident. According to the coroner, who was in the pocket of my ex. Though why the window was open, why a three-year-old was left alone in a room with an open window, is a question I will take to the grave. I've certainly given up getting any answers from her. So you'll forgive me if I'm a little concerned when it comes to the welfare of your son.'

'It's awful, Dave. Please don't be so angry.'

'You're a nice woman, Tessa, but neither of you were look-ing after Joshy that day. I saw you in the bar on your phone.'

Joshy? 'You did? You did see me?'

'And that husband of yours – he was so unconcerned he went to sleep.' His voice had begun to break. 'Children die. It only takes a second. There is only a moment between life and death. Neither of you seem to realise that.'

I was crying myself now. 'I'm sorry,' I said. 'I'm sorry.'

His voice sounded twisted and strange. 'I don't know that you *are* sorry,' he said. 'Not really. If something bad happens to Josh, *then* you'll know what sorry is.'

'Nothing is going to happen to Josh. I won't let it.'

'Neither of you ever understood,' he said quietly, as if hadn't heard me.

'What?'

'I only ever want to help you.'

Him

As the train juddered, my face squashed into my neighbour's backpack, the handles of a bike jabbed into my side.

It stopped at Clapham Junction; a few people got out, more people got in. I was the wrong side of the carriage and found myself pushed and squeezed further away from the door. I shifted my body, lost my grip on the hand-bar. When the engine lurched back into life, I was thrown backwards and then swiftly forwards, rootless, untethered. I needed to get off this train. Now.

At Wandsworth Common, I sat on a bench to get my breath back. In my pocket was a piece of paper, a receipt from lunch with Tilly. I hadn't got round to putting it in the file with all my other claimable expenses. I read it through: chia-seed crackers and the spiced Cornish crab and lobster omelette, chargrilled Iberico pork chop and French fries. The words didn't seem to mean anything, and I tore it into tiny pieces of confetti, and threw them in the air.

I don't know how much later it was that I looked up. Across the empty tracks, on the other side of the station, her hands pressed against the fence, Tessa was standing watching me.

Her

I watched three trains roll in and out before I realised the person slouched on the edge of the bench, on the opposite platform, half hidden by the bushes, was Marcus. His jacket lay crumpled next to him and his tie was askew. Even from here, I could see his shirt was ripped. He was surrounded by little bits of shredded paper.

He looked up. It took a moment for his eyes to focus, and the confusion on his face cleared. He clambered to his feet, started walking towards the steps, and then remembered his jacket and went back for it. He noticed the pieces of paper and he bent to gather them up, studying them before pausing at the bin to drop them in.

I stood at the bottom of the stairs as he quickly crossed the bridge and came down towards me. I felt as if I'd been waiting for him for hours. Now he was so near, fear uncoiled in my stomach. He took several steps at once. He said, 'Sorry, sorry, sorry. It's been . . .'

'I know.'

'Where's Josh?'

'He's at Rose's.'

'Is he OK?'

'Yes.' I'd rung Rose the moment I'd hung up from Jepsom. 'I'm collecting him later.'

It was a balmy evening. The clouds had cleared, and the sun was low but still strong. The big sycamores on the common were dark and clearly defined against an indigo sky. Children were playing cricket in the lengthening shadows.

As we crossed the common, I told him about my conversation with Jepsom. He listened: 'So he *is* the guy in the police report from Tottenham? He *is* dangerous.'

'His son died.'

'But we're right to be scared of him.' He nodded a couple of times. His reactions were off. He didn't seem to have registered the tragedy of the dead child.

When we got home, he closed the door and put his bag down on the floor. As he hung his jacket on the peg, there was a weariness in his expression I didn't recognise. He looked tired, defeated. He closed his eyes briefly and rubbed the side of his head with the index and middle fingers of one hand, which he often did when he was anxious. I felt overwhelmed with love for him.

I sat down on the stairs. When he realised I was still there, he looked at me from out of the corner of his eye, as if he were searching my face, as if he were scared of what he might find there.

'Marcus?'

He sounded defensive. 'Yes?'

I swallowed hard. I didn't want to cry, but there was an obstacle in my throat. I dug my fingernails into my thigh. My sentences came out in broken pieces.

'Don't say anything please. Just listen to what I have to say. I have to tell you something even though I don't want to. I don't care what you think of me, but I know it's going to hurt you and I don't want that.'

'What is it?' His tone was flat. He sat down on the stair next to me, as if he couldn't trust his legs. He leant forward on his elbows and scratched at an invisible mark on his trousers. 'I'm not sure I can take anything else. Are you leaving me, is that what this is?'

'I'm not. I don't want to leave you.'

'But you're unhappy.'

'I'm not. Or I am. But I shouldn't be. It's not your fault.'

He let out a hollow laugh. 'That's what they all say.'

He raised his elbow as if he were about to put his arm around me. I made to lean into him, and for a moment I thought perhaps I didn't need to tell him after all. I felt the relief of that, and felt the tension beginning to go. But I pulled myself back. I couldn't meet his eyes.

'Let's go and sit in the kitchen,' I said. 'I'll make us a cup of tea.'

'I don't want a cup of tea.'

'Or some wine.'

'Just tell me what it is.'

I'd spent so much time trying to think of what to say, the best way to phrase it, but when it comes down to it, facts do matter sometimes – sometimes they are all that matter.

In my head, the words 'I've been having an affair' rung plastic and hollow, but in the air they turned sharp and lethal; they landed like bullets.

He was very still. He didn't speak but his mouth was twitching, tiny darting movements.

'I'm so sorry.'

'Been having?' The skin under his eyes looked swollen.

'Had. It's over.'

He was biting his lip, over and over, almost methodically as if dividing it into different sections. Tiny dots of blood had appeared.

Abruptly he stood up.

'Look at me,' I pleaded. I put my hand out to touch him, but he threw it off.

At the front door, still not looking at me, he said, 'Who? No. Don't tell me. Who? No, don't.'

And he slammed it behind him.

Him

I walked round and round the streets until the soles of my feet hurt.

I didn't sleep. Birdsong made 2 a.m. feel like dawn. Poor blackbirds. Maddened by the light of the street lamps. I sat at the kitchen table, looking out at the bleak garden. Orange clouds chased across the rooftops. A breeze shuddered through the shrubs. The flower beds were as dark as spilt oil.

The pain was sharper and deeper than I knew what to do with. It was suffocating. I was used to fixing things. But I couldn't wind back time. I couldn't make it not have happened. The frustration was unbearable; there was nothing I could do. A scalding fury burnt up inside. I wanted to yell, to shout, to hit something or somebody, to get in the car and drive for miles, but I could do none of that. I could only sit there, trapped, on that chair, in that house, because I loved her.

I thought of her absences. The lunch with that friend from the temp agency. The suppers with friends. The times I'd come home unexpectedly and found her not in the house, not there where I'd left her. Had she been with him? And when she wasn't with him, had she longed to be? I thought of the occasions when she had seemed 'elsewhere', the times I had tried to initiate sex and she had turned away. I thought she was shy about her body, lacking confidence after Josh's birth.

The joke was on me. It turned out she wasn't shy. She was happy to be naked with someone else, with *him*. She just didn't want to sleep with me.

I didn't want to know who he was. I didn't want to put a name or, worse, a face. My mind began to work at it, but I forced myself to stop. I couldn't have stood knowing any more than I already did. All the worries at work, my failures, the hatred and fear I felt for Dave Jepsom was nothing compared to this. I pushed Dimitri and his threats out of my mind. When my thoughts wandered too close to the fact of this man, this stranger, I was aware of such acute jealousy I didn't know what to do with myself. I also felt a hot physical desire for her that was just as painful, just as vicious.

I could hear her upstairs, small creaks, shifts of the floor-boards. I stayed down, pacing the kitchen, the hall, the sitting room. I hurled my body onto the sofa. Anger pulsed through my veins. I felt numbness and disassociation, swiftly followed by rage, and a bolt of uncontrollable panic. I was an idiot, a loser, a failure. She was a bitch. She deserved everything that was coming to her. And him? I didn't want to think any more about him. She was *my wife*. I felt emotions I didn't like myself for. I hated women. They were all the same. We'd cancel the holiday. I couldn't spend another minute in her company. She deserved everything that was coming to her. She had betrayed not just me, but Josh too. Our life was over. I would never touch her again.

I stared out of the window on the way to work, noticing the rubbish on the tracks; the plastic bags, food cartons, tangled clothes, a shoe. A train hurtled out of nowhere and blocked my view, faces looming close, juddering with the pulse of the train. A man with sunken eyes stared straight back at me and was gone. The air-con pulsed.

Cranes and fallen chimneys, the bowels of the earth opened up and spilling its innards. Battersea Power Station was being pulled apart. Victoria was juddering, dismantled – a giant excavation. Nothing was finished. Everything was chaos.

I'd left the house when it was only just light and yet somehow I was later than anyone else into the office. I must have spent longer in the McDonald's at Victoria Station than I'd thought. Or maybe in M&S.

Gail looked shocked to see me. She got to her feet and came towards me. 'Marcus,' she said. 'I didn't think you were coming in.'

'Why? Tessa call, did she?'

'No – I just . . .'

'I've got my meeting with Richard Taylor at 11 a.m. Unless he saw the *Mail* and cancelled?'

She took a step away from me. 'No, he hasn't, actually.' She considered me for a second, put a hand out to wipe something from my lapel – a dab of ketchup? 'Sit yourself down. Jeff and Mary will be out any minute.'

I didn't appreciate the implications of what she said until later. I sat down in my chair. Basty waved his hand at me across the office, but Emma didn't seem to want to catch my eye. I had several new emails, including one from Dimitri. I stared at the list, finding it hard to focus. 'Right,' I said loudly, standing up and clapping my hands. 'What's the itinerary for today? What's our new plan of action?'

They were all too busy to respond. Phones were ringing. Gail put a cup of coffee in front of me. 'It looks like you need that,' she said softly.

The doors to the meeting room slid open and Jeff and Mary came out. They paused, also surprised to see me. Mary put her head down and scuttled away. I got to my feet. 'What are you two doing in there?' I said, louder than I meant to. 'Plotting?' I laughed. 'Basty, Emma: what do you think?'

'Fuck me,' Jeff said, coming towards me. He put his hands on my shoulders, holding his face away, and steered me back down. 'You been drinking, mate?'

'A small bottle, a miniature,' I said.

'You stink. You wearing the same clothes as yesterday?'

I looked down, feeling my chin disappear into my neck. 'I think so, yeah.' I pushed his hand away. 'Why, what is it to you?'

Gail seemed to have disappeared. He swung her chair round and sat down in it. His voice lowered, he said, 'I can understand how upset you are. This isn't the way to handle it.'

'So you know, do you?'

'Yup.' He nodded. 'We all do.'

'How? Tessa been on the phone already this morning, paving the way?'

He frowned, half shook his head, leaving it at an angle. 'No. I'm afraid we all got it.'

'Got what?'

'The email. He sent it to everyone – certainly everyone in the office. Maybe a few of your contacts, too. We've had a lot of calls this morning.'

'What email?'

Jeff leant across me, ran the mouse down the pad, and then clicked. 'This email?' he said. 'I was assuming you'd seen it.'

I spun round, forcing my eyes to focus on the screen.

It was a photograph, dark and blurry, blurred streaks of light, bodies. The focal point was the back of a woman's head, which was odd really because she was scantily dressed, and the chest of the man she was going down on was naked, his shirt gaping open.

'FUCKING, FUCKING, FUCKING HELL.'

'All right, calm down, language.'

'You can fucking talk. What the fuck? What the fuck?'

I was on my feet and slamming the keyboard into the screen, with pathetic little thuds that didn't even crack it. Everyone in the office was looking at me.

Jeff had put his hand on my shoulder and was steering me towards the lifts. 'Go home,' he said.

'I don't want to go home,' I shouted. 'I've got a meeting at 11 a.m. A new client. We've got to keep going.'

'You've got your holiday next week. Take the rest of this week off, too. We'll discuss what we're going to do when you're calmer.'

'You and Mary have planned it. You want me out.'

He still hadn't raised his voice. He nodded at someone across the room. 'Go home to Tessa,' he said. 'You need to talk to her. She's your first priority.'

Tessa. *Tessa.* TESSA.

'I can't,' I said, broken. 'I can't go home to Tessa. I can't leave now.'

'I'm not asking you,' Jeff said, holding me still a moment with his eyes. 'I'm telling you.'

Her

I heard him leave, as a grey light began to seep into the room, the door slam.

It felt like letting go of a breath I had been holding for months. It had been a long, ragged night. I felt as devastated, as exposed, as naked as I'd ever been, as if I had nothing left to lose. Adrenalin had got me to the point of disclosure, but afterwards, once the words had been spoken, when I saw his grief, mortification flooded my chest, my gut. A tug of pain jarred loose the very deepest part of my heart – a place so secret I never went there myself. I had felt so ashamed. When was it that I detached myself from my marriage? How had I let it happen?

I knew I had to get up, to get the blood out of my head and into my limbs, before Josh awoke. So I went downstairs, and tidied the sofa cushions and put the mugs in the dishwasher. I made a cup of tea. I felt relief when he left the house, but now I wanted him back so much it hurt.

When I heard the email alert, I rushed to find my phone, hoping it was him.

In a way it was.

Marcus in a red room, receiving a blow job from a prostitute.

Someone asked me recently if I was 'furious' when I saw the photograph. But anger was so far from the force of my response as to seem irrelevant. I felt horror. Disgust. I had a physical reaction: an awful tightness in my throat and a tremor through my shoulders. I dropped the phone, because my hand was shaking too much to hold it. Almost immediately, these emotions were followed by something quieter and sadder: a crushing loss, and shame, because I knew I was implicated in this too, that this wasn't just about Marcus, it was the pair of us.

Him

It was late by the time I found my way home. I was beyond speaking. I knew from the look in her eyes, the pity and revulsion, that she had seen the email. She asked me if I was all right, and I shook my head. I lay on the sofa, staring at the wall, and at some point in the evening, she covered me with a rug.

I must have fallen asleep. I woke to the sound of footsteps on the stairs. I didn't turn my head. It was getting light out; the street lamps had flickered off. At the top of the shutters, a pearly pinkness streaked across the sky above the houses opposite. She had come into the room. I could hear her skin move. I sensed her breath in the air. She crept onto the sofa and lay down next to me.

In the morning we talked. We both cried. Marriage guidance came up. It would be a good idea, we agreed on that. Rose had mentioned a counsellor to Tessa once. The woman was local, and good. I said we'd be bound to pass everyone we knew trooping up and down the stairs, and she laughed. I said I was beyond sorry that I had no memory of the events in the photograph. She said we had both done things we regretted. Life could be horrible and chaotic and messy. But it didn't mean you gave up trying; it didn't mean you walked away. We'd try again; we'd make it work. I began to believe her. It helped to make me feel better, anyway.

Josh got up and we gave him breakfast. My eyes were raw, my head throbbed. We let him watch television and we talked again in the kitchen. I tried to think about the future. She wanted to go back to work, didn't she? She was lonely at home. I had stopped confiding in her about the agency. I hadn't listened to her properly. I would support her in anything she wanted to do, and that would make a difference.

Tess didn't want to be absolved. She wanted sackcloth, ashes, everything. I was glad she was talking like that. Yes, I had done a terrible thing. But I didn't want my mistake to slip her off the hook. I wanted her to take responsibility, and if she had taken a step back from it, if she'd said, 'Yes, yes, you're right. It's all down to my mother,' I think I'd have found it harder even to begin to forgive.

It wasn't easy, the conversation. She kept her eyes on mine the whole time, and I didn't know what to do with my face. She hadn't looked at me properly for months. Every movement of my mouth felt awkward. A blink seemed to take a lifetime. I could feel each smile or grimace create a canyon in my cheeks. Once or twice she put her hand out and touched me – my knee, my arm, the back of my hand. I had to force myself not to flinch.

There was a time limit. It turned out Josh would only watch television for so long. Who knew? In the afternoon, we did normal things. We cooked lunch and filled up the paddling pool and played a mini-game of football. Around Josh we made nice. We didn't talk about the holiday. We behaved as if it wasn't going to happen, though neither of us had mentioned it, so maybe it would. I didn't have the heart to make a decision. Could we be together for a whole week?

★   ★   ★

Was it that day, or the day after, that we walked around to the local shops? They merge in my mind, those few days before we drove to Suffolk. I had switched off my phone. It might have been the Friday, or the Saturday. We had begun to pretend hard that everything would be OK. Maybe I had even begun to believe it.

It was late in the afternoon, early evening. Josh was on his scooter, and wearing a blue helmet decorated with dinosaurs which Tessa seemed to think was important. He also insisted on the new yellow armbands she had bought, which he now wouldn't take off.

We were walking side by side, only a few inches from each other. But it felt as if a solid object separated us. I had been feeling numb for most of the day, but as we went round the corner and I saw her look out over the common, taking in the early-evening light, turning her face to it, apparently appreciating the beauty of the dappled grass and reaching trees, I was aware of feeling a new surge of white-hot anger at the fact that she was able to do any of that: walk, look, appreciate. I needed her own guilt and her horror at mine to be absolute, I suppose.

Josh was scooting some way ahead. His whole shtick at that time was to try and get away from us. I called after him to slow down, but he sped up, one foot bashing the pavement, giggling maniacally. I shouted at him to stop – too aggressively. Tessa put her hand on my arm in warning. I felt close to tears. He kept turning round. Any minute he would crack into a lamp-post. But he didn't. He skidded, in a mini-slalom, to a halt by a group of people outside the cafe. He threw the scooter aside and started running down the street with another child. A group of adults were standing there, looking on. I wanted to open my mouth and groan, but we walked calmly towards them. There was nothing else we could do.

Yasmeen had turned and was watching us approach. 'Marcus,' she said, nodding. 'Tessa. Lovely evening.'

Simon's hand came out and slapped me on the upper arm, just below my shoulder, an act of greeting that felt like an attack. His voice was loud as he introduced us, 'our new neighbours', to their old friends, a thin, angular couple who were visiting from another part of London. They made a joke about crossing the river. I smiled thinly.

Tessa spouted banalities with them for a few minutes, and then Yasmeen, who had been trying to catch my eye, drew me to one side. With a polished charm I wanted to scratch, she said: 'No hard feelings, I hope?'

'Not at all.' I smiled with the force of my profession behind me. 'You've got a job to do.'

'It was too easy a target, you do see? It was irresistible.'

'Absolutely.'

'And I'm sorry about Maura's article in the *Mail*. I can see you could have done without that. That intern sounds like a piece of work, though. What a little minx. I can just imagine! She probably looked about eighteen. A lot of them do.'

She was smiling, but her gaze was ripe with calculation. I knew what she was playing at. She was building a little trap, stick by stick, for me to fall into. At least, I thought, she doesn't know about the photograph. At least the news of that hasn't reached her.

I said: 'Actually I think we deserved it. You have to take safeguarding seriously these days. We were too casual. We've learnt our lesson.'

She looked disappointed. She had wanted so much more from me. More material. More fodder.

'So . . .' she began, and then she seemed to see something in my eyes, and she changed tack. 'Anything nice planned for the rest of the weekend?'

I felt suddenly unable to speak. My throat tightened. I felt a pricking in the corners of my eyes. And then Tessa was standing between us. She picked up Josh's scooter and held it over her shoulder at a strange angle, the handlebars pointing at Yasmeen like a weapon.

'Actually we're off on holiday,' she said. Her hand lightly clasped my elbow. I let it rest there, and leant into her like a dog leans into his owner for comfort. 'We've got a lot of packing to do so we'd better get on.'

'Somewhere nice?' Yasmeen asked. She seemed to be talking with her teeth, not her mouth.

'Yes,' Tessa said. 'Suffolk. A staycation. There's a lot of it about.'

She called Josh to us, with a sharpness in her voice I hadn't heard before, and I let her lead me away, her hand still cupping my elbow.

LAST

Her

We left early on the Sunday morning.

It was silent in the car. Talking had exhausted us; had exhausted itself. We were left with facts, with the sinking realisation there was only so much talking could do.

It seemed extraordinary to me that we were going. I felt, at a distance, the possibility of relief: something we had planned before was still taking place. As we drove through south London, I thought about Dave for the first time since Tuesday. There had been no further contact. I tried to remember what he had said about Josh, the exact wording, but the detail had faded. It had been his grief speaking, nothing more. It was over. Whatever threat he may or may not have presented, we were leaving it behind.

Tower Bridge was closed. Marcus followed a diversion sign before I could stop him, and in seconds we were sitting in a jam heading in the wrong direction towards London Bridge. I had to work hard to breathe normally as we drew close to Richard's building, the air caught at the back of my throat. I scrambled through my phone to find a playlist of children's songs, plugged it in and pressed the controls on the dashboard until the car was flooded with cheerful tambourines and twanging guitars. When I looked up again, my heart still banging in my ears, we were no longer near the end of his road, and the danger had passed.

Had Marcus guessed it was Richard? Had he chosen this route on purpose? Or had he driven this way blindly, too stressed and exhausted to think clearly? I had no perspective, no sense of what mattered and what didn't. Packing had been an act of madness. I had written lists, adding items, crossing them out and writing new ones. I laid our suitcase out on the floor of our bedroom and made piles of clothes. Did I need a cardigan to go with that dress? Did Josh need new plimsolls? I thought I could plan away the unknowns. There seemed so many of them. It might rain. It might be fine. The cottage might have games and toys, or have nothing. Marcus and I might have sex. Or we might not. Calpol and dental floss. Whac-a-Mole. Cards. Beach towels. Fleeces. Wellington boots. Crocs. We might stay together. We might separate.

I looked across at him. His hands gripped the steering wheel, a muscle twitched in the side of his jaw. I fought to get the image of the prostitute out of my head and to remember all the things I loved about him. I thought about his need to be liked which was also a form of kindness; that he changed his accent to match the accent of the person he was talking to; that he considered women his equals; that he would buy a stranger a £300 pair of shoes. Tenderness flooded me. I remembered when we first met, how he was the first person in that office not to make jokes about my lack of education; he'd respected me for who I was and what I'd achieved. That moment in the street the day before, when Yasmeen was talking at him, when he leant into me like a dog leans into its owner for security, I realised I would do anything for him, anything to make it right. But nothing was straightforward. There were moments of connection, and then we locked each other out.

Josh started playing up, bored and fractious, as we fought our way out of London. He was determined to eat the sandwiches we'd packed for lunch and I didn't have the strength to resist. The car was cramped and messy. An empty bottle of water crunched under my feet in the foot-well; a wodge of kitchen roll was stuffed in the space between the handle and the door.

Once we had had reached the A12, as the road began to unravel beneath us like a piece of string, I said: 'It's a bit small for a long journey, this car, isn't it? Maybe we should think about trading up.'

'We can't afford a bigger car. Not now.'

'Of course.'

I looked hard at his face. I wished he would say something. One of us could say sorry again; we could start it all up. In search of some kind of confirmation, I said: 'Maybe it is a mistake to go away.'

He didn't demur. 'Yes, I think you're right. It *is* a mistake to go away. But we're going now. It's too late to do anything about it.'

He kept his eyes fixed on the road. I noticed again the tension in his knuckles. His anger was coiled. For the first time it occurred to me that, after this, there might be no going back.

Him

The cottage was at the end of a long narrow road that led across a flat marsh to the sea. It was National Trust land and there was a car park above the beach where we had been instructed to leave the car.

I pulled in and parked at the far end. It was quiet with the engine off. Josh had been asleep since Ipswich, and we sat for a moment or two in silence. I could hear Tessa breathing next to me. We hadn't exchanged a word since leaving the city. I opened the door and got out to ease my back and shoulders. Shingle crunched beneath my feet. Pale yellow sand was piled at the base of the pay-and-display machine. It was cooler than London. The sky was high and white, with wisps of blue, and there was a stiff breeze. I couldn't see the sea – the sand dunes were in the way, grass-tufted waves of them – but I could smell it: ozone and salt, fish on oil, rotting seaweed, salt.

It was a remote, lonely spot. The car park was half empty. Voices carried faintly from down below. Or it might have been the wind, or birds. An ice-cream van sat on the other side of the car park, but it was empty, or if there was a person inside they were sitting down. A seagull picked at an empty sandwich wrapper, flicked it and tossed it.

I hauled our bags from the boot, locked the car with a click and then strode ahead, without waiting for her, up a path on which PRIVATE was written in white paint. I could hear them straggling behind, Josh whingeing in a just-woken-up kind of way. Once out of the dip of the car park, the house became visible just ahead. It was made up of three coastguard cottages knocked together, quite ugly despite their wash of white paint, angular and plain with their small windows and row of symmetrically officious chimneys. No garden to speak of. It was just there on the cliff-top in a patch of grass and shingle, the occasional clump of sea kale or campion.

We approached the front door from the back, through a small porch, standing there in silence as I found the key. It was under a pot containing a straggly lavender – lopsided like a hawthorn on a blasted heath. No one had watered it, and the earth in which it sat was cracked.

Inside, it smelt of pot pourri, and old curtain material warmed by the sun, and below that a musky odour that wasn't exactly human but had the same stale heaviness to it. The door opened into a large lounge, a heavy beam across the ceiling to indicate it was a couple of rooms knocked together; at one end was a neatly swept fireplace, a sofa and two armchairs, at the other a small dining table. A kitchen led off to one side – quarry tiles and scrubbed secondhand surfaces, a scattering of missed crumbs under the toaster. In a folder on the counter was a list of suggested activities. I stood, flicking through it. We could drive to Southwold. We could explore Aldeburgh. There was a farm with a petting zoo not that far away, and a little further up towards Norfolk a camel park. If we kept busy enough we wouldn't have to confront the darkness of our marriage.

'Tomorrow,' Tessa said, looking over my shoulder, 'we could take Josh crabbing at Walberswick.'

'Yes,' I said. I had crabbed with my father. Hooks. Bait. Equipment. *Can't you do anything right? You stupid boy.*

I left Josh and Tessa unpacking the groceries and took the bags upstairs. There was a bathroom and three bedrooms, all newly carpeted, a freckled biscuit-coloured pile, and a view: an ochre and beige stretch of sand, an expanse of green-grey sea, polished and still, and above it, a huge dull sky with the blotchy texture of skin. The house was perched on the edge of a low cliff. The bank of grass outside ended abruptly, a frayed tufted lip and then a perilous eight- or nine-foot craggy drop down to some boulders beneath. Down below, at the base of the rocks, the water squirmed and frothed.

I stood looking out, overtaken by the same loneliness and panic I had experienced in the villa in Greece, an almost dizzy disorientation, of having been plucked from a life in which I knew who I was. It was just a holiday house and yet it was more than that; I felt as if the walls of my person had been dismantled, as if it was the inward pressure of my job, and my home, my daily routine that made me who I was, and that without them, I had no borders, no outline. I was nothing. And this was worse than Greece because at least then I had had a job, and a wife, and now I wasn't confident I had either.

I tried to unlatch the window to bring in some air. It was a simple window, which should have opened out, but it had been painted recently and after I unhooked the catch and pushed, I met resistance. It opened only a small way and a piece of wood in the frame splintered. When I tried to close it, I found I couldn't get the peg in the stay; they wouldn't fit together so I left it as it was.

'This'll do,' Tessa said, coming in behind me. Her voice was cheerful, upbeat, several notes of false. She was putting on a brave face for Josh. There was no way of telling whether she felt the same as me, that the week stretching ahead of us was an eternity. There was no way of telling if she felt as scared.

Her

It rained in the night, and the wind shook the windows, hurled handfuls of rain against the panes. All around us it seemed, waves churned and roared. I kept my eyes shut, clinging on to the edge of the sheet, but when I woke it was calm, a dull light infusing the curtains. It was a surprise to pull them back and find the view as it was – to discover, after all, the cliff-top still in place, the house still standing.

Marcus was already up, and at the table in the living room, eating breakfast with Josh. He looked at me when I came in. I told myself his face was more open than it had been, his eyes less hooded. Josh was chattering about going to the beach and building a sandcastle, and we slowly got ourselves together, collecting a bag of things to take: a picnic rug, bucket and spade, waterproofs.

The air felt newly washed, the grass springy, as we made our way back down the path to the car park. A track led from the other side up and down through the dunes, and we followed it, across a dilapidated wooden bridge over a trickling waterway, and then on a tufty incline down to the beach. The strand was longer and wider than I'd imagined. To the right loomed rocks and a rising cliff, our house somewhere over there in the distance; to the left a long dappled stretch of shingle and sand, littered with weed, as far as the eye could see; the sea a distant sluggish glimmer. The folder of instructions had said you could make out Sizewell B; I couldn't tell if that was it on the edge of the horizon or whether it was an illusion constructed of clouds. The sand was pitted with drops, criss-crossed with footsteps and the engravings of birds. It was early still, no one else around.

'I hadn't realised we would be so isolated,' I said.

'No.'

A seagull picked its way across our path, and then as we grew close, opened its wings and wheeled away.

Josh ran ahead. We walked without talking. There was a new quality to the silence between us and I didn't try to break it. I thought back to a cottage we'd rented at Land's End one January when we were first together; it was freezing cold but we didn't care. We spent most of the time in bed.

Marcus was holding the beach bag over his furthest shoulder and under the weight of it his body was tipped slightly towards me, his hand trailing close to mine. I almost reached out to hold it, but I didn't.

We chose a spot a couple of hundred metres up, on a bank of shingle, and laid down the rug. The ground smelt of fish and wet concrete, and something spicier like tarragon. The sky was a mottled grey, but there were a few cracks of blue, spilling slivers of light onto the water near the horizon. The air was brusque, cold almost, but there was promise in it. I called Josh back over and found the sunblock at the bottom of the bag. I rubbed some on his face and arms.

Marcus said, 'Do you really think he needs it?'

I gave a final wipe across his cheeks. 'Better safe than sorry.' I dabbed a little on my nose, and handed the bottle to him. 'Want some?'

'No.'

Josh picked up his bucket and spade and walked off, waddling in his waterproof trousers, in the direction of the sea. His head was bowed. He was searching for something on the beach which he seemed to find, because he suddenly crouched, shoulders hunched in inspection. I sat down on the rug and hugged my knees into my chest, and after a few seconds Marcus sat down too. I felt a tiny gust of warmth from his body. I had to force myself not to lean into him; it was an effort not to actually, the movement felt innate. For an instant, I longed for his touch, before that image again, red, blurred, dark, flooded in.

We both stared ahead, watching Josh as he dragged his red spade in circles across a patch of sand, making ineffectual swipes.

There is no such thing as silence on a beach. Gulls, wind, the scrape of the spade filled the void.

He made an effort to make conversation. 'It's only a few weeks but it seems months since we almost lost him.'

'I know.'

'It was so . . . just awful, wasn't it?'

I began to speak. I said out loud what I had hardly dared think. 'In that moment, when I came out of the taverna, and I thought he was dead, I had an instant of stillness. The worst had happened; I had nothing more to be afraid of. I had nothing left to lose. It felt almost like relief.'

I was aware that he had looked across at me but I didn't yet turn my head.

'I'm left with the terror of keeping him alive.'

I thought about what Jepsom had said. It's a fine line between life and death.

'If anything happened to him . . . I just love him so much. It's awful.'

Marcus took a deep breath in. It sounded like a shudder. 'I know. How can one ever relax?'

I began to laugh and then stopped. 'I don't know.'

'You just have to try, I suppose.'

Josh stood up then, and began slowly continuing his path away from us. The sea was still stretched several hundred metres ahead, small waves on the shoreline breaking and swirling in low circular washes. I watched Josh move closer, the distance between me and him growing, as the distance between his body and the water shortened, and I felt a sort of dizzying agitation. My breath quickened. I was still holding on to my knees but tighter now. I was about to push my weight forward, and be on my feet. I was about to run. A shout, a yell, was growing at the back of my throat.

'He's OK.' Marcus's arm fell heavy across my back; his hand reached for my far shoulder. It was a restraint, but also a support. I forced myself to lean back into it. 'Nothing's going to happen,' he said softly.

I turned my face to touch his hand with my cheek. I felt him flinch.

'Not with me here,' Marcus said.

We ate out that night in a pub, The Ferryman, which was recommended in the information pack. It was low-eaved with a Farrow & Ball elegance, run by Londoners, I think. We sat in the garden, under a patio heater, and ate crab gratin with sourdough crumb, and locally sourced honeycomb ice cream. Josh, who had eaten at home, was happily occupied in the small play area. A local was tinkling on the piano: 'On the Sunny Side of the Street'.

I bought a packet of Silk Cut and a box of matches at the bar. A man with a shaved head had his back to me; he was leaning forwards, elbows out, talking to the barman. I couldn't see his face, but you could tell he was in late middle age by the reddening wrinkles of skin on his nape, the white bristles. At the base of his neck, just to one side, was a tattoo of an anchor.

Outside, I handed Marcus a cigarette. 'Shall we?' I said. 'For old times' sake?'

A current of amusement passed between us. 'I have to say I occasionally—'

'Yeah, me too.'

'Go on then.'

He lit my cigarette and cupped his hand to light his own. The smoke he exhaled looked creamily delicious.

As I exhaled, watching Josh climb the wooden slide, I said: 'I feel bad about Dave Jepsom. To lose a son . . . I mean, it would change you. It would change your relationship with the world.'

'He's certainly unbalanced.'

'But he hasn't been back.'

'Not yet, no.'

I thought over all the moments when I thought I'd seen him – the most recent in Peter Jones. What with everything that had been going on, I hadn't even told Marcus about that. It seemed so insignificant now. I'd summoned Jepsom to life at points of tension and high anxiety. I had an image then of that first moment, when he rescued Josh from the water, when he carried him safe to the shore. I remembered the strength of his body, the tension of his muscles, the bulge and pull of them, the sun bright behind his head, and then as he turned, that great tattoo across his shoulders, those enormous spanned wings.

'Maybe he was a guardian angel,' I said, 'and not a threat.'

'What do you mean?'

'It's just he was there, wasn't he? First, obviously, when Josh almost drowned, and then at other times when our life was . . . most endangered.'

What I could have said: I 'saw' Jepsom after I'd visited Richard at his flat, in the Tube, in the street where I'd left the car; I'd summoned him from the depths of my subconscious when I was with Richard in the Turkish restaurant; in the department store when he had intruded again into my thoughts. He'd come as an apparition, a warning every time I was most in danger of losing what mattered.

Marcus was looking puzzled. 'You mean, you think he's been looking out for us, or for Josh? It's quite a frightening thought.'

'He said this thing on the phone last week – that I should be careful nothing bad happens to Josh. But I think I misunderstood. I think it came from a place of pain. I don't think it was a threat.'

'What?'

He made me repeat it.

He picked up a beer mat and tapped it a few times on the table. 'I don't like that. I don't like that at all.' I'd agitated him. He threw it down.

I put my hand on his arm, and felt the muscles rise and tense. 'I don't think it's real is what I'm saying. It's more in our minds. Does that make sense?'

He didn't answer.

I wish I hadn't said it now.

Him

In a way it was good the house was so isolated. For those few days, there were no distractions. There was no Wi-Fi, no signal, but also no other people to watch, or wonder at. The car park filled at certain points of the day, but whoever had driven there seemed to dissipate, to disappear, to be swallowed whole by the sand, or the sea, or the dunes. Occasionally, you'd see a dog and its owner in the distance, but they never got any closer and after a while you'd stare at the space where they'd been and wonder if it wasn't a post you'd noticed. Or a patch of seaweed.

It was the weather, I suppose.

We walked as far as Josh would let us those first couple of days. We were trying to tire him out, but also perhaps ourselves. I found the more I walked, the less likely I was to dwell on what had happened or what was going to happen, concentrating instead on where to position the tread of my trainers, how to avoid the treacherous swathes of slippery seaweed, which combination of shingle and sand and pebble was most stable underfoot.

I found I could begin to pretend, too, that neither of us had done anything wrong, nothing had changed. Whole moments passed in which I believed we were still exactly as we had been.

On Monday we stayed near to the house but on Tuesday, which was even greyer, we got in the car and drove further up the A12 to Southwold. The folder in the kitchen had promised us 'a charming, pretty, quintessentially English' seaside town and it was all of those things, even in a mild drizzle. It had that architecturally patchwork feel of the best British towns, pastel-coloured houses next to red brick, roofscapes that rose and fell, a church spire, a town square, a proper butcher's. We ran Josh along the pier, into the wind, and then we dried off in a tearoom. It was bustling with a combination of locals and tourists. The windows were steamed up. We ate slabs of chocolate cake and drank milky coffee. A shaggy brown dog under the next table was pulling on its leash, stretching out its tongue to try and reach the crumbs we had dropped. Josh clambered down and let the mutt lick his face. Its owners smiled benevolently.

Tessa was worrying about germs; I could tell from her expression.

'Shall we move to Southwold?' I said.

She looked up quickly. Her eyes grew bulbous, then I realised they had filled with tears.

'No.' She looked back down at Josh. She was smiling lightly now. 'But we could get a dog.'

The car park was empty when we got back that evening. Even the ice-cream van had gone. It was like living on the edge of the world. Or as if everyone else knew something and we didn't.

The house felt more like home when we got back to it. Darkening clouds, threatening strips across the sea, and a scatter of rain against the windows made it feel cosier inside than before. We put on the side-lights and made a fire, neither of which we had bothered to do the day before, and the three of us played a game of Whac-a-Mole. I read to Josh, and then he and Tessa constructed a tower with Lego, and then, finally, we let him watch television: a reward to us for having kept him off it that long.

We had bought fresh provisions from the shops in Southwold, and we moved together around the kitchen, pricking potatoes and getting them in the oven, laying out sausages on a tray. I was at the sink, washing up the breakfast things, when she came up behind me and put her arms around my waist. She rested her head on my back.

I was up to my wrists in soapy water and I froze. I found it hard for a moment to breathe. Her hands were clasped across my stomach, touching my forearms. The weight of her head was gentle; I could feel her breath against my back, the slight dampness of her mouth.

I had the old familiar thought: *maybe tonight we'll have sex.* And I felt a stirring, the beginnings of arousal. And then immediately I thought about him.

I brought my hands out of the water, and I shook them, and pulled away from her to reach for the cloth. I dried each finger carefully. She was still standing next to me. I saw what I thought was hope in her face. She was waiting expectantly, I realised. She thought I had turned round to hold her. And there was an instant in which I felt sorry, and compassion for her, but it was too late: there were bigger, uglier emotions in the way. There were images crawling in my head I couldn't get rid of. Panic and anxiety, rage rose up. I wanted to hit her mouth where he had kissed her.

I looked at the floor; anywhere but at her face.

'I'm going out,' I said. 'I need some air.'

I walked back down the path to the car park. Two more cars were here now; a beaten-up estate, with a dog cage in the boot next to a coil of ropes and an old tarpaulin, and a black saloon, parked alongside the Fiat.

I set off towards Sizewell B, the wind buffeting at my back. The sky was low and heavy, the sand looked silvery in the flat evening light. The sea, which was so strangely flat, almost bronze, was seething quietly, rumbling under its breath. A middle-aged couple came towards me, shoulders hunched, a dog nosing in their wake, and then passed. To my left beyond a rough wooden fence was flat land, a nature reserve, strips of water and reed, water-birds. To my right, the sea.

I'm not sure how long I walked. An hour at least. I know I walked as far as I could. I couldn't keep the thoughts out, they started racing through my brain, churning, sending out sparks. I didn't want to know who he was, but the question was getting needier, and hungrier. A memory, an idea, began to fight its way through. I had to push it back, force it away. If I knew, if I saw him face to face, *I'd kill him*. Maybe I should kill her. It was too big, I couldn't constrain it. It was beyond anything I had done. My one-night aberration. A whole affair. She'd said it was nothing to do with me, but how could I believe her? *You stupid boy*. My father's face and Jeff's face – his contempt as he steered me to the lift. He had only ever suffered me. Our friendship: worth nothing. Tilly's: gone. Dimitri's revenge, my own actions. How worthless I was. I hadn't protected my wife, or my son, or my business. Everything was over. Ruined.

I kept spiralling back to that moment on the beach. It began then. I fell asleep and if it hadn't been for Jepsom Josh would have drowned. *If it hadn't been for Jepsom*. It came to me in that moment, with a blinding logic, that if Jepsom hadn't saved Josh, *I would have done it*. I would have got there in time. I would have dived into the waves and swum towards him. I would have lifted him like a trophy. I would have been the hero. And Jepsom would never have been in our lives. Nothing else would have gone wrong.

I felt invincible and weak at the same time, unrestrained and also needy, lost. Adrenalin merged with an unquenchable bitterness. Muscles in my calves began to give up, my feet ached, and when I did turn round I was walking into the wind and our headland was a low shelf in the distance. I was alarmed when I saw how far it was to walk back. Then I was glad. I hoped the potatoes had shrivelled to nothing. I hoped her face was pressed to the window. I hoped she thought I'd gone for good.

The light was changing, the air thickening, when my feet finally slid and slithered along the path through the dunes. It was almost dark. Clouds had gathered in a strange formation. The sea had come in close and sounded louder now – like an uneasy wind, something urgent, maybe even industrial. The car park was empty. The Fiat was sitting on its own on the far side, a fine layer of blown sand creating a pattern on the bonnet. Tough grass scratched at my ankles. I lengthened my stride on the private path, suddenly eager, panicked, and when I reached the point on the track where you could see the house ahead, I began to run, filled with a sudden desperate surging need to be with my wife, and my son, to remind myself of their faces. I hadn't thought much about what I would do on my walk, but I knew now that whatever it was, I wanted everything to be all right.

The front door was closed but unlocked. I turned the handle and pushed it open. A chair had been knocked over next to the table and I righted it. The lights were on and her phone rested on the table next to an empty mug. In the sink in the kitchen lay a muddle of dirty plates and cutlery. The house was quiet. I didn't see anything odd in that. She would be putting Josh to bed, or maybe she'd already done that. He would have been exhausted by the journey and the sea air. Maybe she was reading quietly in our room.

I took the stairs two at a time. I didn't call out, no. It didn't seem appropriate.

There was a curdled stillness to the air on the landing. The bathroom door was ajar and I called hello. Silence. I pushed it open. The bath had been run, but it was tepid when I dipped my fingers in, covered in a soapy film. Josh's toothbrush floated at the tap end. I took it out and dried it on a towel that was lying crumpled on the floor. The toothpaste was in the sink, with its lid off, a trail of white on the blue enamel. The bath mat was scrunched in a damp heap. Snailed up in the corner were Josh's vest and socks.

Josh's room was empty, too – though a drawer had been pulled out and his pyjamas were laid out on the chair. There was a pile of his books on the bedside table, and I perched on the edge of the bed and picked up the top one: *Goodnight Moon*. I flicked through it, the back of my throat hurting. I'd read it to him in a minute. When I found them.

Our bedroom door was closed, but I turned the handle into an empty room. The duvet had been roughly pulled up in the morning, and I straightened it, laying my hand along the cotton to smooth it.

I went back down the stairs, and checked the kitchen again, opening a door onto a shallow larder lined with bare shelves. I looked in the sink at the plates and the pan, and in the bin in the corner, which contained a curled cold potato skin, two used tea bags and an empty baked-bean tin. The oven was cold. I stood in the sitting room and looked around, searching for anything that seemed out of place. On the floor next to the table was a small pile containing the pad of paper for colouring, the top sheet scrunched up, the crayons and her make-up bag, the fat pink tube of her mascara poking out of the half-closed zip. In front of the sofa, next to the Lego tower they had made earlier, was Josh's fire engine. Had we brought that with us? I didn't remember. I walked over to the window and gazed out, at the bank that ran down to the cliff-top, the blades of grass illuminated in the oblong of reflected light.

Josh's slip-on plimsolls were resting by the sofa, neatly aligned.

Her

Josh was tired and yawned several times. When he asked where Daddy was, I told him he had gone for a walk, that he would be back to kiss him goodnight. He nodded, satisfied with that answer, and I smoothed his hair, and told him I loved him.

When the potatoes and sausages were ready and Marcus still wasn't back, we ate our supper by the fire. I cleared away the plates, and then we went upstairs and I drew Josh a bath. The water gurgled reddish brown out of the tap. It looked like old blood and I let it run for a while before slotting in the plug.

I had packed Oilatum, that weird moisturising oil that creates a light film across the surface of water, and I let him carefully pour in a capful, and then we took off his clothes. I checked the temperature of the water and lifted him in.

He played for a while – pretending the blue Oilatum bottle was a submarine. And then I cleaned his teeth, to get it done, while he was still. He was floating with his head in the water, eyes blissfully closed, his hair fanning his sweet baby face like silky weed, when I heard a noise downstairs, the crunch of the door closing.

'We're in the bathroom,' I called. I was trying to sound cheerful and welcoming. I was hoping Marcus would hear in my voice how much I wanted him to come up. I was hoping we could both pretend to be normal, that this small thing – a shared bathtime – could be the start of *being* normal.

His footsteps weren't as quick as I'd have liked. They sounded heavy on the stairs, slow and ponderous.

Behind me the door opened, a ruffling scrape as it pushed against the carpet.

I had one hand under Josh's neck to keep his face out of the water. Without turning, I said, 'Hi, sweetie. Chuck me the towel, will you?'

Nothing happened.

I waited a few seconds – one, two, three – and then I turned.

And gasped, inhaling sharply, simultaneously through my mouth and my nostrils: a scream in negative, a scream in reverse.

He was smiling as if I should be pleased. I think he even said: 'Are you really so surprised?'

The blood had drained from my face. I suppressed my fear, damped it way down into my chest. 'What are you doing here?' I managed to say.

'I thought you were hoping I'd come. *You* rang *me.*'

Josh had surfaced, wriggling up and forward, pushing against my hand. I gripped on to his waist, with one arm. He looked at me, brows crossed, and then gazed past me, his eyes focusing on the newcomer. 'Hello, man,' he said.

'Hello, boy,' he replied.

I moved my head to block his sight line. 'How did you find us?' I made words form, strung them in a line to create a sentence that sounded as if it made sense.

He shrugged, almost winsomely, the gesture too small for a man of his size. He was dressed for summer, in cargo shorts and a short-sleeved T-shirt. On his feet was a pair of mesh and leather Nike trainers. The bottoms were white and bulbous; they looked new.

'Did you follow us here?' I moved my eyes to his, and kept them there.

'Come on now.' He leant against the wall, raising one elbow above his head for support. A corner of underarm hair was revealed below the cap sleeve of his T-shirt. His hair had grown since I'd last seen him. 'You don't sound pleased to see me.'

'We're on holiday.'

He laughed, and placed his spare hand on his heart. 'What's a holiday without me?'

'You've got to leave,' I said. 'You shouldn't be here.'

'Why would you talk to me like that, after everything I've done for you? You need me.'

'You're scaring me. It's not normal you turning up like this.'

'I just wanted to see you. I wanted to work it out, why you treated me as you did.'

'You're not welcome. I think you've misread the situation.'

I managed to hook the towel with my foot and propel it closer. I got my body in such a position that I could keep my eye on him while raising Josh out of the water and wrapping his wriggling limbs in the towel.

Why didn't I leave Josh in the bath and force him out of the room? All I can say is that my instinct was to protect my son, to remove his vulnerability, to cover up his naked body, to hold him tight, to protect him. And then I would deal with this – whatever this was.

'That's not very nice,' he said. 'That's not very hospitable. I only want to talk.'

Josh was dry in my lap and I cast around for his pyjamas. They were in his bedroom; I'd have to get past him to get there. Josh's pants and vest were in a ball, over in the corner. I could reach his shorts, though, and his T-shirt and I dressed him in those, keeping him on my lap while I did so. My hands were trembling.

'Marcus will be back any second.' I tried to speak as calmly as I could. 'Why don't you go before he does? It's better if he never knows you've been. We can pretend it never happened.'

'I'm not going anywhere.' He shook his head, and gave a small shrug. 'Not now I've come all this way. Not unless you come with me; I might change my mind then.' He blinked slowly like a lizard.

Josh held up his arm and studied it. 'My clothes are back on!' he said.

'Yes,' I said.

I got to my feet and hoisted him onto my hip. 'I'm going to put Josh to bed now,' I said, keeping my voice steady. 'Why don't you go and find a pub and I'll come and join you shortly?'

Irritation crossed his face. He shook his head. 'I'm not going to do that,' he said.

'OK.' I tried to work out my next tactic. 'OK. Well, Josh can stay up a bit longer. Can't you, sweetie?'

'Yes,' Josh said doubtfully. 'When Daddy comes back he's going to kiss me goodnight. Will I go to bed then?'

I took three steps towards the door. He didn't move for a second; then he stood to one side. 'After you,' he said.

I felt the touch of his hand on my arm, smelt his breath. A disc of nausea rolled through me.

Past him then onto the narrow landing, to the top of the stairs, and then down, one step at a time. I could feel the vibration of his feet as they landed a few inches behind me; I smelt his aftershave.

Him

I sat at the kitchen table, trying to work out where they might be. They had gone looking for me. But if they had, I would have seen them on the beach, or passed them on the path down. She was angry with me. She wanted me to worry, to show me. But she hadn't taken the car. It had still been in the car park when I'd walked past. She must have called a taxi to have gone any distance. They were sitting in a pub, drinking hot chocolate, playing I Spy, watching the seconds tick by. That was the most likely scenario, surely. If something serious had happened, if there had been an accident, she would have left a message. She would have time to do that. And there would have been tyre tracks down at the car park, footsteps up to the house. A spinning red light that might have caught my attention, even from far down the beach.

I looked out of the window, staring at the churning sea, and when I couldn't bear it any longer, I left the house. At the back, there was nothing but grass and gorse, disappearing into the dusk, in the distance a flap of trees. At the front, where the ground gave way to the cliff-top, I ran along the ragged edge of it, peering over the lip of garden to the rocks below. But there was nothing but seething sea, scratchy grass, rocks. I called out their names. They wouldn't have come here, I kept thinking. The tide was in. Tessa would have kept Josh away from the edge.

I convinced myself they would be home as I came round the corner of the house. But the door opened to silence. They had just disappeared. Dread, like a stone, settled in the centre of my chest. And then, using a piece of colouring paper and one of Josh's crayons, I wrote a note – 'Gone to look for you.'

Her

I put Josh down at the bottom of the stairs. 'Where are you staying?' I asked. 'Are you staying nearby?'

'Near-ish. I'm a little further up the A12.' He jerked his head to one side. 'It's a nice county, Suffolk. I'm in a hotel quite close to the pub where you had supper.'

'Have you been watching us?'

'Was the crab gratin OK?'

I stared at him. 'You were there?'

He smiled at me.

Josh had crossed the room and was playing now with the fire engine he'd found in the bag of toys we'd brought. He was singing to himself, in his own world.

'Please go,' I whispered. 'Please, please go. There is nothing for you here. We can talk another time.' I put my hand on his arm, felt the muscle tense. His skin felt familiar, warm like normal skin, and inhuman at the same time – solid and intractable like varnished wood. 'I don't know what you think is going to happen, you being here, but it's wrong. Me, Josh, Marcus – we just want to be left alone. Josh needs to get to bed . . .'

He took his arm away. 'Happy families are we now? Is that what we're playing?'

'Please just go,' I said again.

'If you come with me, I'll go. That's all. Simple request.'

I decided to humour him, softening my voice, forcing a smile. 'I can't leave Josh. You can understand that.'

He seemed to consider for a moment. 'OK,' he said eventually. 'I can see it would be unreasonable for you to leave him behind. Though I'm not sure, despite everything, that he's part of the plan. I've got used to a life without children.' He looked almost tearful for a second, then he smiled. 'Whether I'll be able to accept another man's is a different matter. Still . . .' He sat down on the chair, and stretched out his legs. 'Something smells nice. I'm hungry.' He frowned, as if it had only just occurred to him. 'I haven't eaten today. I'll go if you give me something to eat.'

I swallowed hard, tried to bring some moisture to my mouth. 'You can have a baked potato. I put one in for Marcus before he went out. He'll be back any minute. But he won't mind.'

'I'm not sure he will be back. Last I saw he was a long way down the beach, marching off, as if you'd had an argument. Trouble in paradise. Are you sure he even intends to come back?'

'You saw him?'

'Yes. I was about to come up to see you both when he passed me, looking quite upset. I followed him for a while, but he seems to want to avoid me.' He shrugged. 'Then I realised you were all on your own up here and I decided to come and pay you a visit instead.'

I smiled, my heart thudding, and went into the kitchen, trying to take my time. I took the potato I had saved for Marcus out of the oven, and found the butter in the fridge. The sausages were cold, but I put two on the plate. My hands were shaking but I managed to cut the potato down the middle, and then slice a knob of butter and add it. The knife was rounded, like a small palette knife, with a red plastic handle, part of a cheap set. He was standing in the kitchen doorway now; I could sense him even though I had my back to him.

'I'll take that from you.' He had come up behind me. He levered the knife out of my hand and threw it in the sink, and then picked up the plate and walked out of the kitchen and sat down at the dining table. By the front door, for the first time I noticed a black bag. He saw my eyes on it, and he hoiked his feet round it and brought it closer.

'Sit down.' He gestured to the chair next to him. 'Keep me company, why don't you?'

I perched on the edge of it, keeping Josh in my sights.

He started eating with his right hand. With his other hand, he picked my phone off the table and started thumbing the screen. He began scrolling through my photographs. 'That's nice,' he said, holding it up. 'Your day trip to Southwold. Family walk along the pier. Shame it was so wet . . . Hubby and the boy feeding the ducks . . . A kite! That must have been in winter.'

'Please, don't.'

'All this family togetherness.'

I stared hard at him.

He put his fork down, and leant back. 'Does he know you've been having an affair?'

I checked to make sure Josh wasn't listening. 'Yes,' I said quietly.

'Does he know who with?'

The moment of hesitation gave me away. I saw something cross his face; it was satisfaction. I'd given him ammunition.

'Would it upset him to find out it was someone richer, and older, someone so much more successful than him?'

'It depends how you measure success,' I said. 'Can I have my phone back?'

He ignored me. 'You should be more mindful of security.'

'What do you mean?'

'Oh, I don't know.' He chased a piece of potato around his plate, ate it and then used the side of his fork to separate a piece of skin from the flesh. He put the phone in his lap. 'If you're not leaving your house open to burglars, you're leaving your son unsupervised in a department store.'

'You've been watching me.' I was whispering now.

'I'll admit I've been keeping an eye over the last couple of weeks. Planning my next move.'

I could see the car key on the table, next to Josh's paper and crayons.

My jumper was hanging on the back of his chair. I asked him to pass it to me, and the moment he turned to disengage it, I snatched the key from the table, and put it on my lap.

He handed me the jumper and I slipped it on, keeping the key in my lap, and then I stretched, and shivered, and in the process, hid the key in the sleeve of the sweater, pulling the cuff over my fingers as if to warm my hands.

'You cold?'

'Yes, I am a bit.'

He pushed his plate away.

'Right, shall we go?'

'I'm not going anywhere.'

'Yes you are.'

'I'm not.'

'Can you just stop resisting? At every turn.'

He stood up suddenly and his hands reached out in the air, clasping it, his face twisted in a silent roar. He was joking, yes, or trying to joke, expressing his exasperation. But it wasn't funny. He was a large man who spent a lot of his spare time in the gym; he was physically intimidating.

I leapt to my feet, panicked. The chair dropped back behind me with a bang. Josh looked across. I tried to smile at him. 'It's OK, sweetie. Come here.'

Josh came over and stood by me. I put my hand on his shoulder and then I hoisted him up onto my hip. He clung to me.

'To be honest I'm glad you've come,' I said. There was a quaver in my voice I tried to control. 'You're right. I didn't give our relationship a chance.'

He picked up the black bag, hooked his hand underneath my elbow, and led me to the door. He let go of my elbow to turn the handle, and then – either an instinctive courtesy or perhaps, more likely, to ensure I came with him – let me and Josh go out before him, onto the porch.

The outer door was open. He was distracted, closing the door behind him and I leapt forwards, over the step, into the open air, tearing as fast as I could away from him, feet flying, pounding, stumbling only once, Josh clinging, his hands in my hair, his legs thumping against my hip, the wind, the sea in my ears as I hurtled down the path towards the car park. Over the hill and then, in sight, the Fiat, key clutched in my fist, breath harsh in my throat, hair whipped, face bursting, nearly there, nearly there. I was already visualising it in my head – reaching the car, and getting in and driving – but then a shout, the sound of pounding feet, the slam of hands on my back, and I was down, flat. The shock of it, the fear, pain, mouth spitting sand, and then sobbing to Josh, who was next to me, crying, face and body in the earth, 'It's just a game. It's just a game. It's just a game.'

Him

I searched the house for the car key but couldn't find it. I hoped, when I got down to the car park, that the Fiat might be gone. At least I would know that she had driven somewhere then. At least I'd know they were safe. But it was still sitting in its space between two faded white lines, the sand on its bonnet untouched. I took the dune path down to the beach, my feet skittering on the sand, slipping, tripping over myself. The tide was in, and the waves were riotous; roaring like traffic. In the distance, towards Sizewell B, there was a low flickering near the shore-line. I jogged along the top of the beach until I was parallel.

Three dark figures were hunched around a campfire: two men and a woman. They were smoking a joint. The men had goatee beards and the woman had blonde hair coiled in plaits around her face. She was stroking a large dog. They saw me looking and stared back. The dog got to its feet, and stood braced.

'Have you seen a woman, and a small boy?' I called.

'Sorry?'

I took a few steps towards them, down the incline, and asked again.

They shook their heads. 'No, mate. Sorry,' one of them said. 'No one's been along here at all.'

Behind me, as I clambered back up the slope, the dog barked.

Her

I had my arms around him but only for a second because then he had yanked us both to our feet, his grip on my arm rigid, wetness on my face, blood maybe. 'Leave us alone!' I screamed. 'Let me go. Leave my son be!' He had Josh by the hand and I was attempting to twist my arm out of his grasp, kicking out at his arms, twisting, wriggling. 'I hate you,' I kept saying, 'I wish I'd never met you. I hate you.' And then, as loud as I could before flesh clamped my lips shut, I screamed into the air. 'MARCUS! MARCUS!'

'Enough of that,' he said, pulling us the few feet down the path to the car park. There were two cars here, apart from ours, and he dragged me to one of them.

I tugged his fingers away from my mouth. 'HELP!' I screamed again.

Someone might hear me. The driver of the other car might be nearby. Marcus might be just over the ridge.

The wind took my cries.

He opened the back door, holding it open with his knee as he forced us in. The dead-meat stench of leather. 'Don't run away again,' he said. 'You saw what happened last time. It's not a good idea.'

Josh had wriggled up and was sitting upright on the other side of me, his hands tight together.

'Don't hurt my son,' I said under my breath. 'I promise I will kill you if you do.'

I pulled him across to me, holding him, telling him everything would be all right. He said, 'You're bleeding, Mummy, you're bleeding. Why are you shouting? Where's Daddy? I don't like that man. I don't like this.'

'It's a game.' I held him closer. 'We're playing chase.'

'I want to go home.'

And then his face at the window, the front door opening and slamming, and the key in the ignition, the back of his head, and his eyes in the rear-view mirror. I could hear the heft of his breath, the catch of his inhalation; his fingers tapped a beat on the steering wheel. He was agitated. 'I didn't want to do it this way,' he said. 'I don't know why you have to make it so hard. I know when you calm down you'll see it's for the best. You're overwrought and you're making me behave in ways I don't like. I'd apologise but it's your fault.'

The car reversed, a roar, and he spun the wheel and pulled out of the car park.

'Where are you taking us?' I tried pleading. 'Please let us go.'

I held Josh low in my lap, stroking him, trying to cover his ears. He was barefoot; mud was crusted below his knee. Blood smudged the seat next to him, but it had come from my leg, I think. I was aware of it throbbing. Josh seemed unhurt, thank God. He was still holding a piece of Lego. His eyes were open wide, his face pale. I stroked his hair.

The car jolted down the lane. Dark green shadows through the window. Branches scraping. He wasn't paying attention to the width of the car. The wheels kept hitting the bank. The windscreen tilted, righted. Scraping on the undercarriage, a stone thrown to one side.

'Where are we going?' I said.

He didn't answer.

'Are we going back to your hotel?'

'What hotel?'

I know I could have stayed in the car, that I could have let him drive wherever it was he thought he was going. People have told me it was wrong to do what I did. I've heard them muttering. I should have stayed put, used diplomacy. Everyone has an answer, don't they? If only. If only. In retrospect, there is always a better way out.

We were nearing the end of the lane, close to the A12. I knew once we reached it the car would speed up. He'd put his foot on the accelerator. Tarmac out of the window, and road signs, lorries, other speeding vehicles. There would be no escape then. Perhaps I could have waved for help out of the window, gesticulated to other drivers. I didn't think of that. But what would they have done? In those few moments, before we hit the main road, I just wanted to get away.

I could remember a gate off to the right. We'd held over on the first day, to let another car get by. I pulled Josh close, watching the hedgerows pass. 'Get ready,' I whispered into his hair. My right arm was across him and my right hand was clasping the metal handle. It was hot and slippery beneath my fingers.

I saw the gap in the hedgerow approach, the gate out of the window, and then the blur of hedgerow resume. The moment went. He was slowing down. Up ahead was the road. And then a wheel hit a bump, and he braked suddenly, and in that split second I pulled the handle towards me, pushed the door open and, still holding Josh, leapt out.

Earth and weeds and stones. I fell forwards, pushed by the velocity of the jump, falling onto my knees, rolling forwards, clutching Josh, trying to keep him safe, as I rolled on the road, bumping and scratched by brambles, scraped arms, stinging hands. My knee throbbed. Josh let out a scream.

A few yards ahead, the car stopped.

I grabbed Josh, got to my feet and ran away from the car, stumbling, back down the lane the way we had just come towards the gate. Behind us the engine started, and there was a scratching, a scrape of wheels, and then the engine stopped. We had reached the pull-in, the bars of the gate just ahead. I put my foot on the bottom rung, steered Josh up, and then clambered up after him, both of us then dropping down onto a path the other side. The car door slammed. I said, 'Hurry', and took his hand, and we ran, along a short track. It was dark now, with trees on either side. We ran into a clearing, an old boatyard or something. A dilapidated shed loomed ahead, a low wall covered in brambles, a rusting car and a lopsided grey-white shape, the hulk of an old rotting motor boat. I scanned, then pulled him down a bank, behind the first ruined building. We crouched down low. The tarmac at our feet was rough and uneven, cracked with weeds, broken glass. Under Josh's feet was a rope gnarled into a solid shape, ending in a rusted pulley. 'Sssh,' I murmured.

Him

How still and impenetrable the country was at night, the flutter of unseen creatures deep in the hedgerow, a dark swoop between branches up ahead, the shadows on either side of me inky and black, the sky the lightest thing in sight with the moon flickering between clouds, a sheath of brightness glowing on the left – the lights of what? Ipswich?

I stumbled a bit, tried not to think about Josh's little shoes next to the sofa.

Was I crying?

It seemed so far to the main road, so much further than I had realised. When I reached the A12, I would look for a pub. I paced along the narrow strip of tarmac, already imagining the scene: yellow lights dappling through the glass in the door as I pushed it open, the warmth and fug of a country bar, locals turning, raising their pints in greeting as I entered, and in the corner my wife and son, her face lifting from a game of cards; in sequence across her face, annoyance, relief, love.

My teeth were chattering, my heartbeat slamming in my head. Had she left with her lover? Is that where she had gone? Taking Josh? A blackness rose inside me. What did he have that I didn't? Was he *a proper man*? Was he the kind of man my father would be proud of – a lawyer, a scientist, a businessman? Not a namby-pamby, but a man who could run a company. Satisfy her in bed. Save his own son from drowning. The tears dried on my face. The cold air chilled my gums as I bared my teeth. Once again, I remembered Dave Jepsom. Ever since I'd met him my life had imploded. He had been there, in the background, as everything had been destroyed – my business, my home, my marriage. My arm swiped at the hedgerows. If I saw him now, I thought, if he was here in front of me, I would destroy him too. I would tear him apart, limb from limb. I would annihilate him. This time I would show him what a proper man was.

I was nearing the A12. I could hear the whine of the Tuesday night traffic ahead. It wasn't much further now.

The road bent round a corner, and then I realised that ahead of me a car was parked close on the verge, so close to the hedgerow the bonnet was half concealed by greenery. I wasn't sure another car could even get past.

I got closer, and peered first through the front window – a black bag sat on the passenger seat; and then through the back. It was empty, but there was a circular blotch on the pale seat, which ran in a line, over the edge, like a teardrop. Was it blood? Next to it was a little block of Lego, two bricks stuck together. I felt an ice-cold shiver, terror and disorientation. My insides twisted, my mind blackened.

Her

The chain on the post rattled, the struts moaned, the rungs clanged. 'Don't do this,' he called at the top of the gate. A thump as he landed. 'Don't waste my time.'

There was an oily, peaty, damp smell. Water trickled nearby. Through the cross-hatch of trees, I could see a string of car lights, pinpricks.

We leant against the outside wall of the building. His footsteps were coming slowly down the track. I could hear his breath getting closer. A stumble, a clank of metal, and a pained cry. And then he seemed to move off. He sounded angrier now. 'Don't mess me around.' He was the other side of the hut from us. His steps moved away. Torchlight slammed against the trees across the yard.

Josh's mouth was hot beneath my palm. His eyes were looking up at me intently. 'Sssh,' I said again.

I lifted my head to peer through a crack in the cobwebbed window. Through the glass, it was dark and shadowy inside, a dusty workbench, the looming hull of a rotten boat. He was holding his phone, the light from the torch swooping and darting. I could see through the broken cracks in the window on the other side of the building. I moved away to the side, flattening my back to the wall.

'I'm going to find you,' he shouted. 'You might as well come out.'

326

He was pushing at a door, rattling the handle. He swore under his breath, walked away and then I heard him come back. There was a sliding growl as the door opened to the side on rollers.

Josh pressed into my legs. 'I don't like it here,' he said.

'Sssh.'

He was inside the shed. I heard him stumble. The torchlight threw circles onto the walls, hit the window, bounced away.

My breathing was too loud; Josh was sobbing.

I gripped his hand.

'I'm scared,' he said. 'I don't like this game. I want to go home.'

I took a step away from the window, up to the bank. I could still see the lights on the A12. We should double back, I decided, use this chance to get away. Any minute he would hear us. There was only so long before he found us.

I took another step, still holding Josh tightly. We edged slowly round to the corner of the building. One step, and then another.

A creak inside the shed.

And then my name.

Him

For a moment or two, I stood in the middle of the lane. It was quiet but for the rumble of traffic in the distance, or the sea, or both.

But then?

I strained my ears.

A water-bird let out an urgent cackle; a beating of wings like riffled cards, and then silence.

An owl, way off over the marsh, shrieked.

Had it been an owl?

I felt fear beginning to press.

I began walking down the lane in the direction I had come and stopped when I saw the gate in the layby.

There was sandy mud on the bars; I noticed that. It was wet under my hand.

Beyond the gate was a short narrow path. It might once have been a track, but the trees had grown in, the grass had grown up – chunks of tarmac disappeared into hefty holes, brambles reached out at either side. The track ran downhill for 200 yards or so, on one side was a bank, with water beyond, on the other a row of trees; all around a stretch of flat marshland. It smelt brackish, an industrial version of the sea, of fish, salt, fuel, oil. Branches above my head thickened and darkened, and the track widened out into a yard. The moon shook itself free, and I made out a rotting upturned motor cruiser in the bushes, and beyond it, some derelict buildings.

I took a few steps forward. Several hundred metres ahead was what looked like an old boat shed: long and low, dilapidated but intact, made of blackened wood with a corrugated roof. I imagined I had seen a movement in the window, a ripple against the glass. But when I stood still: nothing. It must have been the moon passing over it, a shadow of the racing clouds. I looked away. It was getting colder. A slight rain was scratching in the air. It was damp on my hands, and cheeks.

And then, just in case, I shouted.

Her

'TESSA!'

'Daddy!' Josh was out from under me, and running towards Marcus's voice.

I was running too, but he had come out of the shed now, and he was there in Josh's path, and he swooped down on him.

'Leave him alone,' I said. 'You leave my boy alone.'

But he bent and hoisted Josh off the ground, reared upwards, holding him around the waist with one arm while warding me off with the other. Josh's face collapsed, his arms reaching out for me, twisting his body, trying to get free . . .

Him

No, I don't remember anything else.

I don't remember bending to pick anything up.

I just remember running towards Josh. I was aware of his voice but I didn't process it. I was zoned in on the broken pieces of Tessa, her muffled shouts, Josh's broken cries, of it filling my head, of seeing the shape of him ahead of me, my son stretched in his arms.

And my head was full of light then, the sun glancing off the water, and the heat rising from the ground, and the size and shape of him, and the way he held my son up above his head like a trophy. Across his shoulders stretched a pair of angel's wings – intricately ink-drawn, da Vinci-like in their detail – a patchwork of webs that looked like tracings of his own muscles.

Her

... and I was pulling and pushing, trying to get my son out of his arms as he backed away, holding Josh higher and higher, further and further from me, screaming at him to let my son go, kicking at his bare calves, screaming, 'Richard! Don't do this, Richard!'

Him

There was a brick in my hand, and there was a shaft of glass in the other. The heave of Tessa's breath was in my ears, her deep ragged sobs, but no words because my ears were ring-ing – just white noise and air as, finally driven to action, finally in time, I rushed at him, hitting him again and again with what I thought were my fists, but which I now know were a brick and a piece of broken glass, and I kept on hitting even as I registered the expression of surprise on his face, as he fell to his knees, his eyes slithering, his head changing shape. I kept on hitting, even as I began to know something was wrong, that his eyes had darkened, his hair was longer and flecked with grey. I kept on hitting as the blood burbled from his mouth, his shoulders shaking, even as Josh had scrambled free. I kept on hitting as blood soaked his football shorts, as it seeped through his hoodie to what I knew was a da Vinci angel across his shoulders, as the blood blotted out the tattoos on his arms, as he slid sideways to the ground.

The rest is hazy – though hazy is the wrong word. It is blood red, and orange and purple if I try and piece it together. No football shorts. No tattoos. Not Jepsom. No, not Jepsom.

He lay there, this other man, drained of all life, silent and motionless.

I looked up for Josh and Tessa. They were sitting huddled, his head buried in her neck, his frame shaking in silent sobs. She had her arms around him, holding him tight as if she'd never again let him go. I searched her face. I didn't know what I hoped to see: love, relief, awe? But her expression was impossible to read. When she didn't speak, I found the words myself.

Her

'I saved you,' he said.

IN THE CASE OF CROWN V MARCUS ARTHUR
NICHOLSON
Case number BB238/3D
Hospital number GP4403847

PSYCHIATRIST REPORT

We declare that Marcus Arthur Nicholson was evaluated at
Springfield Hospital, London under Regulation 38 of the
Mental Health Act 1983, according to an order dated 5
August 2017 by the presiding judge.

We hereby certify and report as follows regarding the
mental condition of Marcus Arthur Nicholson, hereafter
the accused.

A. The examination consisted of clinical interviews with
the accused and observation of his general behaviour. He
was physically examined. Special investigations, including
blood tests and an electroencephalogram were done.
Psychometry was done, and a psychological report was
compiled.

B. Psychiatric diagnosis at the time of the alleged offences.

At the time of the alleged offences, the accused was not
suffering from a mental disorder or mental defect that
affected his ability to distinguish between the rightful and
wrongful nature of his deeds. A mental disorder or mental

defect has not affected his ability to act in accordance with the said appreciation of the rightful or wrongful nature of his deeds.

We consider the patient fit to stand trial.

Signed:

Peter Kitchen

Dr Peter Kitchen MBBS BSc MRCP MRCPsych

S Speigelman

Dr Susan Speigelman MBBS BSc MRCP MRCPsych

Some actions, you could argue, are beyond the powers of communication. Someone saves a life. Someone takes a life. The difference is immutable. And yet, the machine keeps moving, it never stops. The lawyers have taken over now, with their more expensive narrative power. They have their own ways of presenting a story (the bullying father, the pressures of work, the wife's affair).

It leaves me confused, all this: the talk, the reports and interviews, the spin. It doesn't seem to touch what matters.

You can hate someone who saves a life.

And you can love someone who takes a life.

It's all I'm left with, really.

Acknowledgements

It's easy for a writer to forget what an office is like; thank you to Ann Morgan for letting me spy on hers, and to Elsbeth Smedly for her glorious inside information on the world of comms. Ben Smith, as ever, was an invaluable guide to police procedure. Thank you, also, to everyone at Flotsam & Jetsam for allowing me to pretend that the table at the back is actually my place of work.

The book would be nothing without my wonderful editor Ruth Tross and the rest of the team at Mulholland, especially Cicely Aspinall and Veronique Norton. And I owe boundless gratitude to everyone at Greene & Heaton: Kate Rizzo, Rose Coyle, Holly Faulks, and the unmatchable Judith Murray.

To Giles Smith, my deepest thanks, as always.